PRESS

2026 ANTHOLOGY

Editors & Staff

James McNulty
Managing Fiction Editor
Visual Arts Editor
Interior Designer
Copyeditor

Sara Moore Wagner
Managing Poetry Editor
Copyeditor

Fiction Editors
Claire Agnes
Rachel Phillippo
Michael Hugh Stewart
Danielle Barr
Charlie Watts

Poetry Editors
Christen Noel Kauffman
Ben Kline
Erin Carlyle

Social Media Manager
Olivia Farina

Copyeditor
Jessica Maple Holbert

Cover Image & Content Illustrations:
Io Wuerich

Cover Design
Sally Franckowiak
James McNulty

Independently published by *Driftwood Press*
in the United States of America.

Fonts: Sifonn, Josefin Sans, Agency FB, Bembo MT Pro, & Merriweather

Published in March 31st, 2026
ISBN-13: 978-1-949065-41-1
Please visit our website at www.driftwoodpress.com
or email us at editor@driftwoodpress.net.

Table of Contents

SECOND EARTH FISHERMEN

Ajith Thangavelautham

That morning I decided I would steal from Father. I slept on the small boat while he worked in the fog of dawn. The boat rocked and a splash of cold water woke me up. Father jumped into the net like a madman, lost amongst garbage, weeds, fish, and crustaceans, lifted out a battered chest the size of my torso, heard the clink of coins, and smiled a smile I did not recognize. I did not think that the warmth and ease of that smile suited his face, but it was the first truly enviable thing I had ever seen him possess—the smile, that is. In that moment we thought we were rich men.

His gambling debts followed us to the new country, so we fled East, away from the big cities everyone landed in, to a small fishing town, as far East as we could go without crossing back over the ocean. Father was a fisherman by inheritance and now circumstance. Unsatisfied with its simplicity but averse to anything more, he turned always to pleasure—alcohol, sex, violence—a different kind of simplicity, one more befitting a man, he taught me.

Stealing the chest was an exercise in independence: change for the sake of assumed personal growth. I was at the age when one wanted that—to speed up the transformation from child to man by any means. I had gotten it into my head that I deserved better and he deserved worse. A son is not a donkey or a hammer. A son is just a boy. But just a boy is weak. A son is not weak. A son is a father and a father is a fisherman or a priest or a farmer or a thief. The chest was my chosen inheritance since I refused to inherit the work of a fisherman. Father thought I was useless because I didn't man the net or steer the boat or gut the fish, because instead all day I swam and read English books and watched the pale boys and girls chase each other and fight and kiss and touch.

That night, chest already hidden in the forest, I sat cross-legged, hidden in a bush at the back of our home, a lone, run-down fishing shack, by a crack in the wood planks that were our walls, just big enough for me to look into without being seen and watch Father's reaction. I felt my cruelty was earned after all this time by his side—the cruelty of observation, like watching a wasp first swim then drown in honeyed milk.

I rolled a cigarette to pass the time. I usually rolled Father's for him and sometimes mixed in dirt and stole bits of tobacco for myself. It seems I had always been a thief. The fruit trees I used to climb with friends long gone were not ours, nor was the faulty radio we found and sat in front of to eat our stolen bananas, which when we were lucky sputtered Balu or Bob Marley or Madonna. Apparently Father's Father's Father's Father stole the piece of that island we called home. It seems we had always been thieves. The ocean that Father plundered now was not ours, nor were the women he slept with. Neither the patch of infertile earth that our latest something-like-home swayed on, nor what the bush that I was now hiding in grew from, were ours.

Father would say to my concerns that ownership is only ever momentary, that trees are owned by whatever is perched highest, a bird or a boy or a gust of wind, a body of water by whatever is sinking fastest, a home by whatever is sleeping deepest, and a woman by no one.

The door scraped open. I watched Father walk inside, glowing, sweaty with a low-eyed smile, a senseless smile that was more common for him, followed by a woman I recognized and dreamt about, having been forced to share our one thin mattress with him and her and other women before. I would strike a dead body pose, limp and unflinching, taking up as little space as possible so Father would leave me be. I would only ever briefly open my eyes to see his hairy body in prayer, the beast of man so annoyingly obvious, enveloping absolutely the young woman underneath. I then realised that I could sleep outside and let the more easily understood bugs crawl all over me instead.

He had probably spent all night drinking on credit and bragging to anyone who would listen about the treasure that he recovered, still unopened, exaggerating its possibilities, like gold and textiles and art and artefacts or, once he had drank more, a mermaid's heart beating god's bell-adorned drum. The whole town must've been out for blood, we were already being watched. There were whispers of foreign terrorists of which we were assumed to be the leaders. A week ago, two lifeboats full of our people fleeing our faraway home had been rescued nearby. They were currently being investigated but would most likely be given asylum.

When they were dumped adrift the coast, I swam out and watched them bob in their lifeboats from a distance. Father heard what was happening, came home early that day and shut himself in, while some of the other fishermen prepared to help them. The lifeboat people looked like me but I did not feel like them. A few wore orange life jackets or yellow rain ponchos, the rest were bundled up in sweaters and scarves. They were mainly bearded men and a few women, one holding a baby. There were oars but the current was too strong to paddle. They waited. The baby cried but there was calm amongst them. I was jealous of their existence out there at sea.

Water is formless, or more accurately every-form, its shape and memory is infinite and overwhelming. In those moments, they were anything and everything. I was homesick, but not for the fishing shack and Father—maybe one day if we ever left I would be—nor for the cities out West and Mother, though I did miss her and her baby way of loving me and her fat arms like pillows and her laughter and her cooking and her—though I did miss her I could not be homesick at my age for a mother—nor for the fruit tree sputtering radio days—I could not be homesick for a place that hated me—but for the eternally bobbing, formless lifeboat, something like the heaven the people here prayed for.

When we first arrived three years ago there was an unsettled interest because of our dark skin and unknown origins, maybe we were Black or West-Indian, something vaguely familiar, but our English was different and those groups did not claim us. Father bought the shack and a boat from an old man with a wad of cash and promised a cut from all future sales. The old man's grandsons, twins, both also fishermen, disapproved, especially when we started selling fish at a massive discount. The old man died recently and the twins wanted his land back. They came to our house one night and found me sleeping outside because Father was drunk and had a woman. The twins had survived a house fire as children that killed their parents. One of them was scarred from head to toe like a moon. The other was unscathed and everyone except for his brother thought that he was responsible. I barely understood their accent, but the burnt one yelled about their land and their business and their fish and their ocean. His flesh swirled as he spit. The not-burnt one was quiet and smiled a thin smile that made me believe the rumours. He cut off the tip of my right ear with a pocket knife and they left. I returned inside the house because of all the blood but I did not cry or make a sound. Father thought I was useless because I did not fight back. That same night we broke into the twins' walk-in freezer and pissed and bled all over their fish fillets.

I assumed Father would think the twins had stolen the chest. I doubt he thought I had the mental or physical strength for that sort of heavy betrayal. He was still noisily preoccupied with the woman and hadn't noticed the robbery. I put my fingers in my ears and looked up at the stars. Father constantly made excuses for his life, like the preordainment of all things, duty as the only path forward, obedience to those before and penance for those after. Penance in the form of pleasure as punishment, his overindulgence of vice a strained apology to me, but why bother trying to make sense of it for his sake. A fisherman's son can never escape the ocean, he said.

Fate had created this man who I would not become, this man who was so much only pretending to be simple. Fate had brought him to the edge of this distant second earth, alone and lonely with a son who would take everything from him without hesitation. A man's dream perhaps.

I often wondered what he dreamt of. Not while he slept—the man did not sleep unless blacked out. He did not dream when he slept, so his subconscious was instead forced to cohabit with reality. I would sometimes hear him in rambling unintelligible conversation with the fish he caught. I wondered about his waking dreams from youth. His dreams as a father had soured and atrophied into fate and duty and obedience and penance, but in youth dreams are grander, uncompromised.

Despite (or more likely in response to) his inner turmoil, a violent pleasure-seeking conscious and an undreaming leaky subconscious, he was always pristine and exact-looking on the outside, hair parted and slicked with saltwater, clean-shaven, teeth straight, body and clothes scrubbed every night. He was constantly distracted by his reflection in the water. I could picture him as a child with the dream of being a famous actor. He had the confidence and work ethic and indulgence of a superstar type, and above all an unwitting desire to be loved and liked. Even here he tried to woo the women and make friends with the men, but only I loved him because I had to and the women he paid only liked him because he was generous and lively and clean.

Adrenaline waning, I fell asleep and dreamt of performing a romantic dance number in the Swiss Alps with the woman Father was laying with. I woke up to yelling and scrambled to my knees to find Father on the ground being beaten by the twins. The woman sat legs-splayed on the floor against the wall, picked at her nails, and watched. Why had she stayed, for entertainment maybe or perhaps she had not been paid yet and would take her share from the chest. The twins were trying to get Father to reveal where it was. I had missed Father's reaction and was not prepared for such a large audience, but I rubbed dirt on my clothes to indicate struggle, ran in and yelled, "Father, I stopped the thief!" His face was puffy, probably a few broken bones, but he seemed okay, and through the puffiness I could see confusion. The twins grabbed me and I said, "I'll show you, follow me."

So the twins, the woman, Father, and I walked through the forest late that night. The twins were impatiently tripping over tree roots, threatening me, and pushing Father forward as he limped slowly at the back. I hummed a made-up song to distract myself from any sympathy I might have felt for him. The woman whispered excitedly to the twins, making sure she would still get her cut; she did her job perfectly, she said. There was a grunt in response and she looked at me excitedly, as if she wasn't trying to rob us.

But of course, there were no great riches in that chest, just mould and still water and broken glass bottles that clinked together like coins. Earlier that day, I ventured this deep into the forest before thinking to open it. I had given in to Father's delusions—that he was a man so deserving he considered it heresy to even check its contents. I looked at him now, trying to catch the moment when his dreams died, but he was unreadable, composed, almost normal. He stood solid despite his bruised legs and I tried to stand like him, moving my shoulders back and inhaling deeply into my ribcage.

The twins laughed, the scarred one quietly wincing, his peeling cherry lips pulled back to reveal perfect teeth, he couldn't help it. The other twin laughed loud and bassy for the both of them at Father's foolishness. Their laughter was full of relief, treasure was rarely worth the trouble; it was clear that they didn't really care for it, they just didn't want us to have it. I had felt the same kind of relief and I hated that we had that in common. When I smashed the lock with a stone and saw what the chest held, I realised I had no plan and no idea where I was going to go with the money; if there even was any, what would I do with gold and textiles and art and artefacts? I was relieved to walk back empty-handed and be a boy for a little longer. The only one who was truly disappointed was the woman. I wished I could've given her something.

The unscarred twin told Father he needed to leave town, glanced at me and then to my ear, and walked back the way we came with his brother and the woman. I didn't know if Father believed that someone else had stolen the chest and I had somehow chased and fought them off, but he didn't question it. He insisted that we lug it back but besides that was completely quiet. He shrugged his injuries off, walking straight and strong and fast. This was the reaction I truly needed to see—not to the theft, but to the worthlessness of his dreams—and his reaction was to walk straight and strong and fast through the forest with his useless thief of a son.

The shack was on fire when we got back. No one else was around. We threw the chest into the flames and I waited for it to explode but the sodden wood only smouldered. Father was seated on the shore. I told him I had taken the chest. He said he knew. I don't know when he knew, if it was when we were in the forest, or when I showed up with dirt on my face, or had he already noticed the missing chest when he got back home that night, or maybe he saw me watching him smile that morning and knew then, but regardless I felt a hint of pride in the words when he said he knew. It was a foggy night with not much to see, so we listened to the ocean, the noisy bugs, and the eventual pop and shatter of the glass inside the burning chest.

THE PRACTICALITY OF DREAMS

A Conversation with Ajith Thangavelautham

James McNulty: Welcome to the pages of *Driftwood*, Ajith! And congratulations on winning our In-House Short Story Contest this year!

Ajith Thangavelautham: Thank you. I'm grateful!

JM: Talk to me about your journey as a writer.

AT: In my early twenties I was looking for ways to express myself creatively, purely for the sake of sanity and joy. I always wanted to be a painter, so I painted a little. I made some music, I cooked, I experimented with clothing. All of these things stuck to some degree, but I eventually tried writing stories, having been an avid reader of fiction since childhood—mainly YA fantasy and whatever was on my Mom's bookshelf: medieval historical fiction, Dan Brown, Salman Rushdie—and the connection was instant and singular. I knew I had found something to commit to.

JM: How did this story come to be?

AT: I wrote the first version of "Fishermen" on a three-day train ride from Chicago to San Francisco in July 2024, and the story is brimming with that energy. It really was a joy to write, so much so that I wrote maybe four or five more versions of it during the remainder of the year, each too different to be called drafts. The one that's most fully formed and intelligible is the one being published by *Driftwood*. I think it's the third version.

A real-life event that played a part in the story was the 155 Tamil refugees who landed in Newfoundland in 1986 after travelling on a cargo ship for months and being left off the coast in lifeboats.

JM: I love the unconventional rhythms, surprising shifts in language and tone on display here. It often reminded me of the work of Marlon James. Please talk to me a bit about the process of sculpting the voice here.

AT: Thank you. I love Marlon James' work. The way he writes so many distinct voices so well and, of course, his bright and brutal imagination. I'm obsessed with his podcast *Marlon and Jake Read Dead People*; I've been listening to them talk about all the Victorian authors I never read.

The voice for the protagonist of "Fishermen" came fairly naturally. I've been some version of that boy, the one on the cusp of that unreachable thing called manhood. He has a calm, intelligent rage common amongst the boys I write, but he's also heavily influenced by the drunk and violent philosophical mind of his father in the story, a person he is conflicted about and painfully takes after.

JM: *Marlon & Jake Read Dead People* is a great podcast! I've listened to a handful of episodes as well, despite not generally reading too much of that genre either.

This story is very much about transitioning to a new phase of life & the hopes and hopelessness of dreams. Talk to me more about these themes. What are your dreams?

AT: The story being about a father and son—sons are very attuned to their fathers' once-dreams.

Immigrants & refugees focus on survival, so their children may find it difficult to hope for anything more than prescribed success; they inherit loss, but it is the child's job to remind the parent of the importance and necessity of dreaming hopelessly.

Having said that, the dynamic in "Fishermen" is interesting because it's somewhat flipped: the father, despite his many faults, is a dreamer, and the son, per an earlier draft, "gives into [his father's] disillusions." The son tries to dream further but doesn't know how; the son is hopelessly practical.

I think you're asking me what my waking dreams are but that feels maybe too vulnerable and difficult to answer, so instead, my dreams at night are interestingly and excessively mundane, so much so that I often have difficulty telling them from reality, especially during cold Toronto winters when I sleep lots.

JM: For a story like this—with so much emphasis placed on voice and rhythm and language—the punctuation is appropriately idiosyncratic. Talk to me about the thought process behind punctuation decisions.

AT: I actually don't think I've ever consciously thought about punctuation until you just asked. Punctuation for me is completely intuitive, for better or worse. I punctuate how I feel it's meant to be read, how I read it under my breath; the rhythm needs to feel good in my gut, almost musical but not quite.

JM: I noticed during our revisions and interview process that you have a penchant for comma splices; many of them within "Second Earth Fishermen" work beautifully. What do you feel comma splices add to the rhythm that isn't available via other forms of punctuation?

AT: I find commas to be nimble and inconspicuous and uncomplicated. Commas feel expansive in that the writing has a chance to breathe but not rest. I think words just flow more readily for me with commas than other punctuations like periods or semicolons or dashes. Truthfully, I only really like run-on sentences when I'm writing, not as much when I'm reading other works, and that is why writers need editors such as yourself. Thank you.

JM: Rhythm can be somewhat subjective; as an editor, an errant comma splice or overused use of one type of punctuation can disrupt my internal rhythm, whereas it might feel entirely smooth, consistent, and poetic for someone else. It sounds very much like you listen to your gut while writing, so I'm curious: what does your revisions process generally look like? Do you re-write from scratch every time?

AT: As you've experienced firsthand during our revision process, I am extremely volatile when it comes to my opinions of my own work. This usually leads to a complete dismissal of anything previously written and a subsequent re-imagining, for better or worse.

This is intensified when there is significant time between revisions, since I feel my writing changes so frequently. While revising "Fishermen," I've learned to trust my original intuition while in the heat of writing a story and living in it; editing and refining is important, but rewriting tends to remove a lot of the magic.

JM: What do you think draws you to re-imagining old work from the ground-up rather than embarking on new journeys with new work? Asked another way: when is a piece of fiction *finished* for you?

AT: This is probably the most difficult part. It's not necessarily difficult to make it to the ending, but when you're writing, you're making so many decisions and opening and closing so many pathways. It's difficult to not explore at least some of them. I think that's where the re-writing comes from: what if this happened instead of that, what if they were like this and not like that.

I think a piece is ideally finished when everything feels inevitable, but to me that's impossible when the writer is too in control. Writing intuitively—meaning, in relationship with the story, at equal footing—while easier said than done, leads to that desired inevitability. I think.

JM: Do you have an outlining process? If not, what does initial idea creation look like to you?

AT: I've learned not to outline; instead I try to find *things* that are powerful enough to work as a starting point, not necessarily the chronological start of the story, but the *thing* that gives me energy and momentum to build a story from. This can be an image or a place or a person or a relationship or a dream or a scenario, the more specific the better. For "Fishermen," it was *son steals from father.* After that, I brainstorm the bare minimum that I need to start, like the general setting, and basic information about the main characters, and I start to write. I know I'm ready when I can't bear brainstorming any longer. I've been learning to trust the story and the process of writing by not over-preparing.

JM: Ah, so your outlining is mental and only sets the basics that you need to begin. As such, do you often sit at the computer for long periods mid-paragraph imagining where to go next? Do you take breaks to brainstorm where the story will go next, or does it all tend to flow out at once? What does your actual drafting process look like?

AT: Ideally, the thing I've chosen to use as a foundation is generative enough so that words will flow and story appears, but there are definitely going to be moments of stuckness, usually around a character's emotions and psyche and resulting actions; the writing of the first draft is when I usually discover the most about them.

I love to use a first draft as a way to get excited about a story and write anything and everything related to it—the plot, sure, but also the feelings and the history and the sensory elements of the place.

If I'm stuck for too long during a first draft, that means I've probably regressed into a state of control, a panic response, maybe I'm focusing on the wrong thing, let me backtrack to where I felt free-er, or let me close my laptop and walk to the park and listen to music and read a book.

JM: Who are some of your favorite writers? Which ones inspired "Second Earth Fishermen"?

AT: Marquez is my go-to answer for favourite writer, and he's definitely present here, I think specifically in the way the town feels.

The story was directly inspired by R.K. Narayan's short story "Naga," about a boy who is abandoned by his father, a snake charmer, and is left a cobra as a means of providing for himself.

I was reading Akil Kumarasamy's novel *Meet Us By The Roaring Sea* while writing the first version of "Fishermen." I would read a chapter and then write, and then read another chapter. I couldn't sleep because my seat on the train was uncomfortable, and maybe it was for the best: I read her book and wrote my story. The first version of "Fishermen" feels like her—I don't know what specifically—but I think I felt a kinship with the way she wrote her sentences. It is my favourite thing I read in 2024.

Over subsequent versions the story became my own, but all of their energy is still in there somewhere.

JM: Do other mediums influence you at all?

AT: Hip-hop is foundational to my writing practice; it taught me the craft and power of poetry and storytelling, but also, and maybe more importantly, that the root of all things is movement. Hip-hop and beatmaking is where I discover my own rhythm that I then fold into my writing and living.

JM: Do you listen to music as you write? Any particular bands if so?

AT: When I first sit down to write, yes. Music (Coltrane usually gets me fired up), sugary milky black tea, incense, a fidget spinner. For the first thirty minutes, an hour, hopefully not longer, I try to get back into whatever I'm writing. I engage all my senses and get my brain firing, then the words come and I know they're here when the music has become distracting and the incense has burnt out and my tea is cold.

JM: What are you working on now?

AT: I'm working on a collection of linked short stories thinking about the migration journeys of my family, life in Scarborough and Toronto, & the emotional consequences of landlessness and capitalism. Mavis Gallant has a compilation titled *Varieties of Exile*, and I wish she didn't so I could use that title for my own book; the other option at the moment is *Headless Heroes of the Apocalypse,* after Eugene McDaniels seminal album. Is that allowed?

JM: Anything is allowed if it makes sense. Any parting words to leave with our readers—either about "Second Earth Fishermen" or writing in general?

AT: Drink water! Write stories!

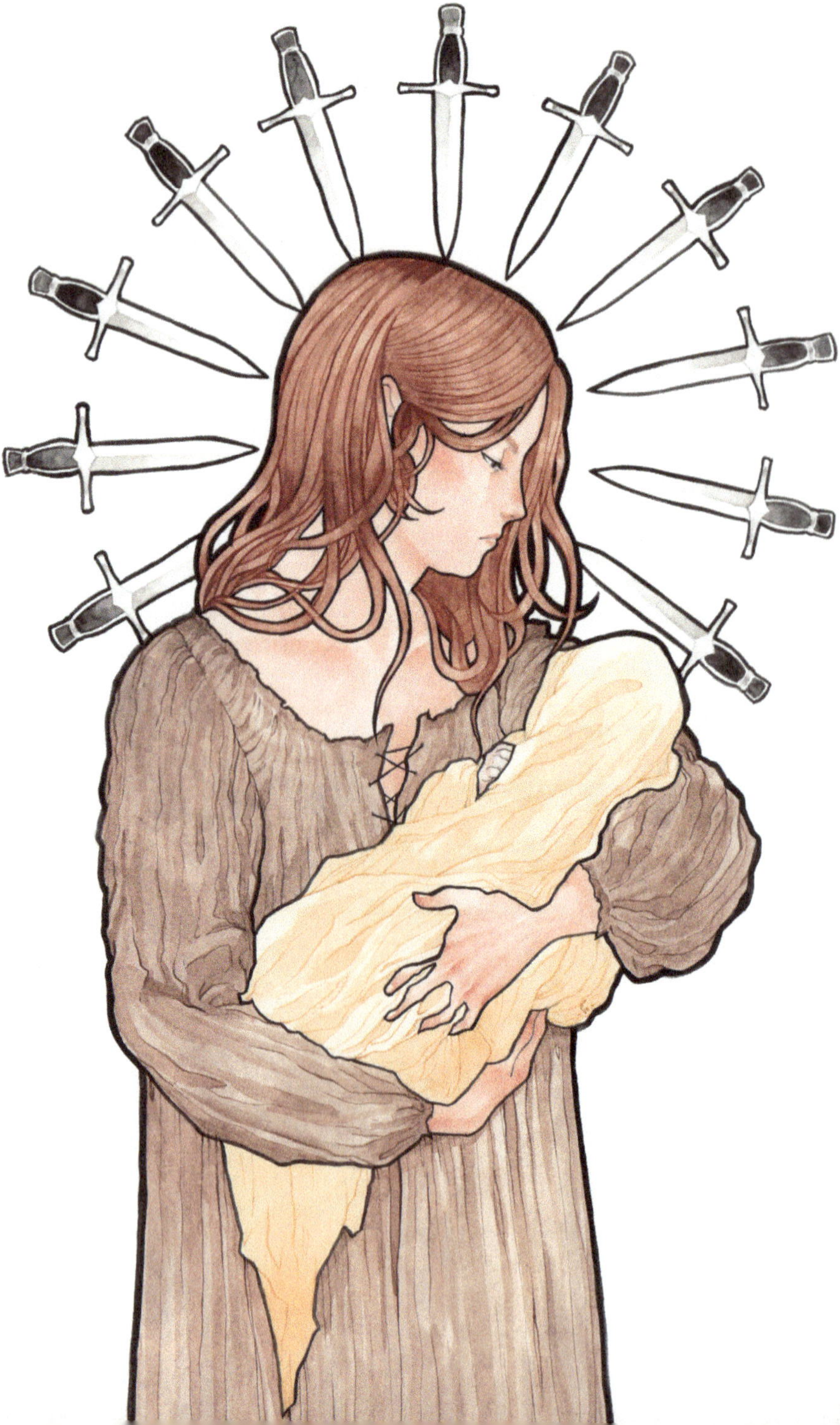

MERCY

Devin Choudhury

On the final day of the final fast I wake before the sun. Something is moving in the corner of my cell. I sit in the darkness and listen to it scrabble. Probably it is a ghost or some wild beast; to me it makes no difference. Fear seems only vanity. So I rise and pray and then pass water, and when dawn strides in from the balcony it reveals a shrunken bluebird. I watch for a while as it limps through the rising heat. It rustles its wings and tucks them back in. Poor thing, I say. To think that you are trapped. I spit and turn away, and as I do the bell begins to chime. I do not hesitate. I fill a bucket at the pump. I haul it onto the balcony. The procession is passing through the narrow wooden gate. I watch as they mount the winding path between the towering firs. When they reach the stilts of the cleansing house I raise the bowl and tip it gently forward. Water pours down the rough slanted surface of the balustrade. It falls in a curtain on the bowed capped heads below. For a moment it seems that they will raise their eyes to mine, but they cling to their oaths. They gather themselves and continue on as if nothing has happened at all. Hunger burns and gnaws; only rage holds me upright. Still I stand and watch until they withdraw through the gate. Just as I turn to return to my mat the bluebird makes to flee. It passes close; I feel its wings caress my cheek. For a moment I think to follow it, but I know that I cannot. Now they will come for me. For him. So I creep into my endless dusk and sink onto the floor. I lay my head on my two hands. All that remains is to wait.

⋆

Not long after we found each other he told me a story from his youth. We had just made love, and he whispered in my ear as I ran my palms across his shaven head. His mother had worked in a factory that made the mainsprings of clocks. After the army crossed the ocean the mainsprings were abandoned, and the factory began to manufacture a small metal cap for the mines our soldiers used to encircle the enemy's villages. One of the women on his mother's line objected. She told the overseer that she would not murder babies. The overseer said nothing, and no one stopped the woman leaving. When his mother returned to their home in the company town she did not mention the incident; she did not speak at all. Later that night they woke to screams outside. The objector's house was on fire. He and his mother rushed from their room and out among their gawking neighbors. He remembered the scene in great detail. Ash arced to and fro as it rained down on their heads; dogs fled the choke of melting plastic. But most of all he remembered the relief in his mother's eyes as she watched the burning roof collapse from the safety of their small dirt yard. When he began to cry she seized him by the shoulders and shouted in his face. Son, this is what happens. She has three children in there with her. She chose the children of strangers who what's more want to kill us. His voice rose as he recited his mother's words, and he rolled away from me to face the open window. When he spoke again he was calm. My mother told me, God will not stand for it. God will not let it stand.

★

In the early afternoon a crowd begins to gather just outside the gate. Word has spread, and the locals have come to see me for themselves. They point and exclaim at the building's rough exterior; they imagine passing glimpses through the opening to the balcony. They think that I have lost my mind, and they are waiting to see what happens next. I lie inside unmoving on the thickening muck.

★

When I found her she looked more peaceful than she ever had in life. She was lain below a spreading oak by the creek behind the encampment. She was hidden in the roots, and if I had not stopped to catch my breath against the trunk I would not have seen her. At first I did not recognize her. I was still weak from the labor, and the miles to the well and back had left me barely conscious. I dismissed her as a child's doll forgotten for some other game. Only when I leaned in close did she offer up her shape. There was no mistaking it. All I could do was stare. She was alight with the soft rain falling from the cloudless sunset sky. She was a spray of golden drops beside the rushing water. For a moment it seemed to me that God had brought her there to soothe the pains that wracked her tiny body. For a moment I bore witness to His tender stroking hands. Then the moment passed, and I fell to my knees with a wild shriek that clove the air itself.

★

At last I see one coming. The crowd has grown so large that the saint must announce himself to ensure he is not touched. There is no light within the compound but what falls from the streetlamps that rise beyond the fence, and when he steps through the gate and into the forest the night swallows him whole. I listen to the gentle scrape of his feet against the path, and then the hollow clangs as he climbs the spiral stairs. The rusting padlock whines. When the door swings wide the stench rushes out to meet him, and his silhouette recoils. He steadies himself and enters. He places an electric lamp on the floor and turns it on. By now he is prepared, and the sight that greets him causes no reaction. I sway faint with hunger in a full moon's sweat and dirt. The floor is thick with bird and squirrel droppings; a soft green fuzz is forming on the walls. Still he lowers his gaze and utters the chaste sorrowful greetings I am due. I do not offer the response. I offer nothing. He glances up astonished, then closes his eyes and shakes his head. You have accepted the right to vengeance, he says. If you do not plan to use it then you must give it back.

★

When I became pregnant we did not know what to do. News had reached us of work to be had in the mines that scarred the foothills, and we had joined a caravan crossing the plains. There was no room for the trials of bearing a child. No one would let a baby's home go beneath the earth. He told me he would work enough to feed the three of us, but we both knew there were not enough hours in the day. So when we reached the rises and the first of the great stepped pits I hid my belly as best I could and went down by his side. We got our cards and joined a line of filthy panting workers. We hacked at the thick red sludge until late into the night, and when beneath the floodlights the bottom of the mine broke open in a storm of rock and fire they sent us into the breach before the dust had cleared. In that shapeless haze there was only glow and shadow shifting. After a while the company men came and burnt a bright blue liquid. The air was lightening in my lungs; it settled thick upon my skin. But we got our scrip as soon as we reached the surface. We found spots free in the bunkhouse, and the guards did not beat us. It was as good a place as we had come in all our time together.

★

He stares at me with eyes deep-set in a head almost perfectly round. He is young for a saint; his beard is barely patches. But he has given his body to be God's vessel, and I cannot help but tremble. He gestures at the floor beside the lamp, and I sink down on my haunches. He watches me from the edge of the ring of light. After a moment he says in the same calm voice, Only a human being can exercise the right. Only a human being can return it. You were so eager. You wept and beat your breast. Why then have you made yourself a beast? Why do you wallow in this filth? He steps forward, and the light on his starched white shirt is so brilliant that I must shield my eyes. Daughter, I am not come to accuse. I am not come to condemn. I am a guide. I would take your hand and lead you to the altar. I would hold you steady as you take the knife or leave the task to us. But I cannot help you if you do not break your bonds with the world of lesser beings. So wash yourself clean, child, and when the procession passes tomorrow morning you will step forth from this halfway house and into the light of the Lord. You will put an end to all this suffering one way or the other.

★

When I fell down by her body I had the feeling of falling into death, and darkness covered all. It was a few young boys who found me. I woke to jabs from a long thin stick and my name in a child's voice. My bucket lay overturned beside me, and my clothes were soaked right through. She squelched against my breast as I wandered from the woods and through the rusting trailers. I held her close past families huddled round their fires, and when a careless welder cast his sparks toward us I tried as best I could to take off at a run. We had made our place on a gentle rise just past the edge of the camp. I found him sprawled beside the cart watching the stars pierce the sky. That was his way; I thought nothing of it then. Maybe his smile as he rose to greet us was wider than was normal. Maybe he made sure that he did not lay eyes upon her. But if so I took no note of it, and I hurried toward him crying out again and again, She is dead, her throat is cut, I found her by the stream. Someone has taken her from us. Someone has killed our daughter. After a moment of indecision he let a dread show through him. He rushed toward the cart. No, he said in a trembling voice, no, I left her here asleep, she is safe and warm, but when he thrust aside the blanket lain between our bags of food we found only emptiness. She was gone; she was in my arms. By then the boys had spread word, and the camp had gathered. A murmur swelled. He began to stalk the edge of the crescent formed around us. Who? he screamed. Who among you? She was innocent. Just a broken little baby. He raged until his voice had gone to pieces. When the only sound was the pale cool wind a voice rose from the crowd. I saw you, it said. I saw you do it in.

⋆

I tell him, No.

⋆

In the end my stomach betrayed me. Guards came in the night and led me to the overseer's office. He loomed behind an iron desk with sorrow on his face. A woman from my work-gang squatted by his side. I took my seat on the stool across from them; she spat and passed a hand before her eyes. Her voice was thin and high. I saw the child in the bunkhouse, she said. I glimpsed its home as she stripped down to bathe. I did not mean to look. It only happened. But I will not stay silent while she forces it into work. She spat again and whispered, Slaver. The overseer stood, and a guard lifted the woman by the arm and pulled her from the office. We were left alone in the stale pinched quiet. After a moment he said, You know that I could call them here to do to you what they would. At least the saints would clear your stench away. But you are lucky. I will not have them at the mine again after what they did the last time. Days of work lost to righteous talk and rules no man could follow. No. You will leave before the sun, and you will take the man that did this to you. He shook his head. I should not be surprised by the things you poor beasts do. But a child. I had not thought it possible.

★

The young saint lowers himself and takes a seat beside me. I recoil as I must, but he does not accept it. He edges toward me across the risen filth. Waste smears his trousers; I am seized with shame at the smell of my own body. He raises a thick white hand and takes hold of my arm. Fear scorches, and I cannot keep me in. I pitch forward and vomit across my lap. I have not eaten in days, and only water comes. He sits unmoving as it pools dark around my legs. When I have finished and fallen to gasping through my tears he says, You must understand. For now he is just a shade. We have gathered his life from the Lord, and we hold it in abeyance. Do you see the debt that we have accepted for your sake? Do you see that we have asked God to withdraw that vengeance might be taken? You must obliterate him, or you must return the right to us. We cannot simply take it back. It is only freely given. His grip tightens. Daughter, this is no small thing. Until he is dead the world will remain misshapen. Godless. Would you be the cause of that? Would you condemn us all? I do not speak. I will not give him the relief of meaning. I let myself fall limp. He holds the full weight of my body aloft for a long while, and then he lays me on the floor. I hear him stand and then his voice. We cannot make you choose, he says. But you cannot leave until you do. He walks slowly from my cell. He carries the light away with him.

★

They bound him and hauled him to one of the working trucks. I followed forgotten with our daughter in my arms. Between the moonlight and his fear he was deathly pale. He sweated and squirmed; he tried as best he could to pass denials around his gag. Close to the center of camp a small sharp rock came flying from the crowd and struck him on the cheek. He raised a muffled scream, but no one moved to wipe the blood that poured into his mouth. A child leapt out and seized his leg. She sank her teeth into his calf. Laughter rose. The mob pressed in. One hand tore his shirt from his body; another took hold of his hair. For a moment it seemed that they would tear him limb from limb. Only when a woman pulled a poker from her fire did one of his captors cry, He is not for us. There is a sanctuary close by. The spokesman turned and pointed at me. She has earned the right. They will offer her the choice. But if we take this man from life we will rob the Lord and turn His gaze on us. Even a child-killer belongs to God. Even an infanticide. When the camp shrank back they bundled him into a truck, and then they returned for me. It's alright, sister, they said as they dragged me along behind them. We have him. He will not escape.

★

The night is full of rain. I lie awake and picture the forest sprouting moss and steam. Soft green life drowns and blooms in the darkness. Three times through the tapping on the metal roof I hear him at the door, but always it is only an animal or a trick of rising sleep. Morning pours a rinse of kneaded gold. The drain is clogged with hair and leaves, and pools of water muddle the floor. Outside the bell is ringing. I make no move to go and see. He will pass unheeded; he will live and wonder for at least another day. A faintness passes over me, and I steady myself against the wall. My stomach turns and seizes. I listen for a while to the footsteps down below; I check the pump and find that it still runs. For a moment I am tempted to take up the bleach and scouring pad, but I clench my teeth until my weakness passes. I kneel and pray until the gate squeals shut behind them.

★

We had only walked a day or three when I felt a wetness down my legs. It was much too early. My child was not ready for the air, and we were all alone. That morning a passing family had told of a camp beyond the coming rise, but even after we mounted the ridge we did not see a sign of it. My feet shone red with bloody spume; I could not go on. He lowered me down to the bare dark earth. He was frightened, but I had no strength for comfort. The child was a mass of pain pushing through my sex. Is it coming? he asked. Can you give it life? I tried to answer, but I could not cling to thought. For minutes or years I dissolved into the pulse of sky and land. I woke to a thin pale girl crouching just beside me. He sat huddled by a windswept shrub; I could only see his back. The girl leaned in. I know you have to push, she said. I know you have to breathe. I'm sorry, miss. There's a doula back at camp, but you're not fit to make it. I stared at her without understanding. Are you from God? I whispered. Are you come to offer mercy? She smiled. I don't know, miss, she said. I'm only a forager. But I'll stay until it's done.

★

I realize I am close to my end. I am not sure how long it has been since I ate; I have lost my grasp on time. I only know that I can barely cross the cell to the toilet or the pump. No one has come since the young saint. They are waiting for hunger to grind me down. They believe that I will come onto the balcony in skin scrubbed raw to breaking with my choice upon my lips. And yet each morning when the bell begins to sound and I struggle even to raise my head I feel that they have given me a gift. Left to myself I do not know that I would have the strength to endure it. I would hold firm for months or maybe years, but in the end I would give them an answer. I would take his life or hand it to God's agents; I would let the saints set the world in its proper place. Instead I welcome death like a weary stranger come searching for a bed, and I leave him still a specter. Instead I lie in my puddling urine and let my stomach kiss my spine.

★

The sanctuary was a narrow warren cut into the mountain. After his captors forced us over the threshold we found ourselves in a chapel lined with desks stacked high with paper. One saint sat writing; the other paced the chancel. My daughter's father knelt bound before the altar with his forehead on the floor. Please, he whispered. You cannot call it murder. Our child was not alive to begin with. This world was a Hell for her. I only sped her to the Lord. I even left her by the water so to give her one last beauty. I did not mean for my woman to find her; I did not mean for her to be found. When he fell silent the pacing saint approached him. He crouched and placed a calming hand on the back of his subject's head. God's mercy is infinite, he said, but He knows that ours is not. At our request He averts His gaze that we might make a medicine of vengeance. The saint turned to me; he lifted the bound man by his hair. For a brief moment the two seemed nearly twins. Daughter, said the saint, look into his eyes. Their light is forfeit. The wrong he did has sundered him from God. Now he is only an animal, and it is our duty to dispose of him. Or it is yours. Our knife or yours. For a child's death we always give the choice. The two men watched me; the pen fell silent. I looked down at my daughter. Save for her cool stiffness she might have been asleep. I bent and laid her on the chapel floor. I smoothed her patch of hair and straightened her limbs as best I could. I slipped my shawl from my shoulders and laid it as a veil upon her. Maybe from that holy place she would find a way to God. Maybe his light had entered her through the wound he laid across her neck. I rose to face them as the pen resumed its scratching.

★

I decide I will look down on him one last time. I spend the night dragging bit by bit from my mat to the lip of the balcony. The summer is ending, and it offers up its final heat in a dark wilting gasp. I make a pile of my bones and let it spill against the balusters. I shed my clothes long ago, and my body is red with sores. Some fester; it does not touch me one way or another. I just sprawl and drink the wood's dense toil. Somewhere a bird is singing, and a memory tries and fails to form itself inside of me. It does not matter. He is suffering; I am here to witness it. I blink, and he is trailing up the hill somewhere in the long white ribbon. I do not need to make him out. Each bowed head can be his if I let it. Still I try as best I can to cry out his name, and after a moment I manage a shapeless moan. I am not sure it carries over the rustling leaves; I moan once more and louder. A ripple runs through the procession at this sign so long in coming. Many heads half-rise, but only one cannot hold its oath. A face near the rear turns to mine. I strain my eyes, but it is only a collection of lines and colors. A broken arch; sunlight on a rough stone wall. As quickly as it rose it falls away again. The procession passes. I am left alone.

★

My child came in silence. I had no more screams after passing so much blood; her father just lay and gazed up at the sun. Even the wind quit coming down the mountain. Still in that stone-carved world the forager pressed on. She shimmered and gleamed between my thighs; I felt each grazing finger as God's own touch. I was so intent on her that I did not realize it was done. Only when she rose did I feel my body empty. She looked down on the bundle in her arms. She shut her eyes. I raised myself to see; all that appeared to me was a twisted fleshy club straining to unfold. I'll get someone, said the forager. If I run I'll make it back in half an hour or so. Just hold on, miss. Lie back. I'll leave it with your man. I could not even thank her before she went. Through my daze I saw him take the bundle. His face was turned to Heaven; a mute prayer was on his lips. He rocked our daughter back and forth. Did you take her name? I whispered. If the child is a girl we should call it after her. He did not respond. What is it? I asked. What's the matter? Still he did not speak, but he turned toward me and took a short step forward. I could hold no longer. As I slid once more into void I saw a searching look on his face. I saw in his arms a limp dull knot.

★

I do not have the strength to return to my mat. For days or weeks I lie flimsy just inside. Sometimes I close my eyes and find myself floating in a round and starlit pool; others I listen to my breathing bottom out. I hear in my straining heart the footsteps of the procession passing below, and I am never alone. I wonder how long it will take the saints to find me. Perhaps a day or so, or until the smell becomes unbearable. Or perhaps they will leave me as a lesson for others who beg the choice. Perhaps I will slip into the darkness of this swamp that I have sunk, and he will rise each morning and wonder if I still wait hidden in some corner of the cleansing house to redeem my promised vengeance. He will rise each morning and think on our daughter's face. Meanwhile the beasts of the forest will consume me, and those that stomach my poisoned flesh will carry me into the canopy. They will spread me on the forest floor. As the procession climbs the hill each day I will spring up all around them in tender saplings that will still be young when he falls to his wizened knees and passes from this life. I smile, and as even my bones begin to give way I whisper, Yes. I have touched the days to come. They would dig a pit for you; I will grow a world.

CONSTRAINED POSSIBILITIES

A Conversation with Devin Choudhury

James McNulty: Welcome to the pages of *Driftwood*, Devin! I loved this stark slowburn, which gradually lets you into the world it builds while utilizing surprising language and a unique structure. Please start at the beginning and tell me how this story came about!

Devin Choudhury: Thanks, James. It's very exciting to see this little experiment hit the page, and I can't think of a better home than *Driftwood*. The story began with an image, a question, and the uncanny feeling that the two must be connected. The image is the story's opening scene: a desperate woman pouring water from a balcony onto a solemn procession that is passing below. And the question: are there moments in which mercy functions as an act of violence, even as it remains mercy? That is, a sort of inverted mercy killing (if a mercy killing is a moment in which violence functions as an act of mercy)? Certain things came to mind—those instances in which a terminally ill patient is kept alive against their express wishes, or the experience of living on with the psychological torture of having awaited one's death, as in cases of a suspended execution, similar to what Dostoevsky describes in *The Idiot*—but none seemed quite right, they didn't offer me the footing I needed, and I still didn't feel as if I could formulate anything approaching a rigorous answer. The a-ha moment, as it were, came when I realized that the woman pouring the water was the one who was, perhaps, perpetrating this violent mercy. I wanted to tell her story, delve into her psychology, describe and explore the system of justice that would put her in this position and produce this foundational image. "Mercy" evolved from there. It grew to encompass a number of other things I was thinking through as I was drafting it—the meaning of bodily autonomy in the face of extreme exploitation and environmental destruction, the exertion of agency through self-deprivation or non-action—and in the end, it's come quite a way from its roots. In particular, and as perhaps must be the case when transmuting abstract ideas into fiction, the protagonist's actions and motivations are far more ambiguous than in my initial vision. So my question remains unanswered, but it's still at the core of the piece.

JM: You reference here how "Mercy" reflects many of the things you were considering while drafting. I noted during our revisions process how there were a few anachronistic lines in the story, and you addressed that those were fully intentional. Is incorporating anachronistic elements an intentional tactic to wink at the reader that the story isn't so removed from time as it first might seem? What specific personal or political topics were you thinking about as you crafted "Mercy"?

DC: I was struck, actually, that you took the lines as anachronistic. "Mercy" was in part driven by the conviction that the notion of history as necessarily progressive is a myth—and an extremely destructive one at that. With that in mind, this alternate world defined by the coexistence of a religious system of justice, an extractive economy reliant on scrip-based wage labor, and the presence of a number of "modern" technologies—plastic, explosives, motor vehicles, chemical-reliant open-pit mining, etc.—did not strike me as anachronistic or as unmoored from historical time. Rather, setting the story in such a world was an attempt on my part to depict and defamiliarize some of the predominant forces at play in our present.

That brings me to your second question: as I drafted "Mercy," I was thinking in particular about the peculiar powerlessness that I think many people feel right now. I say "peculiar" because I do think that there's something new about it. Certain elements of our current situation are continuations of long-standing forces, and I've incorporated those into the story as well, albeit in denaturalized forms: the government's attempt to exert direct, coercive control over women's reproductive systems and the labor of prisoners, for instance, or indirect forms of power such as the maintenance of a political economic order in which so many are compelled to subject themselves to degrading and dangerous forms of work simply in order to subsist. Nothing is new about these, although of course their forms are slightly altered in the face of changing historical circumstances, whether our current circumstances or the ones that I've outlined in "Mercy." But there is also—and this I think is the main distinction of our 21st century feeling of powerlessness—a sense that not only is history not progressive, it has in fact assumed a sort of downward arc: a sense that, due in particular to anthropogenic climate change, things will only get worse from here. This really is a "sense": pushed to articulate a cogent position, I would reject hopelessness. Still, that sense, that feeling, permeates my relation to the world. I think it permeates "Mercy" as well, even in those moments in which we encounter something like hope. This is by no means an endorsement of that feeling. I just think it's something with which we need to contend.

JM: "Mercy" struck a chord with me personally because I often think of the US justice system as primarily concerned with doling out retribution rather than rehabilitation (though of course there's the private prison's profit motive and other complications and factors to this reductionist sum up). The protagonist refuses retribution, a kind of mercy for her partner, but what does rehabilitation look like for someone like her partner, who was arguably providing his own form of mercy via his crime? If one doesn't believe in retribution as being effective or helpful for anyone, what do they do with the people who commit one-off crimes based on circumstance that would not benefit from rehabilitation?

DC: I am very wary of the idea that the narrator entirely refuses retribution against the father of her child. Certainly she refuses the form of retribution demanded by the religious order that controls the state, but the father isn't getting off the hook entirely. He will continue to live in this suspended state on the brink of death; he will do so, what is more, with the full knowledge that he has killed his child. Despite her refusal to further the cycle of mortal violence, or even to allow others to further that cycle, the narrator maintains an ambivalent relationship to the father's continued suffering. I think that we disagree—or at least are not in perfect accord—about what precisely she feels toward him. That is good. There are no easy answers here. And this I think is the product of a system of justice, as well as a metaphysics and a system of ethics, that disallows such answers. Mercy, at least what we tend to conceive of as mercy, is not possible in this situation: the father will not be released back into the world to live a normal life; that would make permanent God's absence from the world. What, then, is mercy? In the face of these constrained possibilities, how far can it truly extend, not just in its material effects, but even in its conception? These are some of the questions I hoped to pose—questions that I take to be quite relevant in our current historical conjuncture.

This brings me to rehabilitation. It's a great question, and I think it gets at the core of the story. One of the things that I hope "Mercy" does is ask us to question the fundamental presuppositions of our penal system: this means questioning not just whether retribution is an appropriate response to wrongdoing, but also whether the ideal rejoinder to retribution is necessarily rehabilitation. Rehabilitation continues to place the onus for crime entirely on the individual. Earlier I mentioned powerlessness and compulsion: the narrator and the father are subjected to a number of structures that vastly exceed their control and are largely responsible for creating the situation in which the father kills their child. By no means do I intend to excuse him; still, I think there is value in these situations, if one is genuinely committed to justice, in turning our attention to the structures that produced the situation in the first place. In an ideal world, perhaps those who committed one-off crimes based on circumstances beyond their control would be enlisted in an effort to change the deleterious structures that produced those circumstances. Of course this is essentially impossible so long as the penal system is controlled by an entity—or, as in the United States, entities—that benefit from these same structures.

JM: With the amount of care & intention clearly paid to the writing here, I imagine the initial drafting & revisions took you quite a while. How long did it take you to draft this story? What was the revisions process like?

DC: Drafting took about a month of late-night sessions in total. It had a very specific rhythm to it; it was a bit like learning a language. There was an initial period in which I moved painstakingly, feeling things out, but once I'd accustomed myself to the flow of the language, once I'd understood the way in which the fragments of narrative related and cohered—or didn't relate, didn't cohere—then suddenly it all rushed out. Revision mostly focused on clarifying the intricacies of the situation and the world, particularly familiarizing myself with the dogma of the religious group that controls the system of justice so that I could express the narrator's dilemma as precisely as possible.

JM: I love what you say here about writing this story being a bit like learning a language. I often say that the best writers have to teach you to read them; I wouldn't start with *Absalom, Absalom!* as my first Faulkner book, for instance. On the flip end, it's wonderful to hear that the writer has to proceed with a good bit of trial and error to learn the language themselves. Talk to me more about this process.

DC: It was mostly a matter of understanding the world of the story. The precise manner in which the narrator phrases things, the rhythm of her sentences, the way in which she arranges the plot, or plots—all of it is formed by her circumstances and by the larger forces operating in this world, which are at once radically different and subtly similar to our own. The pleasant difficulty came as, after some initial planning, I attempted to capture her voice and found myself uncovering a world that was not as I had initially imagined it. This was the first, painstaking period: writing within a world that was changing by being written and, in turn, that was changing the voice in which I was writing. I've had this experience before—I think I have it every time I write—but here it felt especially acute.

JM: The story has a beautiful structure—but one that isn't necessarily intuitive on a first read. On a second read, the chronology is very clear, but on the first, it may take a minute to notice that we're jumping around between three timelines—not two. (The present, the pregnancy, the death.) The story expects some mental work on part of the reader—and that's one of the many things I personally love about it. What do you make of challenging your readers?

DC: I don't think one should hesitate to challenge readers if the challenging elements—here, the narrative structure—are central to what the story aims to accomplish. And I don't mean simply producing the pleasure of encountering a particularly well-wrought aesthetic object, although I enjoy that as much as the next person. The challenge, both in its specificity and in the more generalized additional attention it demands, should produce a radically different relationship to the material than if that material were "told straight," as it were. The initial opacity should lead toward some greater shedding of light. I hope I've accomplished that here.

JM: Fully agreed, and I think you well accomplished your goal here. Talk to me more about the benefits of not telling this particular story in chronological order—or even chronological order with two timelines.

DC: In this case, I wanted to express something of the experience of living under conditions of such extreme subjugation that it is difficult (or more difficult than usual!) to hold together a clear, well-ordered sense of self. I turned to the figure of the fragment: that shard of narrative that does not lend itself to coherence. Very quickly I confronted the classic problem of attempting to express incomprehensibility or chaos within an aesthetic object. Some order was required. I ended up landing on this sort of interwoven narrative structure, where each section takes on meaning not just through its insertion into some master narrative but also through juxtaposition, surprising resonance, and etc. And while I wanted to express a certain degree of abjection, I also wanted to create a sense of possibility. Adania Shibli recently put it well when she said that linear narrative structure resonates with the grand narratives that underlie dictatorship or tyranny; the narrator of "Mercy" is precisely someone who, upon encountering various forms of authoritarianism, throws sand—or, rather, her own body—upon their gears. In this sense, a fragmented structure seemed appropriate.

The other reason for this particularly puzzle-like narrative structure was that I wanted to produce for the reader the sensation of discovery, of unveiling. This is what the narrator is going through: the slow, always only half-finished process of encountering the contingency that underlies these seemingly natural structures on which her society is constructed. This process takes work; it's often painful or unpleasant. In real life, at least, it's usually worth the effort; again, I hope that the reader finds that it's worth it here as well.

JM: The sense of discovery & unveiling is such a wonderful sensation for the reader, too; putting the pieces together from context clues, intentional & precise phrasing, guided intuition, etc. is like placing puzzle pieces—but far less boring. Talk to me more about this process on your end.

DC: I've always enjoyed the process of piecing together a work of literature, uncovering hidden resonances, understanding the machine humming within a plot—I think that it's a wonderful way to train your mind to think critically, and it's something that I often try to reproduce with my students. But it's also insufficient in itself. The novels and stories that I find myself returning to are those that find the perfect balance between that more mechanical process and larger ethical, social, or political questions, a balance that, ideally, pushes me to reflect on both the process and the questions in a new light.

JM: At risk of delving too much into the minutia of craft, I want to talk about your punctuation decisions, and how they enforce your narrative's tone. Often enough in grammar, there are instances where the comma is optional. In stories like this, the absence of those optional commas contributes to the tone. Why do you think that is?

DC: I wanted to give the narrator a somewhat flat affect, something to express her peculiar combination of trauma, abjection, acceptance, venom, and courage. The absence of commas, particularly insofar as it aligns with the story's rigid, constrained sentence structure, contributes to this flatness.

JM: Who are some of your favorite writers? Which ones inspired "Mercy"?

DC: I'm never sure how to answer the question of my favorite authors—it always strikes me as demanding a knowledge of myself that I don't think I possess. The best answer I can give right now is that whenever I'm going on a vacation on which I'll have ample time for uninterrupted reading, I bring an Iris Murdoch novel. As to authors that inspired "Mercy," three immediately come to mind, maybe just because I've been returning to them recently: Nadine Gordimer, V.S. Naipaul, and the Bengali-language writer Mahasweta Devi. This in terms of the prose, the way these three authors capture complex and often quite unflattering psychological states without resorting to stream of consciousness or other, more straightforward attempts to mimic the workings of the mind; and also in terms of their ability to give expression to extraordinarily violent social and political arrangements in various states of disintegration. But then my move away from any reference to an actually existing context, my turn to something like fabulation—that's a departure from these three authors, all of whom are such remarkable observers of highly specific historical circumstances. That isn't to say that "Mercy" has no relation to such circumstances. It's just that the relation is much more opaque. Here, I think, the main (albeit distant) influence is Jorge Luis Borges' short stories.

JM: Do other mediums influence you at all?

DC: There was a time I would have said music, particularly very harsh and repetitive music that does a sort of violence to the listener. These days, though, I'm not so sure. If anything I would say photography and painting have become much more important to my writing. The way that a single, bounded, unmoving scene discloses an entire world, as much through what it does not depict as what it does, as much by being static as by gesturing toward some type of movement in time—I'd like my work to do something similar. And there is a part of me that wants to take this to what I see as its logical extreme. I remember hearing when I was young that famous Edward Hopper quotation, you know, "Maybe I am not very human. What I wanted to do was to paint sunlight on the side of a house." That made quite an impression on me; I feel similarly. Right now, though, that type of transcendent simplicity seems impossibly ambitious. Certainly "Mercy" feels quite far from that ideal.

JM: What are you working on now?

DC: I have a novel in progress. It's very different from "Mercy"; that's all I'll say about it for now. A few short stories and essays in various stages of planning and drafting. And then a book and several essays in my role as an academic.

JM: Any parting words to leave readers with—either about "Mercy" or writing in general?

DC: Just another enormous thank you—to you, to the rest of the crew at *Driftwood*, and to everyone who took and is taking the time to read the story.

ANASTASIA

James Gianetti

Her pointer finger shoots up at the sky. "Look, Daddy!" In a few moments, the figure in the sky will be a small dot. They always form themselves into a lowercase "t." Arms out. Stiff back. Two vultures soar counterclockwise around them as they rise. One eye closed, she measures them with her pinch. I tell her to be respectful. It's rude to stare too long. They go up at different rates. Sometimes quickly. Sometimes slowly, like balloons the day after your birthday.

"Would you ever let go of Mommy if it happened to her?"

"Of course not," I tell her.

"Are you going to come live with us again?"

A "soon, sweetheart" stutters out of my mouth.

"Maybe they didn't quit smoking those bad cigarettes like you." She points to the nicotine patch on my arm. She doesn't seem to notice or care that the ice cream traveling down her cone has reached her fingers. "Maybe they had a lump on their brain like me. Owen in my class said his uncle had what I have, and he went up two weeks ago."

I clutch her shoulders, halting her next "maybe." I wipe her lips, dried and waxy with vanilla.

"That's why it's super important you keep taking your medicine. It only happens to the people who don't."

Some swear it to be a divine, Darwinist phenomena, only happening to the "weakest ones." The Catholic Church believes there are two governing rules to follow to prevent it: Have faith in God and repent. Scientism says to be of good health. Atheists advise us to live in the moment and embrace the universe operating according to its natural law. However, the many instances are as mysterious and random as the occurrences themselves. IBM and the elite universities across the world are chasing their tails trying to find the patterns. Cheap opinions of "first-time callers, long-time listener" types flood the cultist radio stations. Before it happens, it's said that your body weight doesn't drop, but you seem to get very light. Then your feet rise off the ground—so slightly at first that you'd never notice. The space between your feet and the ground grows by millimeters, enough not to leave footprints in the dirt. By that point it's only a matter of time. Evangelicals state that when it happens to you, you are granted a coveted—or perhaps even your greatest—desire. They call it the "divine rising" and give credence to it bringing peace and prosperity to your loved ones. When it first started to happen, people clung to their shoes or clutched onto the hemlines of their pants. They say you can measure the love of a couple based on how high they get before one of them lets go.

"Daddy."

She presses her hands to her forehead. An uncontrollable amount of *it's okay*'s flow out of my mouth. I scapegoat the ice cream. "Just a brain freeze," I say loud enough to alleviate the concern of the few people outside the ice cream shop. When she kneels, her knees meet her elbows, and my fingers disappear when I run them through the grain of her hair. I squeeze her into my chest and tickle her ribs until her giggling vibrates my collarbone. She smiles with her whole face. Her freckles stop where her nose begins to curve. I guide the crown of her head with my palm toward the sky that we sometimes like to call the upside-down ocean.

"Imagine whales and manatees and monkeys."

Her face scrunches. "Monkeys?"

That's when I know she's okay. Her forehead is warm against my lips. She doesn't know she's running a fever yet. I roll her bicycle over to her. "Time to go back to Mommy's." I fasten her helmet. The buckle pinches the skin below her chin, but she's too nervous to bellow an "ow." The early August afternoon brings the first autumn whispers and the final rattling from a choir of cicadas. We keep a steady pace beside the curb. Her knuckles go white when she squeezes the handlebars. My one hand covers her left, the other pressed onto her back, controlling her wobbly body until she straightens out. Her first time without training wheels.

"Don't let go."

"You can do this. I'm not going to let go." Her knees rise with each pump against the tension of the pedals, occasionally grazing my elbow. My hand swallows her grip. The calluses fill the spaces between her knuckles.

Glittery pink tassels dangle from the handlebars like the blonde pigtails from the side of her head, both barely fluttering. We pass under a towering maple tree, and I lose sight of the small dot in the sky through the blue gaps between the leaves and branches. There are strict orders for me to not let her fall into the concrete lava—and the next block it's the hungry asphalt sharks. As the day begins to dim to yellow, the golden clouds lower and swim gracefully just below the sun in the upside-down ocean.

"I'm too tired to do this anymore. My legs hurt. Can we just stop?" Her pink sneakers touch and skim the asphalt.

"Are you coming to my gymnastics recital?" The hopeless optimism in her tone makes me choke on an excuse, but her tongue is already fluttering through the gap in her lips between my reciting of, "I have to work again, sweetheart," and "I promise I'll be at the next one." I flick her kickstand down with my toes.

"Want to show me one of your moves?" She swings her leg over the seat and hops onto the curb with one foot, beginning a pirouette of sorts. She tiptoes out of my focus as I gaze upward at the lonesome, now microscopic dot. The vultures must have grown bored with them and veered off. When a figure gets that high, it could be anything. A plane. A star. The little dot remains still in a cloud, like a single black seed in a clump of cotton. My gaze is disrupted by the giddiness of her voice.

"I did it! I made it all the way. Did you see?"

"Of course I did!" I lift her up from the armpits and hurl her into the air a couple inches. I pretend to be a thunderous crowd cheering her name in unison. *Anastasia!* Emphasizing each syllable.

"Are they going to put more blood in my arm next time I go to the doctors?"

My thumb caresses her knuckle. "I don't know," I tell her. "But it makes you stronger."

"I hate doing it. I don't want to do it anymore." I pull her head into my stomach.

"I know. We're going to go back next week one more time for a little surgery, so you won't have to do that anymore." I'm quick to assure her it won't hurt.

"So I won't go up into the sky?" I kiss the top of her helmet before looking up again. The dot has vanished. Drifted out into the deep sea.

Just two blocks from her mother's, we pass by the Turner's house. The baby blue Dutch colonial with banana-yellow window shutters always makes me crave something sweet. It's not until we are right in front of the house that I hear the stifled sound of a hollering voice, as if someone is screaming underwater. Inside the house, through their living room window, I can see their two rottweilers jumping from the couch, barking madly at something on their ceiling. I grip Ana's hands tight again.

"Ana, can you pedal faster for Daddy?"

Kathleen Turner's husband Patrick's head emerges first from the over-sized chimney flue. Then his torso. He winces in pain as his hips emerge.

"Come on, Ana!" Her head twists halfway towards the house before I redirect it forward. I double our pace. "Keep pedaling!"

I can hear Kathleen's scream for help as her husband clings to the telephone wire. A few crows occupying the wire lose their balance as he pulls on it. Their caws sound cantankerous, probably asking one another why he's trying so damn hard. They stab at his fingers with their beaks. His feet flap up and down. Kathleen calls my name, and it feels like a hand clutching my back shoulder. Digging its nails through the flesh, pulling downward. I clench my eyes and hold, feeling the tug in my forehead skin. His flailing body mimics a fish out of water, gradually untucking his polo shirt that reveals his bearded belly. He'll lose stamina soon. Everything he cries out ends with a squeal. It was all the same thing, on and on about how it isn't fair. Ana's head begins to turn.

"Look ahead, Ana!"

"Please don't let go."

Her legs find a rhythm, slowly gaining speed until I resort to a light jog to keep up with her. Her body forms into a right angle. There's no bend in her arms. We reach the part of the road on a subtle decline. She exhales. Twice per second.

"I can't do it."

"Yes, you can, Ana. Keep going!"

She pedals fast enough to hear the whirring sound of the tires against the road. It's just my fingertips grazing her sundress that sticks to the dampness of her back. I can't keep up with her speed. Suddenly, her back separates from my hands. The bike remains balanced.

"I'm doing it!"

I don't see her pedaling on two wheels for the first time.

"Help me, Daddy!"

I don't see her veer right towards the curb and fly over the handlebars onto the grassy part of the sidewalk. My eyes are fixated behind me on the telephone wire. The crows have blood on their beaks.

TV anchors exchange reasonings between cleared throats and stroked ties, every channel the same—even the ones that normally have SpongeBob. All headlines read: "Thousands Ascend." Clusters in every state. The footage is choppy. Blurred. My phone rings. It's Ana's mother. I skip the salutations.

"Are you watching the news, Lillian?" I ask. She demands an explanation about why Ana has cuts and bruises on her arm before getting into my not making it to Ana's gymnastics show.

"Working more and staring at the news all day are not reasonable coping mechanisms to deal with Ana's illness."

I choose silence as a reply. It's what I do when I know she's right. I can feel her pointer finger jabbing at me through the phone.

"You're becoming an absentee father. She's forgiving now. She's too innocent to know what's going on with you. But if she gets older..."

Blood rushes to my face and I feel it in the follicles of my hair when she uses the word "if." I swallow my irate response to diffuse a futile argument before it begins. I speak just above a whisper.

"She had a headache again, Lillian. Worse than last time." We let the silence talk for us. My forehead touches the TV screen. Staticky fuzz tickles my nose. "It happened to Patrick. Kathleen's Patrick. Right from his chimney. And Terry called from her Florida house. Said Henry went up right from their sofa through the window."

She's somewhat affable. Too exhausted to get into another bout.

"There may not be many more of these moments left," she says.

"You have to start being there for her."

Her voice fades from my focus. My eyes are back on the choppy footage. I chew on Nicorette while I stand, slightly rocking my hips. My knuckles brush against my lips like I'm playing a soundless harmonica.

News outlets and major networks always celebrate the famous actors, rock stars, and Nobel Prize winners who "ascend." Sometimes they'll get a prime-time TV tribute commemorating their legacy. Springsteen's *Born to Run* album sells out worldwide. Gerhard Richter paintings quadruple in value. In small town USA, local papers list the hometown heroes and longtime residents in the obituary sections. I find Patrick Turner's name with a short blurb about his volunteer work in town and his recent battle with cancer. I scour other local newspapers, combing through the lists of those who ascended. There were only a few in the surrounding towns: an older couple who ascended simultaneously and a little boy just a couple years older than Ana. I attend their funerals to find out more. I listen keenly when the little boy's father speaks. His diaphragm contracts when he cries, struggling to talk about his son, his "beautiful, healthy, happy son."

I rush to buy plywood at the hardware store. Mel the owner provides unsolicited insistence that I am wasting my time. "You're about the tenth one today stockin' up on this stuff." He brings a tin can to his lips and spits into it. Some of it gets caught in his beard. "Y'know my cousin tried cementing himself to his driveway when he knew. Damn idiot's torso split from his hips. He interlocks his fingers, then separates them. "Right in half, the son'v a bitch."

After I finish boarding up the opening in the fireplace, I get to work on all the windows. My muscles tauten from the hammering and fastening. It's only once the house is deprived of all natural light that I call Lillian and tell her to do the same. Her sigh sounds like static through the phone.

"Stop acting like you can control everything. Ana has a round of chemo this week. She's been getting paranoid. She asked me to tie her to the bed so she doesn't ascend in her sleep."

"I can come by and see her."

"You need to get your shit together and set an example."

My lips move but the words are mute. By the time I get them out, she's already hung up.

On Labor Day weekend, the President is on TV. Every channel the same red tie and blue curtained background. He speaks in succinct phrases, sounding unintentional and nearly speaking in haiku. Lacking his typical visage of optimism, he explains that the "Air Force has detected more 'anomalies' than usual in the past month." He declares it unsafe to go outside for extended periods. My several calls to Lillian go unanswered, my texts unread, voicemails unheard. I pace around my kitchen table. After each lap around, I go the opposite way. I change my course and crack the front door. My head wedges through the gap. I squint against the brightness that causes a tenderness in my eyebrows. Before things come into focus, my pocket vibrates, and I read the text from Lillian.

"Going to pool with Ana. Promised her. It'll be good for her to get out."

"Is it really the best idea after her chemo?" I reply.

"She's been talking all week about jumping from the diving board."

"It's not safe outside, Lillian. You should keep her home."

"It would mean a lot to her if you came."

Denial hides behind the good timing of red, white, and blue holidays, cold beer, and fireworks. At the dawn of summer, parents let their kids run wild around the community pool like dogs off-leash. Mosquitoes have a field day, preying on the slow reflexes of the already tipsy who smuggled wine and hard seltzers in their pool bags. I find Ana basted in sunscreen. Lillian's fingers rub counterclockwise from her feet to her nose until her bronzed skin is visible again. I tell Ana, "One jump, then right back home. No arguing."

I avoid the scowl from Lillian and eye contact with other parents. I overhear their conversations about local restaurants, workout routines, and soccer schedules. I examine the pale line around her biceps when Lillian yanks the floaties off. "She wantes to jump without them," she tells me as Ana rushes towards the diving boards. The water stops at my belly button. I nervously caress the patch on my arm, hoping it doesn't loosen when I clap and cheer. She'll hold me to my promises of snow cones, screwballs, or the popsicle shaped like Super Mario after she jumps and swims to me. A girl in her class dressed in a neon one-piece swimsuit I could spot from the stratosphere stands beside her on the other diving board. Her name eludes me. It is something generic. Three syllables, ending in A. She clenches the shoulders on her crossed arms. The baby blue lenses of her goggles dangle from the broken strap in her hand. Her popsicle-purple lips quiver as they wait for the lifeguard's thumbs up. Both girls are an inch taller from standing on their toes. Their buckling legs go stiff at the sound of the lifeguard's whistle, which is their cue to jump. Blood rushes to their feet, making their toes go red. They count down from three. Three seconds between each second. Ana is one of those pinched-nose jumpers, squeezing it just before she gets ready to rush forward. Four little feet scurry, their toes silent on the board. So many steps, such little ground covered. The end of the board doesn't start to wobble until they're both halfway. Four little heels press down; the edges of both boards give. Two sets of little heels spring upward but only one splashes below. Hundreds of heads tilt skyward. We all stare, even against the sun. It's treated as a spectacle at first. It always is when you see it happen in real-time. Nobody hears the typical panicked calls for help expected of most children at several hundred feet. Our necks stubbornly steady, no one wavers at the baby blue lensed goggles falling and plummeting onto the pavement. Hushed whispers turn into gasps turn into crying women. I wonder where the girl's mother is. If she's looking, too. In a moment, fighting for resonance in the airspace are the howl of sirens, blowing whistles, and the names of every child from their mother's cries. Forcing my gaze away from the sky, Ana crashes into my torso and gasps for air.

"I did it, Daddy! Did you see? No swimmies!" One arm tucks under her butt, the other runs up her back. My hand cradles her head into my chest.

"You're such a big girl." Something brittle entwines around my fingers and tickles the webbing between them. In my palm: a loose chunk of her hair. I panic and plunge my hand into the water and make it disappear, then place it back against the back of her head. It twines around my fingers again—more this time, enough to fill my palm.

Nobody finds any pattern. It happens more frequently across the world. Reports of ascensions come in every day from San Antonio to Johannesburg. The increased frequency keeps people panicked inside their homes. Weeks go by. I resort to desperate attempts, combing through Reddit threads and they-sayer Facebook groups. Gypsies and psychics lead me on and tell me it happened to non-believers this time; they go on about the retrograde of one of the planets. The only people who leave their homes are the Bible readers who gather in circles in open fields and point at the sky and shout that this was inevitable. Down south where school begins earlier, some districts lose more than a quarter of their staff. A few days ago, a whole playground of kids ascended. They continued playing tag in the air. The recess teachers say they could hear them giggling and laughing past a thousand feet. Sometimes my neighbors and I make eye contact, hoping one of us makes a gratuitous comment like how hot it is for late September.

When I have Ana for the weekends I hide her medicine in applesauce. Every Saturday it's Neapolitan ice cream and she guesses which of the three flavors it's in. I find her falling hair everywhere. It clogs the drain in the shower and fills the dustbin of the vacuum. When she finds it in her cereal or in a forkful of dinner, I'm never quick enough to crack a joke before she cries. During the week, I shatter all the mirrors in the house and dispose of the glass. I spend hundreds on whacky hats and wigs. We play make-believe, each day a different theme. Swashbuckling pirate charades, spaghetti western imitations.

Some days we dress up as rockstars and use household appliances as fake instruments. When we run out of fresh ideas, we repeat with different roles.

Fall bleeds into Winter. Daylight is short, the days are long. We'd have to earn the Spring. The perishable foods go quickly. Chinese food and pizza delivery become a delicacy—a hundred dollars or more for an order given the fear of ascension during pick-up. After an hour long wait for pizza, the manager calls me. His tone laced more with annoyance than remorse.

"He's not making it, pal. My third one gone up this damn month."

Even for takeout, her appetite begins to dwindle—and with it her weight. On Christmas Eve, we ditch the Seven Fishes for seven different types of leftover Halloween candy. By February, we get creative with the canned stuff. Corn and Ravioli Tuesdays. Tuna and Eggo Waffle Thursdays. Whatever it takes for her to eat. The heat goes on once a weekend, but we make good use of quilts. When we aren't bundled up, we make them into couch forts. On Valentine's Day, she puts on her ballet gown and we say our vows to a crowd of stuffed animals and Barbies and Ken dolls. It's the little wackiness that keeps us sane.

The Spring part of March brought a blizzard overnight that she begs to play in. I zip her up to the chin in nylon. The only visible flesh is her rashy, red cheeks that are cold on my kissing lips.

Her bubblegum pink coat juxtaposes the infinite white in front of us. I squeeze her arm until I feel bone. We advance forward in unison. Jubilantly, Ana lunges forward. Her feet gallop in place with excitement, boots scraping the garage floor. My feet pivot as I try to maintain control of her. "Hold on, Ana!"

Her arm gets free of my grip. I swipe for her hood, but she's long out of reach as she begins twirling counterclockwise with her arms out, like a spinning, pink lowercase "t" trying to catch every flake on her tongue before they touch the ground.

"Watch me!" All I look at is the sporadic trail of six-inch boot prints in the snow surrounding her like a prayer coming to fruition.

We walk to the hill at the school a couple blocks away, dragging the sled in tow. Front lawn snowmen wave with their twig hands and their charcoal smiles. She names them all "Mr. Marshmallow." When we reach the top, we fall backward butt-first, then recline heavy on the ground. There's a lisping *sorry* or *oopsie* each time her hands collide with mine as we flutter our arms and our legs kick in and out. The rustling rhythm of nylon on snow hinders. Her arms stop flapping first.

"I'm tired. I need a break."

We let ourselves feel the pull of gravity while I tell a joke. "What do you call a snowman in the spring?"

She smiles with teeth. "What?"

I let suspense build. "A puddle." She laughs like her mother. For every four cackles, she snorts, causing her laughter to intensify until it becomes a coughing spree. "You're okay," I repeat, pulling her into my shoulder. Her hacking pulses against my collarbone. When she catches her breath, the excitement returns to her face. She breaks away from my arms and rushes towards her sled.

"Watch how fast, Daddy!"

She plops onto the sled, and I give her a countdown.

"Three!"

She shimmies her body.

"Two!"

My gaze finds my coat sleeve. That's where it stays, fixated on the constellation of blood-splattered dots around it. Some are a darker red than others. Merlot. Some are bigger than others. Dime sized.

"One!"

All I see is red juxtaposing the infinite white around us.

Lillian and I take shifts at her side, quickly running out of ideas and bribes to force food into her mouth. When the iPad runs out of battery, we exhaust her on Aesop's Fables and Roald Dahl. The weight drains from her face first. The bones on her torso push against the surface of her skin. We aren't necessarily spiritual, but whenever the doctors and nurses come in to check on her our fingers interlock against the brims of our noses. My fingers slide across her forehead. Her jaw sags. Her skin is pasty white. Her raspy breaths are periodical, several seconds between each intake. When she wakes, I tell her the nice doctors need to help get some bad things out of her body.

"You're gonna go night-night for a little, then wake up feeling okay. Mommy is going to be right beside you."

Her face constricts, trying its best to salvage a grin. My hand grazes the outline of her ankle beneath the bed sheets. I tickle her feet but don't get the giggle-smile I wish for.

I hear the humming of the vending machine as I slip in and out of sleep inside the waiting room. I get a text from Lillian.

"She's in surgery."

"She's so brave. She's lucky to have you as her mother."

She types a response for a while. I stare eagerly at the three little dots inside the little bubble for several seconds. It suddenly disappears.

When I come to again, I wander out of the hospital. Outside, the break in the weather has turned the snow into steam. The day hasn't thawed yet. Night brought rain, so puddles blend with the concrete of the hospital parking lot to form what my father used to call "concrete mirrors." I plot my move to avoid the sprawling puddle surrounding my car. For a moment, I pretend there are asphalt sharks inside it. Unsure why, I hold my breath before my leaping step over it, then yank the passenger handle. I fumble inside the glovebox and pluck a cigarette and lighter from beneath the rubble. It flutters, then stiffens in the wedge of my lips as I light the tip. My head tilts upward, then it lolls until I feel the bend in my neck. My eyes close as I drag, open as I exhale. High above, two vultures soar clockwise, and I don't realize how far I've followed them until I stumble and notice I've drifted deep into the empty part of the parking lot. I'm on the tips of my toes, standing on a giant puddle. Instinctively backpedaling from panic, I wait for the water to splash against my legs. I take the tension off my Achilles, feeling the weight press against my heels and ankle. There is no ripple, no wrinkle in my inverted reflection. I stomp lightly. Then heavily. The puddle remains still. A text comes through my phone. I see a few missed calls from Lillian before I see her message. When I read it, I feel as if the water and blood have drained from my body.

"She's back in the room resting. I'm with her. She's going to be okay. Please come back up."

The roof of a Nissan Altima passes beneath my ankles. I ascend above streetlights. I hear the brief calling of sparrows in the trees as I float beside their nests. I look through the hospital windows until I find Ana's room. She's awake. Lillian sits beside her bed caressing her head as she checks her phone. I wonder if she tells Ana I'll be up any minute now. Soon, Ana will be a small dot. Once I'm above the roof of the hospital, I can see the whole neighborhood, the sloaping surfaces of roofs, and the swimming pools like aqua-colored rectangles. Ana is big enough to measure in the pinch of my fingers. I feel the heat of the day begin to cool. The air loses density. The horizon is hazy and blurred. I see every neighborhood in town. The water tower and the school and the ballfields all shrinking from my view. The streets are grey tributaries intersecting and merging. I keep my eyes on the small dot in the window until it dissolves from my sight.

THE STRANGE AND THE FAMILIAR: A MARRIAGE OF TENSIONS

A Conversation with James Gianetti

Rachel Phillippo: Hello, James! Welcome to *Driftwood*! "Anastasia" is an emotional and memorable story. I look forward to learning more about it.

James Gianetti: Thank you! To have this story appear in *Driftwood* is an honor. A huge thank you to Dean Bakopoulos as well for judging the contest and selecting it.

RP: One of our favorite aspects of this story is the way in which you weave multiple threads of tension toward one common theme. The external story of the ascensions serves to inform the internal conflict of the protagonist, as well as steadily build the tension. When conceiving of this story, did one of these "threads" come first? Or did you know from the start how these pieces would work together?

JG: So I am very drawn to magical realism and surrealism in stories. That external story of the ascensions came first because that made the story unique and bizarre. It provided that foundation of something strange to stand on. Then I needed to marry that tension with something familiar and grounded in order for it to be interesting. I try to make sure a parity of sorts exists in my stories when blending conflicts of the surreal with ones that are more based in reality.

RP: You make good use of recurring motifs to tie these elements together. One of those motifs is the repetition of circular movement, either counter or clockwise. Can you speak on the significance of this element?

JG: Absolutely. The counterclockwise movements represent the irrationality of this world dominated by this global phenomena that is essentially unexplainable and unpredictable. Perhaps more implicitly, while these ascensions represent the randomness of death, the counterclockwise movements represent time we wish we hadn't lost or the wish that we could reverse time itself and cherish moments we took for granted. The clockwise movements of objects represent a forecasting of "normalcy" and rationality for our protagonist.

RP: Using counterclockwise movement is a really clever way of indicating irrationality. This theme of "randomness and death" is brought close and personal to our protagonist through the illness of his daughter. Childhood cancer is such a tender topic. You do a lovely job of describing the protagonist father's love and fears for his sick child. Were there any challenges in writing on such a fraught subject? How did you balance this to avoid melodrama?

JG: For sure. The challenge was, at least initially, how I was writing this without the empathy of being a parent. However, the birth of my niece helped shape a new approach and provided me a fresh outlook. When writing fiction that deals with a topic like childhood cancer, I make sure to honor those topics by treating them carefully and with respect. It's not a topic to handle lightly or gratuitously by any means. I have people very close to me affected by childhood cancer which served as an additional catalyst for writing this story. Doing further research on it to broaden my understanding was a challenge. I found myself caught up in emotions, you know, by learning more about treatment, side effects, and the road to remission. Knowing parents have to do this kind of research for their own children was often a sadness I had to persevere through.

It can be easy to dig yourself into a hole with overwriting and melodramatic description with a topic like this for sure. Especially when you layer the element of magical realism on top. And that's where that marriage of tensions came into play. It was important to fuse the tensions to elude a notion of them being binary. In fact, a codependency had to exist with them for it to feel real and believable. One kind of takes the pressure off the other and they share this spotlight of high stakes. Working with you, Rachel, helped me craft better dialogue that avoided coming off saccharine and helped me evade any unnecessary or exaggerated dramatics. Your feedback was invaluable and allowed for further dialogue to speak the actions of these characters.

RP: Thanks for that, James! It's been a pleasure to work with you to polish this story. I hope you are as pleased as I am with this "final" version (though I know a draft is rarely final). "Anastasia" opens in late summer and ends in the following springtime, covering quite a length of time for such a short piece. However, the movement does feel progressive (as the ascensions increase in frequency) and natural. I find that sometimes moving so quickly through a timeline can slacken the tension, but that is not the case in your story. How did you use the movement through time and seasons to your advantage when it comes to theme and tension?

JG: I try to include seasonal changes to accomplish a flow and reference for the reader. It's something I use to give them a sense of time and that progression of time to avoid any confusion or ambiguity. Whenever starting a new scene, I ask myself if incorporating some sort of nod to a time lapse is gratuitous or meaningful. It also gives the reader a sense of setting with a four season change within the story. I also like using seasonal changes because it can give the story some scale and make that world feel a little bit more expansive. It's always my goal to make a short story feel extensive while making sure the tension is airtight.

RP: Time—both the passage and the limitations of—is such an important element to this story. Another great strength of this story is the use of striking and memorable images. That of the people ascending as "lowercase t's" is an example. There is an almost photographic quality to your scenes. Do you find, in your writing, that the image comes first, or do the images arise as a side effect of the plot? Are you inspired by any visual art?

JG: Thank you. That means a lot. As I gravitate toward writing stories with magical realism or surrealism elements, I always make it a due diligence to lean into the fantastical nature of it with proper imagery. Typically, the images arise as a side effect of the plot. Well said, because that is exactly how my mind operates. I'll have a general concept such as the ascensions, right? But then I ask myself what makes it unique? Perhaps darkly humorous? Heartbreaking? Once I begin to answer those questions, I have a better shot at conveying that into photographic imagery. Importantly, since we have a story about a little girl, it must be playful with its description. It can't be too punishing or harsh because then there would be a dissonance in a sense. To be honest, as much as I love visual art, I am more inspired by other writers and stories. Whenever I am in a creative rut, I read as much as I can. I try to find stories I wish I wrote. Fiction from places like *Joyland* and *The Normal School* always serve as inspiration. Writers like Kelly Link, too.

RP: The structure and tone of this story is reminiscent of another of my magical realism favorites: "The Ceiling" by Kevin Brockmeier. Were you inspired by any other works of magical realism when writing "Anastasia?"

JG: "The Ceiling" is one of those stories I wish I had written! When writers can stick the landing with a metaphor that is as compelling as the conflict it symbolizes, that to me is magic. It's something I strive and reach for in my own stories and writing. I read another recently called "The Elephant" by Riley Kross which used a metaphor in a similar way. The story "Departure" by Amy DeBellis was a big inspiration for writing "Anastasia." She does a great job of capturing the mystery around these floating objects and the impact it has on the community.

RP: Your story, too, does a very effective job of using magical realism to reflect the conflict in reality. Your protagonist faces both fear and a palpable sense of powerlessness in the face of the inevitable threats of both the cancer and the ascension, yet the story ends on a note of hope that I think readers will find endearing and refreshing. Can you speak a little about the ending of "Anastasia"? Am I on the same page when I say I read the ending with a sense of hopefulness and peace that transcends the inevitable?

JG: For sure. I try to instill a theme or acts of redemption in my stories. It doesn't always have to be so punishing or remorseful for it to resonate. Initially, the ending was quite different, and I scrapped it because it lacked that redemptive quality I strive for when writing stories. It was clear when drafting the new ending, containing that feeling of hopefulness you referenced, that I realized the story couldn't have lived without it. Once it came together it really adhered nicely to the dynamic between parent and child. My hope is that it throws the readers for a loop yet also provides justification.

RP: How long have you been working on "Anastasia," and what does your revision process look like?

JG: I had worked on it for a few months prior to submitting it. I have gotten better at letting the story settle after the first draft. Since growing and maturing as a writer, I will let the story breathe. Almost always, new ideas and ways to improve it blossom in my head and I will go back and make alterations as needed. I always work with the great Rebecca Van Laer on any finished story. I am incredibly lucky to work with and learn from her. She and I go back and forth on what's working versus what needs further improvement. I don't send things out until I get her stamp of approval.

RP: What does the early stage of your writing look like? Do you find that you prepare with a lot of research? Listen to particular music while writing?

JG: Early stages often start with a singular idea, either a specific event or particular character. Then I begin brainstorming like crazy to see if the idea can blossom into something I think can work well with other literary components. You know, conflict, stakes, character transformations etc. At that point, in addition to reading other stories, every room I walk into, person I speak to, lyrics I hear, just about everything I do, I begin to dissect things I think could potentially serve the story well. I try to find plot points anywhere I can get them. The right side of my brain is constantly working. On a more, I guess micro-level, sentence-level, anything I visualize, hear, smell,

I ask myself what's the best way to describe that in a single sentence? What's the very best version or sentence that can capture what I'm seeing? Can that sentence exist in this new story and world? It could take weeks or months of brainstorming an idea to see if it can become a meaningful, impactful, and full-fledged story that is worth writing and most importantly, worth telling. With this story, the idea of the ascensions was first and foremost. Then the conflict that could exist in this world dominated by unpredictability and surrealism. Then the characters. Sometimes, it's the reverse. Once the idea is set in stone and I have a fairly clear idea about sequencing scenes, I do extensive research. My Google searches are often very bizarre. But every sentence needs to have the proper research behind it whether it's a major plot point or something minor. I listen to alternative and heartland rock to further inspire me when writing a story. Bands like *The National, Lord Huron, The Killers, Springsteen, & The Lumineers* always deliver.

RP: Now a more personal note: If you found yourself in the story "Anastasia," experiencing the ascensions, into what camp would you fall? Doomsday preparer? Sidewalk preacher? Or more of a go-about-your-life approach, like Anastasia's mother?

JG: Oh man, I would probably not fare well in that story and world. I would probably lean more on the side of doomsday preparer. I'd likely never let go of my loved ones. Like the protagonist, I'd be the person going to extremes to try and find the patterns and justification in a world overcome by the unexplainable and mystifying phenomena. I'd be a wreck.

RP: I think that very instinct is what makes your protagonist so compelling. Your sense of place, too, is interesting in "Anastasia." While it is specific and crisp in detail, it is also vague in that it feels as though it could be just about anywhere in America, relatable to many readers. This works well to bring the reader more intimately close to the phenomenon of the ascensions. Do you most often find that you write from an unnamed "place"? Or do your settings vary greatly depending upon the unique conflicts of each story?

JG: That was exactly my intent. Yes, I almost always write stories with settings that are familiar yet ultimately lacking specificity. They have the tendency to walk, talk, and look like a specific area or state yet remain intentionally unspecified. My goal is to always widen the embrace. I don't want to alienate readers with a specific sense of place. Instead, why not let them make their own conclusions about where the setting is. Giving the reader some degree of agency and allowing their own interpretations is always something I am mindful of.

RP: We've spoken quite a bit about your interest in magical realism. Do you work pretty much exclusively in this genre? What other projects do you have in the works?

JG: Yes, I do. Unintentionally at first, you know, when I first started writing stories, I was always writing with the primary goal of "write something you would want to read." After writing a handful, the common thread in all of them was the element of magical realism. Having grown as a writer, I realized those are the kinds of stories I want to tell. Those are the stories I love to read. Moving forward, you know, who knows if I'll deviate from that and start writing more grounded stories. Life has a way of altering perspectives and maybe even preference in genre and style. Time will tell. At the moment, I have a novel that's demanded my attention for some time. I continue having affairs on it with short stories because I love writing them. Short fiction gives me more at-bats and allows me to write plots, circumstances, and characters I couldn't otherwise flesh out in a novel. Additionally, I am working on putting together a short story collection.

RP: Will the short story collection follow any sort of theme, aside from a vein of magical realism, that is? More ends-of-the-world, or a motif of floating, for example?

JP: There's another story that is a kind of first cousin to "Anastasia." Aside from the element of magical realism, for the most part, each story will explore a theme of childhood and parenthood. For better or worse, at the center of each of them is a relationship or tension between a child and their mother or father.

RP: I love the concept of a type of relationship as a connection between stories. Thank you for sharing "Anastasia," and for taking the time to discuss your craft! "Anastasia" is full of striking images and heartfelt emotion. I am happy to see it join *Driftwood*. I look forward to seeing your future work in print!

JP: Thank you so much for the kind words and dedication to this process. It is much appreciated.

CREATURE HABIT

Raphael Stigliano

Bridgette wants to spend more time as a stoat. She tells me from behind the wheel of the Volvo, idling outside baggage claim, wearing the same dress as the night I fell in love with her.

"Can we talk about this in the morning?" My nose is packed with St. Louis pollen. It powders my jacket, suitcase, and eyebrows. I sneezed through three days of a conference and a five-hour plane ride.

"It can't wait. I'm living a lie. Every night I practiced what I was going to say in the mirror, like a preteen. Me! Can you imagine?"

Her laughter is the same exact frequency as the hum of the airplane engine. I notice she's not wearing shoes. No force on earth can argue with *I'm living a lie*, but a bearded sage in a neon vest is waving our car out of the loading zone, so I have to wait until we're on the freeway to hear exactly how.

"It doesn't feel right anymore, to be inside my own skin," she begins.

"That probably means you need to stop." I left a pamphlet in the glovebox for a group called *Animals Anonymous*. If she's seen it, she hasn't said anything.

Nor would she. She's shaking her head now with gradually curbing passion. "Do you even hear me? You're miles away, Toms. When did it get this bad?"

I want to laugh, but tears spring to my eyes instead. Or maybe the issue is with my sinuses. "This is what I've been saying. For weeks. Will you take a break? Please?"

"That's not it," she insists. And then she takes her eyes off the road to really look at me, for the first time since I got in the car—maybe the first time in months. "I want you to do it with me."

★

Bridgette might have been satisfied with her own skin if not for her pen pal, an internet resident called *tapir_man420*, who maintained a blog from his pet cat's point of view.

"He's an old, old friend," she promised. "Who totally respects our relationship. He would never do anything." She puts the emphasis on *do*, as though this is a person with physical presence in our lives, not a series of instant messages. What, exactly, could he do?

What he would do is send her a digital coupon to something called *life exchange*, all lowercase, with a GPS address bordering the Humboldt-Toiyabe National Forest. "I've read about these places," I told her. "There are senators fighting them. Well, state senators."

"Is that so."

I assessed the coupon over her shoulder. "Jesus. That's the discounted price?"

She marked the email *unread* and locked her phone. "Looks like."

A few days after that we made the three-hour drive from Fallon. Bridgette was nonverbal and manic in turns. She stared out the window until a new mountain would swell on the horizon and release a rush of thoughts. "Gertrude said things didn't smell right for days after. But also that it changed her life. Do you think I'll be scared? What if I accidentally wander outside the reserve? Do you think I shouldn't go?"

"Who's Gertrude?"

"She answers the phones."

She leaned her head against the window and powered down. "There's still time to change your mind," was all I could think of to say.

The building was a sleek, alien whitehead against the looming tree line. I parked outside and gave Bridgette a kiss. "You'll be here when I come back?" she asked.

"Always," I promised, and then she was gone.

That night, on the other side of fear, we scrolled through photos of shrews online. "That one!" she sang, her fingernails digging into my chest. "That's the exact one. You think that life is so small. Scaled down. You can't imagine how *big* it is to be that small."

I zoomed in on what looked like a furred, inert yam. While Bridgette burrowed through pine needles, I had spent the afternoon answering client emails from a Denny's just north of the park. They had wi-fi and all the black coffee I could drink. "Vagrant shrews feed mainly on earthworms and other small invertebrates," I read. "Is this just an excuse to try out a new diet?"

Her pupils had been dilated huge since I picked her up. That was one of the side effects. "I'm not saying I ate a worm," she admitted. "But if I did, it wasn't as bad as you'd think."

After the third visit, I bought her a membership. I pretended it was to save money, since her new hobby had already burned through most of our date night budget for the year. But it probably had more to do with the silver bracelet—an anniversary gift—sitting untouched on her nightstand.

The next months blurred together. I dropped her at the gate every other Wednesday and picked her up the next morning. Over pancakes I asked: *What were you this time? Did you learn anything? How does it work, anyway?*

"They have this machine. Like a big laser?" She chased a bite of breakfast sausage around her plate. "The science isn't really the point."

I watched her corner the sausage and pounce. "They should put cameras inside the reserve. Then people could watch a livestream of whatever it is you get up to in there."

Still chewing, she laughed. "Please. You'd be so totally bored."

That winter, a different *life exchange* location made headlines when a customer froze to death as a snowshoe hare. A responding lawsuit failed; their waivers were ironclad. But the Surgeon General issued a warning, and bright red signs popped up outside the building. I asked Bridgette if it made her concerned. "How could you freeze to death as an animal evolved to live in snow?" she asked. "Sounds like poor decisions were made."

One day in February she waited outside the complex with a young woman I'd never seen before. "I was a dung beetle today!" Bridgette exclaimed, her eyes lighting up. "That's how I met Amelie. She saved up for two years to move here from France, to be a part of *life exchange*. Amelie, this is my husband."

I smiled politely. "Were you a dung beetle, too?"

Amelie wore leather boots, a black corset, and mascara as thick as war paint. Instead of shaking my hand, she leaned in to kiss it. "No," she whispered through a heavy accent. "Today, I am a millipede."

While Bridgette made a nest of her comforter that night, I asked her if people ever had intercourse while they were in the reserve. "Oh, I'm sure. It's a very popular date night. Why—are you thinking what I'm thinking?"

I shrugged. She traced a shivery finger across my chest. "Did you know that swallows mate in flight?"

Bridgette wasn't the only one making friends. Within a few months, the entire staff of Denny's knew my name, the details of my job, and how I liked my eggs. An honor guard of six, they covered every stage of life from pubescent to geriatric, each one happier to greet me than a childhood friend. Denny's was open twenty-four hours, but it was the same six people whenever I went. I wondered if they were allowed to go home.

In March a young man approached my booth. "Nobody your age comes to Denny's this often by choice. Let me guess. You're an emotional support human, too?"

David's parents had been coming to *life exchange* since it opened. After a car accident, his mother was paralyzed from the waist down. There was some surgery that was supposed to help, but insurance wouldn't cover it. Now she used a wheelchair. But in *life exchange*, David's mother could fly.

"My dad says every visit is like the first dance all over again," he told me. "Isn't that sweet?"

They were always chickadees. They'd even built a nest in a tree in one corner of the reserve. I asked David if he had ever gotten a tour. "I did the animal thing a few times," he said. "But money is tight. And anyway, I like to give them their privacy. You?"

"I'm scared of what it will do to me." Lately Bridgette couldn't sleep without the windows open. She never wore shoes out of the house. When I could get her to sit down to watch a show, she'd spend the entire episode tearing magazine pages into tiny squares and digging around in the pile. And while I'd never witnessed it, she'd definitely been chewing the bed frame. "Bridgette would never understand," I told David. "But I just *like* being a person."

We met up a few more times after that. We'd share a plate of mozzarella sticks and a few cups of coffee, and he'd tell me what he learned online from support human forums. But a month later, I got a text from him that his mother had had a stroke. *She can't get out of bed. Thought we'd get her out there one last time, but everything is happening fast.*

That's terrible, I texted back. Imagine learning to fly, only to be dragged back down to earth. *Let me know if there's anything I can do.* I never saw him again. It was sad, at first, to go back to sitting at Denny's alone. Then I took on more clients—to pay for an upgrade on

Bridgette's membership—and soon I was so busy I didn't feel lonely at all.

When the St. Louis conference came around, Bridgette mentioned that she would head back to Amelie's apartment after dropping me off at the airport. I interrupted an inventory of toiletries to blurt: "You're friends in real life, too?"

She huffed through her nose, the way a horse does. "Please. It's realer in the reserve than out here."

"Human friends, then. Sorry." I aborted the inventory. One could never remember every toothbrush, deodorant, sunscreen, or shampoo. By giving up now, I could look forward to stopping at a CVS in St. Louis, to browse cool aisles of well-lit bottles in crisp plastic travel sizes.

"Are you going to *life exchange* while I'm gone?" I asked as casually as a person could.

"There's a climate protest thing. But we might go after that."

"Is that safe? I'm your emergency contact. If I'm not around—"

"Amelie's brother can pick us up. He's been a couple of times, so he gets it."

"Just don't stay inside too long, okay?"

She didn't reply. She would probably be a grouse the whole weekend. As I sat on the plane, she'd step into a blue paper gown, waiting for a machine the size of a room to power up around her; the hare; the bat; the kingfisher inside of her clawing to come out. What body would there be for me to miss?

Electric razor. That's what I was missing. "Or do," I added, unzipping the suitcase again. "You know. Just be my person when I come back again, okay?"

★

There is more paperwork than I expected. "That's just because it's your first time," Bridgette explains. All she had to do was scan her membership card and flash her driver's license. Most of it is legal waivers, in case a mountain lion gets into the omnivore reserve and eats me, or something. At the back of the packet, once I have initialed my humanity away, is a dense, three-page list of native fauna. I am expected to check one box, and circle one of the following options:

If my chosen animal is not available, please:

1. Substitute with the next available species

2. Return me to the lobby. (You will not be charged except for the non-refundable deposit.)

Bridgette watches me circle an option towards the top of the list. "Just a regular old squirrel, huh?"

"Douglas' squirrel," I correct her, and hand my credit card to Gertrude behind the desk.

★

Later, safely returned to my own skin, I cannot stop chirping. The whole drive home and into the evening, language falters between my neurons and my tongue and out comes another whistling *chirrup* or *piirk* or *pirree*! Bridgette nuzzles her forehead into my hand and laughs like a fighter jet. "You just need to rest," she promises. "This happens sometimes!" It has never happened to her.

It is just as well that I cannot speak. During our time in the reserve, Bridgette twitched and leapt between bark and moss-crusted boulders while I kept all four squirrel feet planted in dirt. Everything squirmed with dizzy life. The scent of rot and sickening freshness formed a sheer wall—did the world always smell like this? I could hardly look up without trees spinning like falling skyscrapers.

You're a squirrel, barked the human voice inside. *Act like one! Climb a tree or something!* But when I reached out with furred, black claws, the trunk tilted and threw me to the ground. Despondent, I curled between thorny roots and shut my eyes. *Imbecile*, the human voice burned. *Wait it out. It's only a few hours.*

Suddenly a furred warmth surrounded me. Bridgette's stoat body enclosed on all sides. My heartbeat slowed and then raced again with contradictions: *Please stay here with me! No, go have fun! Don't let me hold you back! Don't leave me alone!*

Bridgette nudged my head with hers. I opened my eyes to see a second stoat. Was that a person or a regular animal? What was expected of me? *I can't handle someone else right now!* I burrowed back under the leaves as Bridgette and the other stoat tussled and nipped at each other's ears. Amelie, I realized, with qualified relief.

The stoats detangled themselves. Amelie nudged an object forward. She had brought something shiny and brown. Both stoats watched with keen, black eyes as I inspected it.

An acorn. It smelled divine.

I stretched out my squirrel arms and wrapped them around it. *What the hell are you doing*, the human voice scolded. But the squirrel brain erupted in serotonin fireworks. *Yes! Yes! This feels good! An acorn!* I tried to tell Bridgette again and again, and she bobbed her neck in agreement.

It got better after that. I even made it a few inches up a tree, although it felt more like a few feet. The only true elation came when a sound like a foghorn announced it was time to return to the facility. Bridgette and Amelie tripped and scampered between fallen branches, pausing every few feet to wrestle in the brush. I marched ahead and thought about what I would say over pancakes: *I'm sorry I ruined this for you.* And: *At least I never have to do that again.*

But as it turned out, I couldn't say anything at all.

★

One moment I revisit, again and again: the acorn shell, at first cool, has warmed beneath my paws. I have been working them around the flaky, woody cap, picking at the place where it intersects with the glossy seed. If I can get the cap off, I could place it on my head like a little hat. That might make Amelie and Bridgette laugh. But as I pry at it with my tiny nails, I become certain they will sneer instead. *A hat? How human can you be?*

Round and round it goes. Put on the hat, don't put on the hat. And only minutes ago it was enough just to hold the acorn in my arms.

Mid-cycle the two stoats crash-land on top of me. They have been play-wrestling, hurling their fierce weight at each other like hiccupping children. Now the acorn is thrown from my grip and rolls into the leaves.

The stoats separate and circle each other, panting. Neither of them looks at me. Heavily I rise, to plod after the acorn, when Bridgette-stoat's hind leg kicks out. My acorn disappears into the leaves. Her eyes are oil-black; quick; unreadable as the night sky.

Then she pounces on Amelie. They tumble away into the dirt.

And in a calm, clear voice, neither squirrel nor human, I think:

This creature is not your friend.

★

My chicken piccata is cold; her rosé is warm.

"When did you decide?"

She thinks it over, like she wants to give me a really honest answer. "Last week. But I've been thinking about it for a long time."

The restaurant is *Le Diamant Orange*, the place we met, but instead of my favorite pink dress Bridgette is wearing a t-shirt and shapeless jeans. At least she put on shoes for the occasion. I know her feet inside must be twitching and squirming to get out.

A mutual friend set up our first date here years ago. Over appetizers, a younger, happier Bridgette decorated her fingertips with pitted olives and paraded them between wine glasses. "Here's the difference between us, okay? You walk like this. *Bum, bum, bum, bum.* And this is how I walk. *Leeleeleeleelee*!"

I remember laughing uneasily. "You'll stain the tablecloth."

She nibbled the olive from her middle finger and offered me the index. "Are you even trying to have a good time?"

I was. Even now, I am trying, although this evening can no longer be called anything but a breakup.

"It's not a *breakup*." Bridgette is uncomfortable with the word. Her last relationship enjoyed a *conscious uncoupling*, but this doesn't need to be so formal. "It's not that our relationship is over. Just that my time as a human is over. I will always love you, but I can't live like this." Her expression brightens suddenly. "If it helps, you can think of it like I'm dead."

"It doesn't."

Recently, an *Animals Anonymous* facilitator fell off the wagon and announced he was permanently becoming a possum. His final Instagram post went viral. Soon Amelie and Bridgette joined the movement. Their plan is to break out of the reserve. As foxes, they'll voyage west, pillaging picnics and backyard barbecues, stuffing their cheeks with all the wild cherry tomatoes they can stomach. But the ultimate goal is the ocean. One of their internet friends works at the San Francisco *life exchange*. If they can reach him, he'll help them choose their forever body.

"Don't tell me," I moaned. "*tapir_man420*?"

"It doesn't matter."

"This must have taken a long time to plan."

She blushes, flattered that I noticed. "You have no idea."

I stab a fork into my spaghetti and swirl. Bridgette watches it turn. "I didn't want to tell you this, but I found an article on Reddit the other day." I've been sitting on this one for a while, waiting until I'm out of other options. Besides stealing your data, all these *life exchange* locations are in bed with Congress. Their conservation efforts are a front for the real scheme: to gradually brainwash liberal voters straight out of their humanity. A sandpiper can't vote on abortion. Toads won't go to protests. Plus, there's non-inconsequential proof that they're illegally organ-farming their customers.

Bridgette just shrugs. "They can keep my data. That's all the stuff I'm trying to leave behind."

"You can't leave it behind. The planet is dying. Anything you can call wilderness shrinks by 5% every year."

"It'll kill me either way. May as well enjoy it while we've got it."

"Survival is way harder for animals." The pasta has tightened into a fist-sized lump. I continue to twist. "You can't just go to the supermarket."

"It isn't good because it's easy." She gestures to her body. "I could wade through another fifty years like this. Or I could trade it in for moss and sunsets and treetops."

"And getting eaten by hawks."

"Maybe," she says like she really means it. "And maybe not. But that sounds better than dying in front of a computer, one email at a time."

The fork slips and my pasta mountain collapses. Capers go rolling across the table. All I can see in her eyes anymore is the blank, animal gaze of survival. How long have I been crying?

She reaches across the table to take my hand. "I want you to know. You were the best part of being human."

★

I'm allergic to something in the carpet. Since it covers both the hotel and convention center, I'm once again sneezing through an annual work conference. Maybe it's something in the cleaning product; maybe I just wasn't cut out for this world.

We're packing up after our first presentation of the day when a woman approaches. I recognize her from the opening meet and greet. Earlier, at group trivia, she sat at our table, introduced herself as Devorah, and accidentally took a sip from my glass after we both ordered Negronis.

"Great presentation," she says now. "If you weren't our competition, I'd sign today."

"Thanks." I'm still feeling jittery from speaking in front of a crowd. Even with poor attendance, enough people filled Ballroom E to liquefy my intestines. "Did you have a question or something?"

"This isn't about work, actually," she admits. "I was wondering. One of the local guys recommended a noodle spot for lunch. I don't know if you're free, but would you want to join?"

It's been a long time since someone invited me out. Longer, still, since I sat opposite another human with the express purpose of conversation. I'd promised myself an hour alone with a stiff drink and a bottle of Zyrtec. But Devorah has a way of holding her mouth when she asks the question, a little less than a smile but somehow more, that suggests it wouldn't be so bad to let her get to know me.

Right then a fly, fat as a raisin, buzzes a line straight at her forehead. Devorah scowls and knocks it away. "Dammit. How do these things get in here?"

The fly spins corkscrews behind her head, as if to say: *leeleeleeleelee*!

I zip up the last bag and slide it onto the cart. "Thanks for the offer. But we have another showcase this afternoon. I should probably prepare."

It's my first time on the west coast. The air is different—softer, like the salt from the ocean can't stop bounding at the lightness of being air. "This time of year, it's usually pretty miserable," they told us when we landed. "But you're catching us on a good weekend. Check out the boardwalk if you've got a couple minutes. You won't regret it."

So I do. It's packed with as many people as the conference. They all seem to be yammering into headphones, dragging sticky screaming children past ice cream stands, counting down group photos. A fleet of bicycles zoom past, announced by a chorus of *brrring brrring brrring*! Everyone is bleached and tan and smells of sleek sweat and sunscreen.

Somehow I find myself holding a basket of French fries, sitting on the beach where waves wash away sound. Voices blur, punctuated by an occasional barking dog. If I unfocus my eyes, a few dozen crabs dance over the pebbles. Sea lions pile on the jetty like plump, smooth barnacles. There are fish out there, too, between the boats. It is not quiet. But it is quieter than among the people.

I don't hear her approach. But when I turn my head, there is a seagull.

"Hi," I whisper, not wishing to sound too eager. "It's been a while. Hope you're good."

She cocks her head to one side. The black seeds of her pupils track the fries in my lap.

"I miss you. I try not to. But it's hard. Every time I turn around, I think it's you."

The first month after Bridgette left was the worst. We hadn't concocted a cover story, so I gave people part of the truth: she had become so deeply unhappy with life that she left me and disappeared. I didn't bring up *life exchange*, because I didn't need to. If they knew her, they already assumed. And if they didn't, it was easier to pretend she had run away than explain that she found eating beetles and trash more appealing than staying with me.

So I can't blame her for eyeing my French fries. I dig into the basket and offer her one. She snaps it in her beak, then tosses her head back to gulp it down whole. An empty paper basket, identical to the one in my hands, rides the shoreline.

"I wanted to show you this. Maybe you know already." The article is bookmarked on my phone. I reread it three times on the plane. When they shut down *life exchange*, it wasn't because it was too dangerous, or unethical, or part of some big conspiracy. Turns out it's just massively expensive to turn people into animals. Who could have guessed?

"Right up until I saw this headline, I thought maybe there was still time to change your mind. Like you'd suddenly walk up to my door on regular human legs again. Or maybe I'd chase after you as, like, a raccoon, or a rat. Some version of me you'd like me better."

She tilts her head at my phone screen. It almost looks like she's reading the article.

"Anyway I'm glad I got to try it before it went away. Now it's one of those things, like Blockbuster or cocaine in Coca-Cola, that they're just going to have to believe us was real. Or someone will do something awful with the technology and we'll all be one step closer to species suicide. I guess I understand why you left." My voice breaks.

All she cares about is the fries. "You should have ordered your own." I give her another and eat one myself. "You look good."

As a city kid, I have never been this close to a seagull. So all of it is new: those sharp, intent eyes; the row of baby feathers along a beak tinted red like lipstick. One skinny knee carries a ball of scar tissue. Sand crusts the web between her toes. It's chilly, I realize suddenly. Maybe this time of year will turn out to be miserable after all.

"When they announced the next conference was here, I stayed up all night imagining what I'd do when I found you. Like take you home with me. Or say something dramatic like, *I never actually loved you—I just needed you.*"

Bridgette's interest wanders towards the sky. I'm boring her, just like the old days. She will wait until my French fries run out. Then her body will follow her mind, to soar on cloud gusts and dive through air and find some other French fries, somewhere, that have yet to run out. Does she even understand me? Human speech must lose its meaning after too long in feathers. But I hope that a few words are getting through.

"Mostly, I just want to ask if you're happy."

She shifts her weight from one leg to the other. She twitches her head sideways. She pumps her neck in and out and opens her beak to show off the impressive depth of her gullet.

Something like rain begins to spatter down around me. The French fries will get soggy; Bridgette will choke them down anyway.

If it is actually her. "That *is* you, right?" I ask.

Before she can give me a sign, a second seagull alights next to us. We balk, collectively, at the invasion of our privacy. I wonder how to shoo away the newcomer without frightening her, too. But now the secret is out. We are joined by a third, fourth, and fifth seagull. Soon there are more than a dozen, a mirage of grey wings and white feathers and yellow beaks and pink twig legs fumbling over rocks. There are not enough French fries to go around.

The birds crowd against each other, pressing forward to get at me and my basket. Just like that, I can no longer tell which one was her to begin with.

MAGIC LOST; PAPERWORK FOUND

A Conversation with Raphael Stigliano

James McNulty: Welcome to the pages of *Driftwood*, Raphael! "Creature Habit" is such an inventive, riveting short, and I'm excited to be publishing it!

Raphael Stigliano: Thanks so much, James. I'm excited for people to read it! I'm especially honored to have found a fit for it at *Driftwood*.

JM: I think the premise is a great place to begin, since this is very much a premise-forward piece. Can you talk to me about the origin of this idea?

RS: I can't always pinpoint exactly where a story comes from, but in this case it's actually easy to identify—although not somewhere I usually find inspiration. I started "Creature Habit" after reading a relationship advice forum where this woman's longtime boyfriend had just come out as a furry. She must have taken it well, because right away he invites her to a convention with his friends. And she just has a miserable time. She feels like an outsider. His behavior towards her changes completely, like he's a totally different person once he puts on this fur suit.

Her issue is never that she stops loving him, or wants him to stop going to these conventions. She just wants to never have to go *with* him. But she doesn't want to make him feel bad. He just bared this intimate, personal part of himself that he trusted her enough to share, and it feels like a rejection for her to turn it down.

From there it was an easy jump to the places in my own past relationships that deep differences come up. That's inevitable, right? Some of them you can share, and some of them you can only tolerate. It's hard to say: "I love and accept you, but this one part of you isn't for me." The characters in "Creature Habit," Toms and Bridgette, never quite figure it out.

More than anything, what stuck with me was the image of this poor woman, totally out of her comfort zone, trying desperately to keep cool and remain supportive, surrounded by hundreds of people dressed in full-body animal costumes. All I did was swap them for actual animals.

JM: Although the premise is grounded in absurdism, there's plenty of thematic material here that's grounded in reality. I'm thinking specifically about the political talk about halfway through the story, the idea of pacifying a voter set via new technology. Talk to me about which parts of "Creature Habit" have some basis in reality.

RS: Ironically for the subject matter, I was interested in telling a very human story—so the realest thing here to me is the relationship dynamics. The fantastical element exists to highlight problems between two people in love.

"Creature Habit" isn't a sci-fi story. I'm not interested in how it all works. At one point in the story I nearly break the fourth wall to say so. ("The science isn't really the point.") But it does introduce a very sci-fi element with the technology of *life exchange*. And like all the best episodes of *Black Mirror*, all it takes is a single sci-fi element to dramatically change how the whole world looks. A different story would have taken this further, writing new legislature about how to define murder between humans-turned-animals, watching rival companies create competition, and training CIA agents to perform covert operations as pit vipers. In the "Creature Habit" extended universe, all that stuff probably happens. It's just not what I'm looking at here.

But it's impossible to change that one variable and pretend that the world doesn't change along with it, especially because the ways in which this new technology affects the world also affect the characters. So those political questions were one way for me to say, "If this technology was real, how do people use and abuse it?"

There's another way in which this story has a weird basis in my reality. A friend who read a draft of this told me: "Only you could write a story about magically turning into animals that's about anxiety and doomed relationships instead of being a wish fulfillment fantasy." (I'm paraphrasing.) I grew up with *Animorphs*. My friends and I were those kids daydreaming about turning into animals. But growing up has meant that most of the things that seemed so magical as a kid have turned out to be quite dependent on money, time, and basic logistics. One of the questions behind this story is *how quickly does magic lose its magic*? And I think the answer is: as soon as we have to fill out paperwork to do it.

JM: Along similar lines, what do you make of the idea that content—art itself—is so often responsible for pacifying people?

RS: I think there's a line to be drawn between art and content. To me, art provokes. Wielded thoughtfully, it is a tool for expressing ideas impossible to express any other way. It is often the first mechanism for resisting oppression and communicating rebellion. Art should—and I *do* intend this sweeping generalization—make you think and feel.

But we're all about content now. It's the addicting stuff that keeps us scrolling for more. With content, success is measured quantitatively: how regularly an influencer can post social media, how efficiently AI can generate something good enough, and how big a library of original series a streaming service can produce. Netflix knows perfectly well that most of their users just want shows to have on in the background. To me, *content* sounds a lot like *filler*. The more of it, the better. (It also happens to be a heteronym for the feeling of peaceful satisfaction, which hints that the point isn't to ruffle any feathers.)

These definitions of art and content blur with commodification, since to be an artist you either need to make it your living or find a day job. And of course, the line is flexible. Content can be inspiring to the right person at the right time. And when an award-winning film becomes someone's comfort movie, it probably doesn't provoke any new feelings the 20th time they watch it—but it might pacify negative feelings on a particularly bad day. Those are both great things.

Maybe it's a very personal issue I'm finding here. Both my parents have lifelong careers as artists, so I spent a lot of time as a kid wondering what the point of art is, anyway. If the goal is to pacify, I guess I just don't think that's art.

JM: On a craft level, it's typically difficult to comment so directly on politics or contemporary issues, but you get away with it in a convincing way here. Why do you think that is? Does it have something to do with the premise being fairly removed from reality, so the veneer makes the political talk feel less heavy-handed?

RS: I'm flattered to hear that. I was afraid of this story coming across as heavy-handed. It's never particularly subtle when characters say things like *wilderness is disappearing* and accuse the government of brainwashing voters. But I do think it helps to keep the spotlight on the relationship and the magic. Those things only matter to the story as much as they matter to its characters.

It also helps that a lot of the political talk is being intentionally weaponized. I doubt any of Toms' diatribe at the restaurant is actually true. It's just easy talking points from internet echo chambers, that happen to support his attack on Bridgette. The characters themselves are actually surprisingly apolitical.

JM: How did you outline the plotting & character arc of this piece? Did the story go through multiple drafts?

RS: This is one of those rare stories that felt like it wrote itself, with little authorial involvement. It really only had a few drafts. The hardest thing to get right was the chronology. I liked beginning with this cold open in media res, but that necessitated a hefty expositional flashback. Once we're caught up to the present, things continue chronologically. Hopefully it's easy to track the timeline of the story.

But overall, most of the edits this story has needed have been to flesh out details of the world, not to tweak the narrative itself. David, the Denny's crew, and the snowshoe hare story, were all added for the sake of worldbuilding. I wanted to really emphasize how this world treats its humans, as well as its animals.

JM: My entire first read, I was hesitant to see how you'd end the piece—and was so pleasantly surprised to see you nail it with the seagulls scene. How did you land on this scene?

RS: Thank you! As soon as I figured that scene out, I knew it couldn't go any other way. The biggest thematic tool in play here is Toms' inability to move on. He and Bridgette didn't technically break up (according to her), but she's supposedly got a whole new life while he's stuck in the old one without her. There's been no real closure for him. And he's in a kind of surveillance state, too, because every time he sees an animal he thinks, *that one might be my ex*.

Which, naturally, led to a conversation with a seagull. I particularly liked the animal choice because seagulls are ambassadors between worlds. They live on sea, land, and air. They fly, so they must be a metaphor for freedom, but also they're assholes? Beach pigeons that eat trash and shit everywhere and harass tourists and always have a missing eye or foot or something. And they have this fucked up relationship with humans. They're native to the animal kingdom, but we've trained them on new food sources. When I see a seagull divebomb someone at the beach for their fries, l have to think, well, we came into their house and taught them to do that. They have no sense of ownership. They don't care if I paid $8.99 for just that little thing of fries. They have a foot in both worlds and they don't care about human rules. Kinda like Bridgette.

There's another image that felt like it really belonged in this story. I live in San Diego, and in La Jolla Cove I saw a sea lion pup tangled up in a fishing net. Clearly in pain, clearly unable to disentangle the thing, but just going about its life because it didn't have any other choice. We called Sea World, who has a local animal rescue service, and they said they would send someone out to help.

In "Creature Habit," Bridgette wants to live and die by nature, before humans destroy it all. But there's a different, unwritten ending to this story somewhere in my imagination, in which the last moment with the seagull is replaced by Tom's looking at this tangled up sea lion and wondering if that's her. Even after she escapes to nature, the human world still ties her up. It felt too heavy-handed, but it also just felt *too heavy*. A seagull was a lighter, more comedic take on a similar concept.

JM: Who are some of your favorite writers? Which ones inspired "Creature Habit"?

RS: I was reading a lot of George Saunders when I wrote this. Also a lot of Denis Johnson and Lorrie Moore, but I think they're less on the page here than Saunders. He perfected this blend of comic surrealism that takes wacky concepts and tells these deadpan, sometimes deeply troubling stories.

I love Shirley Jackson. My proudest moment as a writer was when I lent a high school friend my Shirley Jackson collection on the bus, and she said, "I didn't really like it. But it really reminded me of your writing."

JM: Do other mediums influence you at all?

RS: Absolutely. Both in terms of intake and output. I mentioned *Black Mirror* already, which is more of a structural model here than a tonal one. And of course, there's that other story about a doomed relationship ending in permanent animalification. Though I'm not sure exactly what, Yorgos Lanthimos' *The Lobster* must have had something to do with this.

It's also important to me as an artist to produce work across multiple genres. Growing up with two artist parents, making visual art has always been second nature. I spend a lot of time drawing. I also do a lot of theater. I direct, act, and write. It's always helped me to be able to look at storytelling through different media, because that creates multiple pathways to iterate on the same ideas and themes with wildly different results.

My fiancée recently pitched that we adapt "Creature Habit" as a play, which I think is a cool idea. It would certainly give us a chance to expand the world. And I bet there'd be puppets. We love puppets.

JM: What are you working on now?

RS: I'm taking a stab at writing a horror story right now. I love the genre, but I've never felt like I had something new to add. So I'm trying it on, but I'm not sure it'll go anywhere. I think my love for horror might be more effective as a tool for cross-genre work than for explicitly writing horror itself.

I'm also mid-production on a tabletop storytelling game, *Murder*

Gently, which I co-created with a dear friend & writing partner. Over the course of two hours, you and your friends create an Agatha-Christie-style murder mystery entirely from scratch. Since it's entirely sourced from your imagination, the game is infinitely replayable—I've played probably about forty times over several years and never had even close to the same story twice. It's honestly one of my proudest creations, and getting to watch people gasp and laugh out loud every time they play it will never get old. At some point soon we'll be crowdfunding, so if you want to learn more please check us out at murdergently.com.

JM: Any parting words to leave with our readers—either about "Creature Habit" or writing in general?

RS: Would you try out *life exchange*? What animal would you want to be?

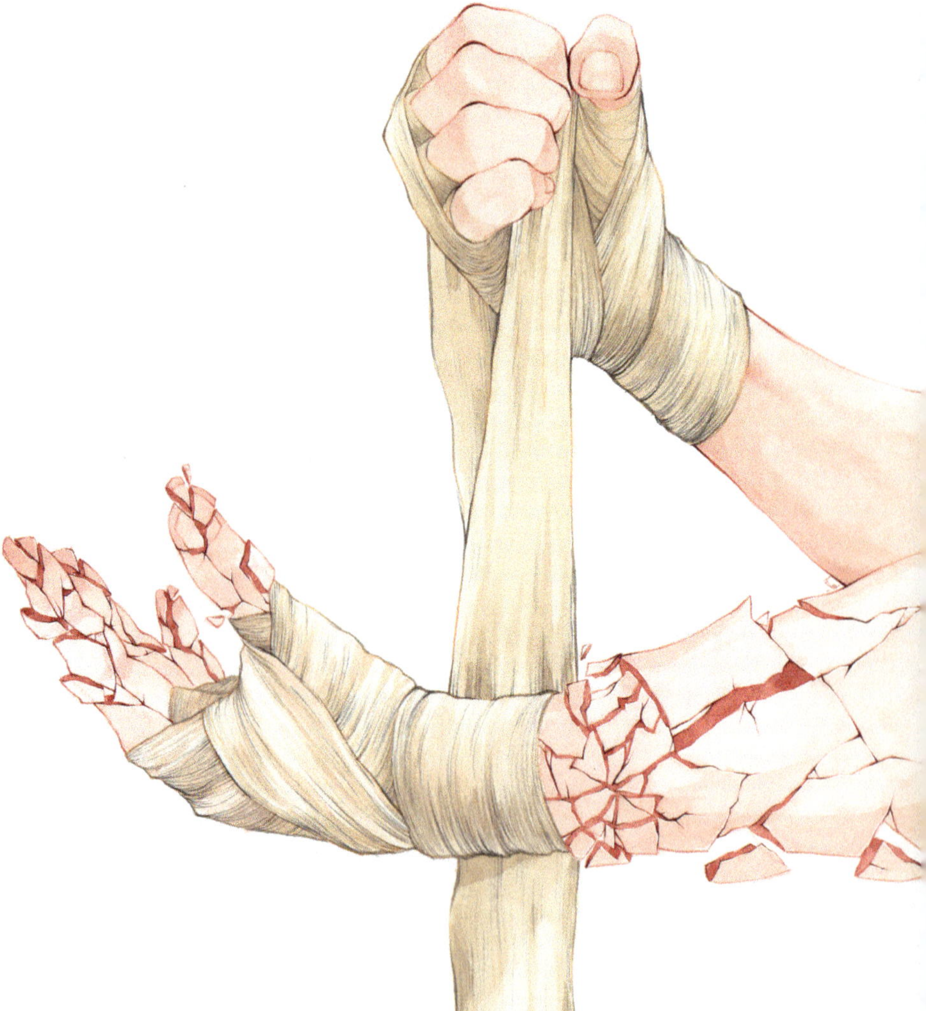

SILENT TEETH IN A BROKEN MOUTH

Joseph Rakowski

Josh called me at two in the morning on the day of his return fight. His voice sharp, each word punctuated by heavy breaths as he threw jabs in rhythm. Then there was a long silence, enough that I wondered if I was suffering a sleep-paralysis hallucination. His voice returned, low and cracked like he'd been whispering to himself for hours.

"Alex is watching me," he said.

"I know she is. We all are." I swallowed, my mouth dry. That feeling of choking on air as my throat moved with nothing in it. Josh took a breath, stretched it too long, caught somewhere between a sigh and a laugh.

"Doesn't matter," he said and hung up.

I felt the lump on my nose. The bone healed over, but even after a year, it still hummed to the touch. The sensation went beyond that; the reminder showed that things don't break—they shatter. I turned over in bed. Outside, I could hear a car playing music, rattling the mechanics apart. Sleeping like this, unaided and clearheaded, was impossible. It's like passing a row of telephone poles, each space between them holding another story. My mind runs the same, thinking about the past. I know all too well how the dark bile can run when I finally peel myself from this bed and return to chasing. I jabbed my nose. Felt the bone fibers crack and the trickle of blood. I decided to head outside and spend the night in a stream of other passing creeps. It would bother me less.

I'd seen Josh a few hours earlier in his hotel room after the fighter weigh-in. He was getting his hair braided, skin slick, desiccated muscles now hydrating and ballooning, his power already returning from the cut. When I saw him again in the morning, his gaunt face and teared-up eyes were rounded in black. I knew he'd spent all night pacing, visualizing Alex as he punched holes in the hotel room walls, the front desk calling him for a second and third time while Josh was calling me, telling me how much he had loved her and how he planned to be buried next to her, about the headstones he'd bought from some quarry in Vermont.

Josh and I started at the same MMA school five years ago, sleeping in our cars in the parking lot. Then on the mats at the gym, and eventually our coach and teammates' couches until we found jobs and were able to get an apartment together. From the jump, Josh gravitated to Muay Thai, and after getting kicked in the thighs a few times and having my eyebrows almost elbowed off my face, I went to studying jiu-jitsu.

Those were the dark days of MMA: schools were popping up everywhere, but no one really knew what they were doing. The majority of us were taught by fans of the sport or by watching Bas Rutten videos and reading Eddie Bravo's *10th Planet* book. Training consisted of shadow boxing, trying to submit someone with the *Twister*, and then standing and banging until someone got knocked out. The idea was to pack eighteen years of knowledge into your first six months, and then if you had the guts, our coach would get you a fight in some shithole barn in Valdosta or a bar in Jacksonville.

My first fight was in Dothan, Alabama. A guy next to the cage was already puking up Miller, while in a row behind him, two dudes squared off on wobbly bleachers over something that happened in the fight before. There were birds in the metal trusses and bird shit caked onto the floors and walls next to a packed bar, yet somehow the place smelled like bleach.

I pissed five times while warming up. I lay down on mats next to the cage, rolling my hips side to side, elevating my torso off the ground. Then I moved into a series of yoga flows and animal movements, getting my body ready. Soon, it would be all-out rounds. My opponent liked to stand and throw bombs—meat hooks aimed to merc me. That's what our coach knew about him. I'd have to avoid standing toe-to-toe and brawling.

Josh came over to work my corner. He told me, "You're a monster, a murderer; you're lovely."

At the opening buzzer, me and the other fighter both came out swinging, looking to take pieces out of each other. The guy tagged me hard on the chin. I felt that terrible urge for destruction, but I didn't chase it. I avoided the incoming fists. He charged forward, trying to make me exchange with him, but I waited for my opening and took him down with a double leg off a left hook. I soaked up every inch of real estate between us. I didn't let him breathe.

He dug in a lazy underhook, trying to get back to his feet, but I put him back on his back and moved to side control, where I pounded his ribs and head. I kept grinding on him until he bellied down and gave me his back. I sank a choke deep under his chin. The guy pawed at me in a last-ditch effort, but I sucked my shoulder blades together, turning the veins in his forehead purple, ready to burst. I felt his body go limp. It was a one-minute thriller that the audience booed, but I felt watched. Josh hugged me, then gave me a friendly dick tap. "Told you, you fucker," he said.

Some people crawled through this insanity, others got injured and shaken. After years of getting dropped on my head—and my neck and limbs cranked on—I quit training and fighting. I got a job detailing cars and only hung around the gym when I was nearly comatose, taking pills and letting my left tricep and arm shrink until it was useless, just a floppy appendage with an attached hand. The jelly discs in my neck were barely trace fossils, my knees not much better, and it all became problems I couldn't keep fixing. My mind was game, but even after all of the physical rehabs and surgeries—the debt piling—my body was still jacked.

I stayed living with Josh but could only watch on as he went up the ladder. He had just returned home from the gym; he had another fight coming up in a few weeks and he limped around, his body bruised in the right spots from all sorts of exacting abuse. He leaned heavily over the kitchen counter with something circling in the microwave above his head. Next to him, nailed to the wall like shot dove carcasses filleted out, were his bloody hand wraps from his previous fights. Our coach had always told us to keep them, *win or lose*, like some medal of honor or a scout badge or a letter from your mother, just reminding you, *you're loved.* But not to come home until you're not like your father.

★★★

I sat on the couch, staring at Josh and the dead birds and listening to the microwave, thinking I was being cooked by it and trying not to entirely melt through my seat. We were waiting for Alex. She was coming over to hang out while Josh took an ice bath and smoked a joint. He texted her, not thinking much of it until she stopped answering him. He kept checking his phone, staring at a postcard on his fridge from the Dalí Museum in Florida. We missed three days of training to travel there, popping caps, looking at melting clocks and elephants with long legs, and the painting where God shot Lincoln, but only if you looked at it through a backward pair of binoculars. The microwave dinged like electrical shock therapy had started, and I felt transported back to my parents' home, to their black-and-white TV, me kneeling on the tile in penance next to my father who had passed out trying to make his way to the couch. That's when I thought I saw her through the window blinds standing in the parking lot streaked in lateral slits of shade. I called Josh, but when he came to look, Alex wasn't there—just empty pavement carved by the shadows of streetlights, long dense lines across its face.

We got in Josh's car and drove in the direction she should be coming from. As we went, Josh reduced his speed, easing the car until we were almost rolling. Then, he sped up again, like a game of chase and retreat, the road accompanying us, the pavement made of black water, and our tires sinking into it. My buzz came in waves and soon I couldn't tell if we were going fast or slow. I just cruised in the passenger seat as God took another honest person.

I saw the flashing lights in the distance like theater, flaming ringlets that staged her and adorned her and reached out to us in weeping globs of menace. I watched him run toward Alex's car; the way steel contained around her body like a metallic candy wrapper drawn tight with low crinkled edges, a glass field of blue and green being flung under his feet as he charged it.

Soon Alex's body was no longer trapped but covered and being loaded in the back of an ambulance. At the same time, they were arresting Josh for punching out a fireman, a cop, and busting my nose and lips with a headbutt. It was stupid of us to try to hold him, but I knew that well before anyone got their face pushed in.

★★★

After what could have been a lifetime of blurred days, tangled in poison, escape, and walls with no doors that whispered the same hour over and over, I sat in the corner, watching them tape Josh's hands. Our coach wasn't really hyped on me being there, being all washed out, but Josh demanded I stay. He told them I had nothing to do with the demolition of the hotel room last night; I wasn't there to aid him this time. I couldn't have been—I was waiting at a bus stop after they'd long stopped running for the night, thinking a chrome-wheeled drifter would materialize anyway and take me to heaven. I felt so good, and it was raining; drops the size of bowling balls were coming from the sky to kiss me.

The camera's light shined on Josh, watching him warm up, hitting pads. He clenched his jaw when he wanted to yell, trying to contain what he could. I patted his shoulder as I left to take my seat in the arena. Josh reminded me again: *she's watching.* And I told him, *I know.*

Josh made the walk to the octagon, his head nodding with his music, flexing his mouth open, his mouthguard with her name on it. His body blurred behind the cage walls as he sprinted back and forth inside. He didn't look across at his opponent, just spit water on the canvas. Mashed his feet in it. Shook out his shoulders. Rolled his neck. Rage like unreasonable horse flanks convulsed up and down his sides as he shifted his weight, Josh waiting for it all to go berserk.

I pulled a pint of whiskey from my pocket and poured the last of it into my beer. Watching Josh, I wanted to be in his place, imagining myself stepping up to the cage door while others sat on the sidelines, cheering on their own made-up visions. Maybe it would take death, or a blood transfusion, or someone to add me in with a fine paintbrush to make this real. I felt a twist in my stomach just thinking it, but the thought wouldn't leave. I took a sip.

My hands stopped shaking so much, and the soreness in my chest went away. The lights raked over the two fighters in one large buzz that held it all, and I wished I weren't made of worthless flesh, even managed to believe I wasn't for a second. That I was strong, capable of being something, anything but crooked, high, junk.

The fight started, and they traded shots right after the touch of their gloves. Josh didn't waste time trying to range up and take the fight right to his opponent. The guy tried to keep him off—moving—trying to survive the hail of leather and bone.

Josh attacked his opponent's lead leg, chopping at it, beating it until the skin looked stained with varnish. He switched stances and took his kick high, his shinbone landing flush to the jaw and side of his opponent's head. Starched him: sent his opponent's consciousness dark and followed it up with a left hand before the body hit the canvas and bounced off it, then rested the way you'd picture a person in a car accident being thrown around the inside of a shiny frame before coming to a hard stop.

The referee shielded the body on the cage floor as Josh turned, as if blinded by the final light. He couldn't believe it, even though he knew it was true. He had made it happen—knockout of the night. The scene replayed on the screen above him, the impact sounding like a baseball bat striking a heavy bag, the crowd's reaction growing louder, fantastic, erratic. Josh dropped to his knees and smashed the canvas with both fists. His whole body seized like he was holding the wires of a downed powerline. He was the prairie wolf of my dreams, ablaze and running out of a fire that had engulfed an entire valley. The charred animal dropping in safety only to be consumed again at rest.

I moved out of the apartment after that fight. I realized now I would just get in Josh's way. He had found himself, found forgiveness for something he didn't have control over. And I was just there, like an old scar white against the skin, the grownup whipping boy from his past. I stopped talking to everyone and focused on my sobriety. I held down a job, making sure not to steal from it for dope money. At night, I started taking adult drawing and painting classes—anything to keep my hands busy. I tried to paint the night Alex died: her texting Josh, the car, her alive. But it all came out wrong: sinful. No matter how hard I tried, I couldn't capture her, couldn't make the unreal glow. I hid the paintings under my bed and slept over them.

One night, in the glow of my phone, I looked under the bed at the scattered mess of paintings. There it was buried under others—the painting from a couple of weeks ago. Not of Alex, but of me. I looked like a fucking watermelon with arms. I would've rather suffered a heart attack with a McDonald's bag in my lap than have anyone find this desperate cry for help. I climbed under the bed, head pressed against the slats, one arm pinned underneath me. I twisted my neck to get the phone in place, angling it toward the paintings instead of pulling it out. My body felt as contorted as everything else: strained, off-balance, trying to make sense of this piece of shit.

I reached for the phone, pulled it close, but it slipped from my fingers and hit the floor. I cursed heaven for such a silly thing, snatched it back up. The screen was slick with sweat; I wiped it on my shirt, but the smear remained, a greasy blur across the glass. I stood, too fast. My knee slammed into the edge of the bed, sharp enough to make me hobble on it as I stumbled toward the window. The frame stuck, like always. I pressed my elbow beneath the lip and forced it upward. Wood groaned. When it finally gave, a slap of cold air punched against my face, scraped along my teeth. I turned back, reached for the mattress. My fingers sank into the edge as I yanked it sideways, dragging the whole bed with it. The frame screeched across the floor. Dust exploded from the floorboards, rising in sudden clouds that danced like startled insects. I dropped to my knees, shoved my arm under the bed, fumbling through the dark until my fingers found the canvas. I tugged at it, dragging the painting into view just far enough to see the corner, the edge of color, the texture of oil. My phone buzzed again, dumb and insistent. I didn't look at it. Just stuffed it in the drawer and slammed it shut with my foot. The wood cracked, close to breaking in half. I knew her absence was pressing into him, an invisible hand long against his chest, dissolving him, dragging that night down harder. I immediately regretted not moving out earlier, not rubbing off on him all my ways of dying.

I called him. I could barely make out his words as he heaved them forward, pushing them over his floating tongue. He was talking about the way that night was supposed to have happened. I stopped listening. I realized the real trap isn't the moment you say yes. It's before that. It's the feeling you get just standing at the edge: the rush, the haze, the voice telling you you've already decided. You're high before you make the choice. That's the trick. No weighing promises, no pause, just a quick, stupid slide into it. And when it hits, you don't flinch. You don't even care. Everything else, the noise, the warnings, even Josh on the other end of the line, faded into that dim, background crowd around us.

I fell off again, found myself driving to the liquor store with a backseat full of whiskey caps and water bottles. I pulled into the shopping center parking lot, where the streetlights cast long, warped shadows that stitched fake boundaries across the pavement—lines you can step on but still feel like you're not supposed to. Like the whole place was built for some game no one explains, but everyone plays anyway.

I sat on the hood of my car and called my dad. My voice was thick, just like Josh's had been—forced, broken, and lost in the noise of something that felt too big to face. I talked about things that couldn't happen, about things I couldn't undo. The same helplessness I heard in Josh's voice now twisted through my own, a reminder that I was still falling, just as I had before. The guilt of it clung to me. I couldn't shake—couldn't fight it off with fists or choke it out.

"I'm an alcoholic," I said. Goddamn, I felt like a coward bothering the old man.

"You aren't the first."

"I'm all fucked up again," I said, thinking this time I'd see rain rolling in over that burning valley Josh created with his return fight.

"I know," he said. "I've always had this dream where I kill a kid driving home drunk. Drag him, finally hear him. Get out and look. But I guess there's still time."

I hung up. I wished it were possible to get someone else's body, use it to bleed. I tried to pray, but I couldn't think of much. I looked around the parking lot for someone to yell something smart to. No one was around, so I just howled to myself. The liquor store's lights went out and I kept singing until I tripped over a parking stopper and chipped my front teeth on the ground, making this half-moon shape in them with tiny fractures that went up to the gums.

I went to Josh's apartment and banged on the door. The streetlight out front glowed awful, dip-bottle brown and orange; it buzzed the fresh cracks in my teeth, and I thought about shooting the light out for him. Josh didn't answer, so I went around back to the sliding window. I found Josh crumbled on the floor inside. He looked harmless. I kicked his feet.

"If you do that again, I will kill you," he grumbled.

I kicked him again, and Josh got up, so I retreated into the kitchen that was littered with bottles and twenty-dollar baggies and stuff we'd used to make ourselves vanish. I took an empty bottle and held it like I'd hit him with it. Josh ignored me and went around to the sink and drank from the faucet. He took a pill bottle out of a drawer, chewed up a few and funneled some more water into his mouth. He offered me one. I took the pill and then regretted it immediately when he closed the drawer.

I was still holding up the empty bottle when he grabbed a piece from a broken mirror on the counter. He pointed the sliver at me, held it out to my eye, then tossed it against the wall, shattering it smaller. He walked by me like a downed opponent.

"We got to get you another fight," I said.

"Sure, dummy. You, too."

"Fuck me. You been training at all?"

"I'm always training."

I followed him to the living room and sat down on the couch. Josh sat sideways in an armchair that made him look graceful. The tattoo of her face on his ribs was skinny, deep set and pale. The black ink hiding her green eyes and brown hair, her always sweaty forehead. The shading of the ink, somehow, still held that detail—preserving it as if the tattoo were a shield, etched with the same care and permanence as Achilles' legendary armor. I tried not to look at it, or Josh, who was staring out the window at the sky that was crawling across the wooden slats that separated panels of cloudy glass. Josh's eyes were far away and drifting. I left him sleeping in his chair, easy and delicate.

A month later, Josh was training again and they'd signed him for another fight. He looked alright moving over the mats, but there were pieces of him missing that no one wanted to admit. You couldn't help but notice them. It was there in the way Josh rubbed his forehead like he saw the crash again with the sound of each landed punch, how he showed up late to practice and then trained extra hard, lay on the ground in a pool of sweat, curled up sort of, stayed down there cradling himself longer than he should have. Alex was weighted inside of him. It influenced the delivery of his body, slowed him down that fraction he needed. The way those things are supposed to.

Josh got mounted early in his next fight. His corner shouted at him to move, but he just couldn't get out from beneath the guy. It looked for a second like he didn't want to. Fists and heavy elbows landed from his opponent. Josh took every bit of the punishment until the referee stopped it. Josh sat up on the canvas, a hematoma growing under his eye shaped like a horse's ear with the horse in full stride.

Josh disappeared after this fight. But he didn't go anywhere, just sat in his apartment with the window shades drawn. Got into gaming and codeine. When I did hear from him, he said he was an outlaw wandering the West in some open world RPG. He'd never been to the boundless plateau that seemed to lean left toward the ocean, he'd never seen the ancient and dried-up great lakes and the once sprawling wetlands, the brittlebushes like drops of paint splattered on mountains that blurred among the layered walls of earth. He had no idea what the West smelled like, what it tasted like. He'd never felt horsehair or cold dust. He'd never held a Winchester or a Colt revolver or a Derringer pocket pistol. But he said it all looked very fine when you're turning into mustard.

I got the news that Josh was making a comeback—not from him, but from our coach. He'd seen me out, walking the streets and punching air in my head as I ate a box of ice cream sandwiches, shoving the wrappers in my pockets to lick later. The coach stopped me, reminded me of my dad standing there, blocking me, waiting a long time to say what he wanted; it'd either be some command or something unintelligible, winding, and long-winded. I used only one eye to focus on him, my other one somehow trapped in my skull.

"You never were the smartest fighter," he said, as I tucked away another wrapper.

"Thanks, Coach." I held back a burp, a rising feeling of nauseousness.

"Josh is coming back. He's putting the pieces together. He needs someone to help pull him back in. Someone who can remind him what he's fighting for." I thought Coach was trying to game me, but I didn't say anything. It's hard to see inside someone, to know just how close they are to barely hanging on. "You think you can show up?"

"I don't think that'd be helpful like you think it would, Coach."

"It would be if you pulled your head out of your ass."

His voice was fixed, but there was something underneath—like he knew how hard this was going to be for me, but that it wasn't really about me. The smell of my dad's cologne ran through the air, and I looked around Coach to nobody standing behind him.

"Pull him in, huh? Like a boat?" My insides ran hot. "Fix it."

"It's not about fixing. It's about showing up. That's all you gotta do. Show up. Be there."

Something my father used to say to me when I was younger passed through my head: *The world's smallest violin plays for you.* For a moment, I thought about asking Coach if he would pay me cash to be there. I knew then I would never change, only get worse.

I shook his hand, my fingers sticky. I could see he felt the goo but didn't say anything. There was a long pause, and I could almost hear Coach waiting for me to say something else, to make a promise I couldn't quite make.

"There is a love between sparring partners, fighters of the same camp. He knows you helped carry the weight. Just show up like that," he said as we dropped hands. "You'll be fine."

I killed some more moments; let the stink fall off me before I went out to the gym, found Josh circling, throwing hands, the dance back in his step. Damn, he was quick. He looked good moving, shifting, loose. Our coach had set up a full training camp this time with a team of fighters to help him prepare. The gym had changed. It was a business, the coach seeing he had something in Josh, that the gym had something. Josh's coach giving out commandments, born again, changed, relieved. I wanted to ask for the cash again.

It was the night before Josh was heading out for his comeback fight that I went to his apartment all mixed up. He was leaving first thing in the morning. I thought about ditching, not wanting to break him off his path. But I just wanted to see him again. Tell him I knew she was watching him. That everyone was watching. I parked my car next to his and sat there with a soda can filled with whiskey and crushed pills. The damn awful glow of Josh's streetlight burning had no business being huge like it was. Flies the size of mice swarming around it, everything was elastic, and the pole flowered, casting its long shadow over the faded concrete. Even at night, these lines stay drawn over blacktops. I could see Josh's apartment window and someone moving behind the blinds.

I waited until I passed out. By midday, the sun had cooked me awake in my seat. Josh's car was still parked next to mine, even though he should've been on his way to the fight hours ago. I knocked on his door.

Then I banged harder. The thought of walking around to the back window never crossed my mind as I kicked it in. I found him in the living room, lifeless, looking like a plank of dark wood. There was another body next to his that looked like it had been kneeling, one leg still tucked under his stomach. Vomit in front of him. It was a guy I recognized from the gym who had just started training with Josh for this fight. I heard the tenor and felt the dry air over the bitter smell.

I called for help and then stood by the window and waited until the emergency lights arrived at the top of the road. As the lights came closer, their whirling held flame like an empty cage in the center of an arena after everyone has gone home. I hollered to Josh, *you fucker.* I turned rotten seeing him lying there. I wished I hadn't come inside. Wished I'd never seen any dead bodies looking up at me. I was afraid, knowing that one day my face would sit among strangers. I ran past their sunken metallic bodies, over the rippling water of blacktop, through the slit in the old quiet. Take me.

SUFFERING & REFINEMENT

A Conversation with Joseph Rakowski

James McNulty: Welcome to the pages of *Driftwood*, Joseph! We're excited to be publishing this visceral, hard-hitting story! Talk to me about the initial conception of this story.

Joseph Rakowski: I grew up immersed in combat sports—initially boxing with my father in the garage. Alongside this, I developed an avid interest in martial arts, consuming magazines and books that fueled my passion. When I entered college, I began training in Brazilian jiu-jitsu, long before it became a mainstream discipline, prior to the widespread recognition of the UFC. Back then, I often had to explain that I practiced wrestling, as most people had little knowledge of Brazilian jiu-jitsu or mixed martial arts. Over the years, I participated in various competitions, including a single amateur Muay Thai fight, and later went on to win the national championship in my division for jiu-jitsu, along with numerous other tournament victories. I trained relentlessly for seven or eight years, spending nearly every day at the gym, drilling techniques and grappling.

However, a week before I was set to receive my purple belt in jiu-jitsu, I sustained a serious neck injury that required spinal fusion surgery (C4-C6), including the insertion of a titanium plate. This injury resulted in the loss of all muscle in my left arm, with my tricep disappearing entirely. The experience of spinal surgery sucked. I found myself grappling with feelings of frustration and fear, realizing the risks of injury extended far beyond the typical sprains or broken bones. My long-held aspirations of competing, teaching, and even owning a martial arts school seemed increasingly out of reach. I watched as many of the fighters I had trained with climb the ranks, with some advancing to the UFC and others earning their black belts. Meanwhile, I found myself sidelined, unable to pursue my dreams as I had envisioned them.

It is this experience that shaped the core of my story: the tale of a fighter who once saw himself achieving greatness, only to be forced to watch others attain what he had longed for. The narrative delves into the psychological and emotional toll of this downfall, reflecting my own struggles with similar demons. While I won't delve further into those personal parallels, it is this complex interplay between ambition, loss, and resilience that drives the heart of the story.

JM: You spoke earlier about fighting being your dream and having to move on from that. What happened post-original dream for you? Did you find a new aspiration, and were you able to accept the results of the first?

JR: I don't believe I ever truly moved on from that original dream. If a dream is genuine, it lingers, continuously present in your thoughts. For me, fighting, particularly jiu-jitsu, remains a significant part of what I think about. My regret was I probably should have got back out there. Looking back, I realize my mistake was not returning to it.

However, in the wake of that regret, I found a new direction: writing. I discovered my passion for writing during law school, which I didn't complete. I remember thinking that if being a lawyer was just about who could tell the best story, I might as well write ones I care about. So I left. I moved from Miami, Florida, to Berkeley, California, and enrolled in the MFA program at the University of San Francisco.

During this time, I became completely absorbed in literature. I didn't come from a traditional English or literary background; I was trained as a criminologist, but that only fueled my curiosity. I asked everyone I met for their favorite book and read whatever they recommended, immersing myself in everything from Noam Chomsky, James Wood, and Michel Foucault to Kurt Vonnegut, James Baldwin, Adam Johnson, to Tracy K. Smith, Louise Glück, Frank O'Hara, and Derek Walcott. It was a period of intense intellectual exploration, where I sought to understand the vast scope of human experience through the lens of both fiction and theory.

While I may not have achieved what I originally set out to in the realm of fighting, this new path has given me a way to channel the discipline and intensity I once applied to combat into something that brings me a different kind of fulfillment. Writing has allowed me to express the complex emotions and themes that still resonate deeply from my past, even as I continue to process the realities of my previous dreams.

JM: Talk to me about the generative process for this story. Do you work with outlines?

JR: I approach writing with a deliberately flexible process, avoiding rigid outlines in favor of a more intuitive and generative method. Much of my work begins in thought rather than on the page; I spend significant time meditating on a story's emotional architecture and thematic direction before I begin drafting. Often, I jot down fragmented sentences or lists—incipient narrative elements that gesture toward tone, image, or conflict—without forcing them into immediate coherence. At some point, usually after a period of distance from the material, an opening line emerges organically, and that line becomes the narrative fulcrum from which the rest of the story unfolds.

While I don't adhere to a formal process, close reading is integral to my practice. I take extensive notes on the fiction I admire—parsing syntax, structure, voice, and narrative rhythm—as a way of remaining in dialogue with the literary tradition and sharpening my own craft. I write as frequently as possible and consider rejection a critical component of refinement; submitting to top-tier journals has helped me identify and discard underdeveloped work before it reaches an audience. For me, the act of writing is as much about revision and discernment as it is about generation.

JM: Talk to me about the revisions process for "Silent Teeth in a Broken Mouth."

JR: The revision process for "Silent Teeth in a Broken Mouth" was both revelatory and deeply transformative, marked by an astonishing blend of thoughtfulness and critical understanding. Engaging with the text through a lens of close reading and reflective critique, the process demanded a slowing down, not just of language but of intention, inviting a more spacious, deliberate exploration of meaning. What began as a raw, emotionally charged draft laced with cheap shots and reactive language gradually evolved into a more nuanced and responsive work. The revisions emphasized tone, subtext, and voice, foregrounding the ethical responsibility of representation and the affective power of restraint. I couldn't thank my editor, James, enough for his close analysis of my work, for his ability to see beyond, to see what I meant, and to help me mean it. In this way, the process became not merely an act of editing but a conversation with the text's interiority, revealing layers of suppressed agency and shifting the rhetorical framework from aggression to articulation. Ultimately, revision was less about correction and more about re-seeing, an act of intellectual and emotional empathy grounded in the poetics of space and silence.

JM: Which writers inspired "Silent Teeth in a Broken Mouth"?

JR: Breece DJ Pancake, Barry Hannah, Terry Southern, James McPherson, Issac Babel, Denis Johnson, Tennessee Williams, and Tobias Wolff to name a few.

JM: What did they bring to this story? Are you able to locate specific things you've learned from some of them?

JR: These writers share a deep affinity for compressed, emotionally-charged storytelling, often through short stories, novellas, or plays. Many of them gravitate toward Southern or American Gothic sensibilities, exploring decay, violence, poverty, and spiritual desolation. Their characters are frequently outsiders: the working class, the disillusioned, the addicted, or those on the margins of society. Writers like Pancake, Hannah, and Williams evoke a raw Southern voice steeped in loss and isolation, while Babel and Johnson bring a hallucinatory, almost mythic tone to lives caught in historical or personal chaos. There's also a strong undercurrent of dark humor and absurdity—particularly in the work of Terry Southern and Barry Hannah—balancing tragedy with wit. Across the board, these authors wrestle with existential questions, often through spare, intense prose that foregrounds emotional and moral complexity. Whether through the spiritual yearnings of Denis Johnson's drifters or the quiet moral reckonings in Wolff's and McPherson's fiction, their work is unified by a relentless search for meaning in the shadow of suffering. "Silent Teeth in a Broken Mouth" engages with many of these same ideas, inviting the reader into a similarly fraught emotional and existential terrain.

JM: Do other mediums influence you at all?

JR: Movies. Movies. Movies. If I had the time, I'd watch three to five movies a day. Honestly, I wish I could write the same way you experience a movie. Well, I guess, I picture my writing that way, and I hope the reader sees it too. But it's not just the writing—it's the cinematography, the soundtrack, all the elements that bring a film together. It's just that something extra. I really love it when a book I've read is adapted into a movie, and it feels and looks just like how I imagined it. Those kinds of adaptations are rare.

JM: How do you think film influences your writing? What do you take with you into the craft?

JR: I'm drawn to films that delve into emotional extremity, moral ambiguity, and richly atmospheric worlds. Stories like *Precious, Biutiful, Manchester by the Sea,* and *Out of the Furnace* resonate with me for their unflinching portrayal of trauma, resilience, and the human capacity to endure. I'm equally compelled by auteur-driven cinema—films such as *8½, Le Samouraï, Inherent Vice,* and *Mandy*—that prioritize visual style, psychological complexity, and formal experimentation. My taste often gravitates toward narratives that blur the lines between justice and chaos, as seen in *No Country for Old Men, Yojimbo,* and *Midnight in the Garden of Good and Evil,* where protagonists navigate ethically murky terrain. I'm also deeply invested in mythic and allegorical storytelling, from the Shakespearean gravity of *Throne of Blood* to the sweeping moral landscapes of *The Lord of the Rings.* Above all, I seek out films that give voice to the marginalized—*Tangerine, The Peanut Butter Falcon*—because I believe the most powerful storytelling insists on empathy and reveals what is often unseen.

My short fiction aspires to evoke many of these same qualities: emotional endurance, existential tension, and the complexities of the human condition. I'm drawn to characters in flux—those navigating moral uncertainty or searching for meaning in a fractured world—and I aim to craft narratives that balance lyrical intensity with emotional restraint. These films have profoundly shaped my sensibility as a writer; they don't just entertain—they illuminate. My hope is that my work might do the same.

JM: What are you working on now?

JR: My immediate goal is to get my short story collection published. At present, thirteen of the stories have found homes—eight with university-affiliated journals and five with independent literary presses. In addition, I have ten more completed stories, three of which I believe are strong enough to either stand on their own or be included in the collection as unpublished material. Beyond that, I have, I think, only one novel in me. I don't say that lightly, nor do I intend it as a gesture of posturing. I genuinely believe that after completing that novel, my work as a writer—at least in terms of publishing—may come to a close.

The writing process, for me, has become increasingly daunting. It asks for an intensity of attention, emotional availability, and personal excavation that I'm not sure I can sustain indefinitely. To write something honest, something with resonance, requires more than just time and craft—it demands a willingness to be changed. If I'm fortunate enough to finish this collection and complete the novel I have in mind, I would feel at peace stepping back to focus on reading, which has always been the foundation of my creative life. Writing has given me immeasurable joy, but it has also taken its toll, and I want to be honest about that balance.

JM: You mentioned Tarantino earlier; he famously said he only wants to make ten films. Why ten specifically? It's a round number, I guess. The statement doesn't make a ton of sense to a lot of artists. Likewise, what makes you think you only have one novel in you? I think many writers take breaks and recharge when work has taken too much out of them, but they aren't quite so definitive.

JR: I suppose I shouldn't say I only *have* one novel in me, but rather that I only *want* to write one. For me, writing a novel isn't just a matter of craft or output; it's an emotional and psychological commitment that asks more than time and discipline. It asks for pieces of the self. I think if you're trying to write something true, something that matters, it changes you in the process. And not always gently. Writing a novel, at least the kind I want to write, takes something out of you that doesn't always come back.

Time plays into this as well. I think about my family, about the people I love, and about how limited our days are. There's a cost to disappearing into a book for years, to inhabiting fictional lives while real ones go on without you. That cost isn't just measured in hours, but in presence, in emotional availability, in memory. A novel can become a kind of private exile, necessary, yes, but still a kind of distance from the world you're ostensibly writing about.

So the question isn't whether I *could* write more than one novel; it's whether I should. How many more times do I want to put myself through that transformation? How many more changes do I have in me, and would those changes be for the better? Writing brings me more joy than anything else I do, but it also brings a kind of melancholy, a confrontation with everything I haven't resolved in myself. It's not just a career. It's a reckoning. So I'm not ruling anything out, but if I only write one novel, and it's the novel I need to write, that might be enough.

JM: Any parting words to leave with our readers—either about "Silent Teeth in a Broken Mouth" or writing in general?

JR: If "Silent Teeth in a Broken Mouth" leaves anything behind, I hope it's an invitation to sit with discomfort, your own and that of others, and to resist the urge to tidy pain into resolution. Writing, for me, is not about endurance, about returning again and again to what feels unresolved. Whether on the mat or on the page, I've learned that discipline alone doesn't sustain you; you need compassion too, especially for yourself. I would also say this: nothing we lose is ever really gone if we find a way to transform it. That's what writing has given me, a place to put the parts of myself that couldn't go on as planned. And to anyone writing through grief, regret, or doubt: you don't have to win the fight to make it matter. Just staying in it can be enough.

HARD SWALLOW

Thea Nguyen

The night we received the lab work from your doctor, you were rolling out a perfect set of cinnamon rolls for our anniversary. I could boil pasta and mince veggies reasonably well—though you would gently point out that my pasta was gummy and my veggies limp and mangled—but yours were the hands that coaxed magic into every meal. The first time we met, at a party for filthy-rich eccentrics, your hands were cold as you arranged butterfly-thin slivers of mango and foie gras on my bare skin. I was, of course, naked and displayed on a table luminescent with pearls, as were the other twelve models hired to be the serving trays for an assortment of hors d'oeuvres. This was your first time catering at a party like this, and despite your skittish gaze grazing me from hip to waist to collarbone, your hands never trembled in their work.

Your hands didn't tremble now as we sat, pressed shoulder to shoulder, and I read the results to you. I spoke quietly, as if the paper in my hands were a vengeful spirit I didn't dare wake, but no matter how quietly I spoke, the words *one year* refused to scatter and be blown to bits in a place far away from our kitchen, the same kitchen we had been dreaming of renovating for eight years, between car payments and the fire that nearly devoured your restaurant, the same kitchen where you had fed me slices of persimmon and I let the sweet, silky juice of it bleed down my chin, mingling with the fragrant tang I had tongued from you, right there on the kitchen counter.

After I finished reading, you merely rubbed my back and returned to the cinnamon rolls.

"Let's eat while they're still hot," you said, as if you hadn't just learned that you only had one more year to live.

It was not that much time later when I found you at the kitchen island, head bowed over a notebook. Chicken scratch would have been too kind to describe the disastrous bramble of your handwriting, and I often pitied the sous chefs who probably spent every minute of prep parsing out your notes. When you set your pen down and slid the notebook over to me, I expected a briar of words. Instead, you had painstakingly written neat, block letters across the top: *Recipes for Holly.*

I peered at you over the top of the notebook. "Leila, darling, what is this?"

Your mouth parted, the rose of your lips ragged from years of habitual gnawing, and the thought of never seeing those lips again, kissing them, rubbing ointment on them, was like a howl set loose inside me.

You bit your lip, and a fresh petal of blood welled from the broken skin.

"When…when it happens," you said, eyes lacquered with unshed tears. My hand, thumbing away your blood, froze at the word *it*. "I want you to eat me."

Your blood clung to my skin.

★★★

As a child, the only time I prayed was during meals. Often, after my sisters had cleared their plates and scuttled off, I sat alone, fork imprinted in the heartline of my palm, eyes screwed shut as I chewed and chewed and chewed and nearly choked on the swallow. I prayed God would transform me into a succulent, a perfect little rosette that could subsist off sunlight and the occasional hard rain. I prayed that everyone would forget the existence of spinach entirely.

I prayed that my father would keep calm enough that I could escape into the safety of my room, that my mother would not have to explain to me again that people in love, no matter what, couldn't help but hurt each other, and that it was a woman's duty to absorb all that hurt.

I watched my mother let my father savor her for years. Chewed on her thoughts and dreams and sucked on her virtues, until all that was left was picked-on bones that he eventually abandoned for another pair of legs. I once asked her if it had all been worth it. The house so far from home, the marriage, even us kids. Laughter escaped from her like a dying wisp of incense. "Your grandmother had it worse," she had said.

Later, as an adult living alone, I would hunch over the sink and devour whole heads of raw broccoli, stalks of celery, shapely bell peppers with waxy sheens that crisped against my teeth. I ate like a hunted animal in short, voracious bursts and quickly grew accustomed to days serrated with an unrelenting hunger, and I carried that into my relationships, first with a long procession of boyfriends whose appetites never satisfied mine, and then into those first, tentative courtships with women who I regarded like porcelain. Far too beautiful and delicate to touch, half-feral as I was. I was always hungry, yet only ever surviving off scraps, preferring to give more than I ever took.

Somewhere along the line, I learned that I could only ever ask for so much, could only take up so much space. At least, until you.

Weeks after we met at the party, I dogged your steps as you solemnly took inventory of my kitchen: a bottle of extra virgin olive oil gone rancid, a half-crushed, half-empty tub of nonfat Greek yogurt, the unspoiled wedge of a Meyer lemon, handfuls of wilted spinach, a small, abused tub of minced garlic, and a frozen chicken breast that had laid crushed under my chilled wine. I swatted away the takeout menus that cascaded from the fridge door, before hurrying to purge the fridge, expecting judgement in your eyes, disgust. All you did was pull out a seat for me at the kitchen counter, where I watched with increasing awe as you tenderly sliced the thawed chicken into bite-sized pieces and lowered them into a bath of yogurt, lemon, garlic, pepper, and salt. I realized then that that was the core of your magic: you could take anything worthless and make it into something beautiful. You hummed as you worked, and the space between you and me at the kitchen counter uncurled like a budding secret.

That night, for maybe the first time in a year, I ate a freshly cooked meal.

★★★

The following nights after your request were dedicated to leafing through cookbooks and your hands showing mine how to slice, chop, mince, sear, poach, shuck, filet. When I was out at photoshoots during the day, you spent less and less time at the restaurant, and more time trussed up in bed with your notebook. You would greet me with flutters of kisses and new recipes to try, new musings. I smiled along with your suggestions, scribbling in the margins of your old cookbooks, but when you finally dozed off, I stared oblivion into my scrawled notes. Here, a recipe for roasting meat on a spit. Would I separate a leg, an arm, give it a dainty twirl over a roaring fire in our backyard, then watch the polish on your nails turn to ash? Plate you on your grandmother's china? Make gumbo with the leftovers?

For cultures that practiced endocannibalism, deceased loved ones were consumed as a way to release their spirits, aid in their passage from one life to the next. Eating your lover meant that they could be free, and that you could keep them close, absorb their smiles and endless goddamn poeticism into your own body. I could take every part of you into every part of me. An intimacy beyond that of a mother and her child. But I couldn't imagine your weight in my arms as I cut slivers of your flesh, like carving shawarma to be served in fresh, warm pitas.

Three weeks into our cooking lessons, my heart still raced when I went to the store. I raked through Meyer lemons, your grocery list folded and unfolded so many times that it threatened to fall to pieces in my hands. My hands skittered over the fruit, acrylic nails tapping against porous flesh. When our lessons had begun in earnest, you were exasperated with my nails, had laughed about how casually I liked to violate every kitchen health code there was. My response at the time had been to stab my nail into a falafel and eat off it like a kebab while you squealed like a wounded animal.

Firm, fat lemons secured, I willed myself forward down aisle after aisle, the ingredients blurring before my eyes even as I snagged them from shelves and dropped them into my already heavy basket. It wasn't until I finally passed through the checkout line and started the short walk to my car, when I stopped, my hands fisted with bulging plastic bags of food that you could barely stomach nowadays. I hovered at the threshold, the automatic exit doors whooshing open and closed, like a mouth ready to fasten its teeth on me, the hot breath of evening stirring the hair glued to my sweaty forehead.

Instead of packing the car, driving home to you, I envisioned myself dropping the bags and walking. Walk where, I didn't know, but I would walk until everything—our house, your voice, your best knife positioned atop my nightstand—dissolved into the evening air. Like these past eight years together never happened.

But then I remembered it was nearly seven, and you would need to take your medicine soon. I crossed the threshold and left for home.

You waited at the kitchen counter as you always did since our lessons had begun, wheelchair pulled up against the granite, cutting board and knife already laid out for me. When our gazes met, fear flickered in your eyes. Like somehow you had seen me standing still in the parking lot, body angled toward the reddening horizon. I set down my bags, leaning into your neck and closing my eyes as you talked, excitedly describing the recipe you wanted me to cook tonight. For a little while, I could pretend you were just discussing our usual meals, that we would one day grow old and gnarled together, the two lesbian grandmas like a pair of intertwining trees.

★★★

You turned toward me, almost shy in just your robe. I tenderly slipped the robe off, the whispering silk puddling at our feet, and met your eyes, waiting for guidance. In the mirror, you were as you always were, willowy and precious, dark hair shorn and vaguely curly like a newborn lamb's, belly button piercing winking in our bedroom's fairy lights. I wanted to brush the cold metal with my lips, let them wander to the tender spot where your thighs kissed. But you frowned at yourself and lowered your eyes.

"Start here," you whispered, gently guiding the marker in my hand toward the smooth expanse of your thigh. The wet tip glided across your skin, and that is how we spent the evening: me, devoutly kneeling on our rug, brows scrunched in concentration; you, shivering as cold ink marked the places you instructed me to circle. It was like those stories, the ones where sorority girls cornered dumb, doe-eyed girls and circled flabby arms, gelatinous thighs, rolls of tummy fat deemed too repulsive.

But instead, you were showing me where to carve when you died.

We practiced with all sorts of birds. Chicken, of course. Turkey, duck, even a tiny, delicate quail that I cradled in my palms. With fresh-caught salmon from the market, still gasping at the gills. Tomahawk steak. Racks and racks of lamb. All of it, bloody and beautiful. I hated how quickly I improved, how steadily my knife maneuvered through sinew, severed meat from bone. Even after all this, you still fretted at the cutting board, wondering if all of it was enough, if we needed to take a trip to the butcher's or to a pig farm.

Maybe, if we were really lucky, we could hold hands while a farmer emptied the blood of his pigs out into rusty metal troughs.

"I'm not," I said, hands trembling, "butchering you like a pig."

I slammed the knife down. My victim for the day, a pale pink snapper, stared pleadingly up at me from the board. For a moment, the only sound was the plinking faucet. Until now, we had both avoided talking openly about what you had asked me to do, despite the lessons, the anatomy textbooks, my late-night excursions through the dark web to determine how best to conceal your body when the time came. I had thought that, maybe, if we never spoke of it, you would eventually let it go. But now that I had spoken it into the room, it was like someone had yanked at a frayed thread inside me, releasing every flutter of my trembling, wet heart.

You picked up the knife and freed the snapper from its skin like slipping off a robe.

"Ask me for anything else," I said. "I could take you anywhere. We could go see the world. Hug a fucking red panda."

You said nothing, only parted the meat into three perfect filets. Even as the rest of your body strained, your hands moved with the grace of years dictating your movements. Your lips were bleeding again, but you would never notice that yourself, because in all the time I have known you, you wouldn't stop for anything the moment your teeth were sunk into a task.

Resting my forehead against your shoulder, I breathed in our combined scent of blood and brine, before letting my hand settle on yours.

Retrieving my knife, I continued the work.

***

"Don't fall asleep on me, hun," the director said.

My eyes snapped open, and I adjusted my pose. Today the lights at work were scathing, the director more irate than usual. The client and his goons milled at the edge of the spotlights, watching me with naked hunger.

After twenty more poses and five other outfit changes, I was finally free. I scurried to the dressing room, where Nat, the other model I shared this room with, already sat, pulling on a pair of red latex boots that devoured her long, tan legs. Her hand, perfectly manicured with pearly white coffins adorning each nail, squeezed mine before reaching into her purse and pulling out a thermos filled entirely with whiskey. She handed it to me, and I tilted my head back and let the burn fill my mouth. We swapped the thermos back and forth, sharing a silence that I didn't dare pierce with any mention of home. Between swallows, I wiped the glitter and foundation from my face, then began re-layering, reconstructing my face into the one you knew and loved.

Nat began to talk as she lined her lips, swapping out the peachy beige from her earlier shoot to her usual deep crimson.

"Have you given it any more thought?"

My heart fluttered. My mother had asked me the same thing over the phone just days ago, when I told her that Leila hadn't wanted a funeral, hadn't wanted family to crowd our house with their tears.

"She wants to be cremated," I had told her, trying to pour belief into my own words. To my Vietnamese mother, the words had been a slap to her face. For her, families spent days with their loved one's body. Washing and clothing them, making sure to perform the necessary rituals to ensure their loved ones could safely navigate to the afterlife. I had to bite back a bitter laugh. What you had asked of me wasn't too far from what my mother expected. I would have to strip you, wash you thoroughly, spend hours preparing your body for what came next.

"Holly?" Nat watched me expectantly.

Warmth prickled my scalp. The other models at work knew what was happening to you, but now I wondered if Nat knew more than I had shared. I took a long swig, my thoughts racing. I hadn't told anyone else about your request. It was impossible to share with any of our friends, who sent flowers and pastel yellow "thoughts and prayers" cards but balked at any mention of your health, and unfathomable to share with our families, who crammed our voicemails full with concerned messages when I spent longer than a day to call and broke into bouts of weeping over family dinners. Even so, I felt the words at the edge of my teeth, like water building pressure behind a dam, waiting to explode into our lungs.

"Given what more thought?" I asked.

"The girls. They wanted to meet at the archery range tonight," she said slowly, as if I were the one declining quickly and not you. The sympathy in Nat's eyes pressed a pebble down my throat. "We thought it would take your mind off things. I promise we won't keep you for long."

A vague memory of Nat asking me a week before surfaced. I let out a flustered laugh and agreed to come, if only for a little while until you needed more of your pain medicine.

As we entered the archery range, greeted the other girls, and picked out our bows, I kept staring between Nat's shoulder blades, my mouth stoppered up with the words I wanted to say. Nat was a new addition at the agency, but she carried a quiet certainty that stood out among the rest of us, who were eager to please, even if we twittered about the director's obvious leering in private. In my smallest, most private moments, I fantasized what it would be like to catch at Nat's sleeve and pull her into a narrow corridor, where our breaths would mingle as I confessed every awful thing. How her eyes might shimmer, her solid hands clutching mine in soundless compassion. In these imaginings, she never responded—didn't have to. She would merely lend her warmth in that close darkness, so different from the clammy cool of your skin, and she would absorb everything—the fear, the love, even the resentment I harbored, that you would ask so much of me. I wondered if my mother had similar fantasies when she was still with my father, until she realized the only people she could still hold on to were her small children.

We strung our bows, counting down from three, and released our arrows all at once. Mine bounced off the target and landed uselessly in the grass. Nat's shot straight, nicking just shy of the bull's eye. She reached down to string another arrow in her bow, and I traced the line of her shoulders with my eyes, noting the tendons there and the stretch of muscle down her neck and along her spine. I imagined you then, standing next to her, a ghost mimicking the movements of the living. The skin peeling off your arms in delicate spirals like a clementine peel as you pull the string taut, your fingers exposing the pink flesh underneath when you release your arrow.

I stumbled against a pillar, my bow clattering forgotten on the ground. Nat turned, concern crouched in her eyes, but I could only stammer, "I'm okay, I'm okay, I'm okay," even as I sank to my knees, Nat's hand reaching but not touching me. I could almost feel your body in my arms, see your face looking up into mine as Nat watched with growing alarm and the other girls scattered to get help for what must have surely looked like a panic attack, but my body felt nothing but a cottony sort of ache. My arms lifted, as if to show Nat your body, more solid now than ever, but there was nothing here but arrows in the distance, puncturing our silence, sinking into bodies fashioned out of metal and wood.

***

You worsened, and despite my pleading to move to a hospital, you stayed home.

I became bosom buddies with the team of nurses who marched in every day to test your fluids and administer your medicine, and I sent them home with packages upon packages of leftovers from all our lessons, where we always made more than either of us could possibly eat. We had reached the point where I could have made you an entire fort out of deli containers, complete with drawbridge and a generous moat of mushroom gravy. The state of our pantry was worse, and I couldn't bear to think of sifting through everything after you had gone.

"So much food," I complained, "going to waste. I've exhausted all my coworkers and first cousins. I may have to start leaving food out for feral college kids. Keep them from rooting through our vegetable garden."

Somehow that only made your eyes brighten.

"Or," you said, your voice parchment-thin but eager, "we throw a party."

Back when you were still healthy, when you spent weekends crack climbing and waving *hello, darling* from the tops of sheer cliffs—and always, I waved *hello, darling* back, topless and sunbathing from the beach below—you loved hosting these huge feasts and inviting all our friends and neighbors over, and it was like one huge gay celebration taking place every month in our tiny one-room apartment. You would spend entire weeks prepping veggies and baking pie crusts for it, while I dutifully chopped, mixed drinks, and held fidgety cheek-chewing vigil over the oven.

"It should be a seasonal menu," you continued, more animated than I had seen you all week. "We can showcase everything that you've learned."

"What is this, a test?" I said, laughing.

You quirked your eyebrows at me, and I lightly swatted your hand, which got you laughing too, breathless as you were. You waved your hand at your notebook, which I brought over and balanced in my lap. You were too weak now to pen anything yourself, so I took notes as you listed off ingredients we would have to buy, people we needed to call.

We planned for a warm day in October, probably the last for the season. I ran back and forth from the store, toting squash and spices and wine, driving with bouquets of flowers clamped between my knees, sprays of pansies and asters framing my view of the road. The morning of the party, you parked your wheelchair at the counter so you could watch me mince garlic and dismantle pumpkins. Ever so often, you grazed from my hands, chewing thoughtfully. With eyes closed, you told me to add a pinch of salt or a dash of paprika.

When you had to rest, I scoured through my recipes, checked

and double-checked my ingredients—brushing aside the scrap of paper where I had written down a list of different tarps, large plastic tubs, black trash bags—making sure that everything was perfect. I frowned at one recipe card for jeweled rice. It was one of the first meals I had learned to make, a birthday favorite you had always made for me, but even though I had followed the recipe exactly, it tasted flat. Something was missing, and the party was fast approaching. I spun toward our pantry, organized in expert fashion with labeled containers detailing the ingredients inside and the date we had stored them. It was initially your system, but as I had taken over the cooking, I had tweaked it so that the ingredients were organized by ingredient type and date. I scanned the shelves, until the bowl of fruit snagged my attention. Perfect, I thought.

Finally, only an hour from our guests arriving, you tasted my food one last time.

"It's lovely," you whispered.

"Really?" I crouched by your chair and looked eagerly up into your face. "You don't think it needs a touch more acid?"

"No," you said, palm enveloping mine. "It's perfect."

I leaned forward and planted a wet kiss on your cheek. You smiled but then frowned.

"What?" I said. "What is it?"

"Did you add something extra?"

I rolled back on my haunches. "I'm sorry. I followed the recipes the way you wrote them out for me, but I did add some of the persimmons to the jeweled rice."

The expression on your face was like the sun bursting through the clouds. "I hadn't thought of that. The addition tastes wonderful, darling."

The doorbell rang, and I shot to my feet.

"They're here," I said, squeezing your hand, before darting off to let the first of our guests in. Soon our tiny apartment was abuzz with voices, laughing and asking after us, the clink of wine bottles settling on the counter and gasps of admiration at the dining room spread. We had built the menu together, each dish a nod to every loved meal we shared in our eight years together: the lemon garlic chicken you first made me, a sweet coconut curry, our jerk chicken tacos we loved pairing with blood orange margaritas, and of course the jeweled rice, glistening and fragrant. We kissed the cheeks of both your mother and mine, and they went arm-in-arm to fill their glasses with sparkling rosé. Early 2000s pop music mingled with Vietnamese boy bands and a slew of Persian love ballads in the background. It was the most noise that had inhabited our apartment in months; between us and your nurses, ours was an inner sanctum broken only by our low voices and soft movements, the caterpillar crawl of your limbs over mine.

Lit candles flickered all over the kitchen and living room, and within their dancing glow, you were incandescent. Despite your exhaustion and the occasional awkward *how have you been* uttered, your eyes were bright and alert. Our mothers flanked your chair, and a circle formed with you at its exuberant center.

I brought over a ginger ale for you to sip as my mother jostled my shoulder, saying, "Can you believe it? This girl used to just eat slices of white bread all the time. White bread!"

She laughed, showing a lacework of wrinkles around her eyes. It struck me, then, that I would never see your face so wonderfully creased.

"Sometimes I buttered and toasted it with brown sugar sprinkled on top," I said, but you could hear the tremor in my voice.

My mother just shook her head in mock shame. "I made so many beautiful meals. Phở gà. Bún bò huế. Bánh xèo. And she just turned her nose up at all of them for her brown sugar bread and cup noodles."

The cup noodles I had eaten over the sink, ears strained for raised voices and footsteps on the stairs.

The evening skipped on like children holding hands. Your body grew heavier with each hour, but you watched every emptied plate with unabashed joy. You pointed out Annie, who had scarfed down so many bite-sized egg custard tarts that the crumbs speckled her long, pink curls. Egg custard tarts were our favorite things to share every time we stopped by Chinatown, sold to us by a little grandma whose mouth puckered at my Vietnamese-tinted Mandarin. There was Gene with his new boyfriend Isaac, who kept going back for extra mouthfuls of sauteed clams served with sesame rice crackers, which was the first thing my mom had ever made you when you two met for the first time—when my sweet, puzzled mother still thought we were just "very close friends" who held hands in the park. I flitted around the room, refilling glasses and slicing more cheese for the charcuterie board, all the while aware of our mothers watching me. I knew on some level that our mothers blamed me, believed that I was the one pushing for no funeral, no formal ceremony with heads bowed down in prayer. I knew that your mother always thought I was dragging you down to hell with me in my Barbie pink heels and bubblegum smile. And maybe I was. Maybe everything leading to your request was a hell of my own making, that I hadn't loved you enough, that somewhere in your mind you doubted me enough that now I needed to prove how much I really loved you. I was a one-woman balancing act actively pedaling with your doubts and the doubts of our mothers teetering on my shoulders, but I couldn't find it in me to blame anyone.

Before, when we still toyed with the idea of bringing a baby into our home, I once told you that there were species of spiders whose mothers let their babies eat them. The mother's body begins to digest itself, becoming a palatable soup of internal organ meat, in preparation for her babies to feed on once they hatch. Some species even make a game of it—guiding their children along on a chase by shaking and tapping their legs on their spider silk, mimicking struggling prey for their children to swarm. Your eyes had taken on a dreamy quality when I told you this, your fingers idly tap, tap, tapping on my knee. That was your idea of love, after all.

***

By the time the last of our guests trickled out the door, toting the carryout containers I had been foresighted enough to supply them with, I only had crumbs to clean up as you dozed in your chair. You dozed as I rinsed our dishes, dried off our silverware, clicked the kitchen lights off and our bedroom fairy lights on. You dozed as I wiped the last of your lipstick off, already cracked and blotchy as it was, wiggled you out of your black turtleneck and cigarette pants, tugged you into your nightgown and a fresh pair of underwear. You dozed as I eased your feet into fuzzy socks and muscled you into our bed, your limbs splaying out like a ragdoll's, your wispy locks crimping against the pillows. You dozed as I showered the last of the day away, the caramelized onions from my hair, the splatters of soup down my chin, your mother's lip gloss on my cheek.

You only woke after I had toweled off and crawled in beside you, my body still slick and hot from the steam. I kissed your cool, powdery forehead, and you whined; as the weeks came and went and you weakened, you whined more often, your voice pitched high like a kitten's. I kissed you again, and when it became clear you wanted more, I gently kissed down your jawline, my lips moving against your throat. I felt you swallow hard, though I knew the medicines made your mouth dry and each swallow painful. I dragged my teeth along your collarbone, which prodded me like an accusation. I worked down each knob of your body, every new hollow. Your skin was stretched tight over your bones, like how I imagined a fattened duck's might be, and I remembered how cold your hands were the first time we met, how even then I had wanted to warm you.

You see, after we met at that party, two or three dates into our relationship, you had explained to me how the foie gras we ate was really produced. With steady, self-assured hands, the farmer gorged the duck. One hand gripped the duck by the neck while the other rammed a funnel delivering high-starch feed down the duck's throat. It either ate or it died. Then it died anyway. Every day to the point of bursting, the farmer gorged the duck until it ballooned to ten times its size—organs swelling against skin against feathers—then slaughtered for its fattened liver, which is carved out of its body and eventually served delicately on the smooth, cold thigh of a pretty girl at a party thrown by people who would never see the farms or the ducks, would never touch that rapid pulse before the slaughter.

Sinking my teeth into your skin, I watched your glossy eyes flutter and your mouth blossom open.

Your eyes left mine for a moment, and I knew without looking what pulled your attention. The knife by our bedside, as common a sight to me now as the empty water glass and the alarm clock shaped like a music box. I felt the magnetism of its pull in every muscle of your body. Your whole face was a delicate emulsion of desire mixed with fear and pain. Even when you were dying, you still wanted to feed me with your own two hands. This was the only way you knew how to love, how to be loved. I took your beautiful hand, trembling in mine, with its tracery of purple veins and the butterfly beat of your pulse, and closed my lips around your ring finger, your wedding ring a cold scrape against my teeth. *Will you take her to be your lawfully wedded wife?* You gasped, like I had siphoned the air from your lungs. *In sickness and in health?* I would have you. I would have all of you, and later, after the sheets have lost your warmth, and the last strand of your hair has spooled down the shower drain, I will remember the way you held on to me, flesh cleaved to flesh, as if you would never let me go.

COOKING, CODEPENDENCY, & CANNIBALISM

A Conversation with Thea Nguyen

Claire Agnes: Thank you for sharing this story with *Driftwood Press!* This was a memorable selection, driven by tangible sensory detail and a palpable, evocative voice. What inspired you to write this particular piece?

Thea Nguyen: A lot of different things inspired this piece. Around the time I was writing "Hard Swallow," my husband and I were marathoning several seasons of *Master Chef*. When I think of this story, I can't help sometimes visualizing a gently frowning Gordon Ramsay standing over my shoulder.

My husband is the main cook in the family, but I'm every bit as obsessed with food and the cooking of it—the inherent creation and destruction attached to the act—and with the people who dedicate their lives to transforming simple ingredients into works of art. Cooks spend hours of training and preparation to toil over a dish that will be consumed in a matter of moments. As a Vietnamese American, I grew up on my mom's phở, which involves simmering beef bones for at least a good six hours to make the broth. It was an extraordinary amount of effort for a kid who would have been happy eating overcooked Kraft mac n' cheese. That's how my mom showed her love for us; we didn't spend time like other families on the beach or playing board games, but we always managed to gather around bowls of phở and let the steam hit our faces. I wanted to express that kind of love—the long-laboring, self-sacrificial kind—and push it to the extreme in this story.

At the time, I had also just read Caitlin Doughty's *Smoke Gets in Your Eyes*, and there's a section in the book where she discusses cultural funerary practices. The Wari' tribe in Brazil practiced mortuary cannibalism as a compassionate act for the community; without the full destruction of the dead body, the community was unable to move on and heal from the loss. All these things together sparked the idea for "Hard Swallow," an all-consuming love mixed in with grief and asking those we cherish to do the impossible for us.

CA: It is funny that you mention the domineering caricature of Gordon Ramsey in *MasterChef.* In examining the characters and thematics of this narrative, I can not help but to also be reminded of the 2022 film, *The Menu.* In it, a sex worker attends an exclusive chef's tasting on a private island with a wealthy client. As the evening progresses, the dishes served grow ever more sinister. The film examines themes of consumption and control through the dynamic between the restaurant's exacting head chef and the young female protagonist. In "Hard Swallow," we see another chef with precise vision, and a model who prefers cup noodles to her mother's homemade meals. How do these choices in characterization and employment reflect larger cultural perspectives surrounding work, identity, and autonomy?

TN: By characterizing Leila as a head chef and Holly as a fashion model, I did want to differentiate the degrees of autonomy each woman has in their professions. While Leila oversees her restaurant's whole staff and is able to make decisions at every level to create perfect meals, Holly herself becomes part of a commodified object that viewers will consume. For models, very little is within their control. A whole team of professionals determine the model's outfits, makeup, photoshoot locations, their poses, and the overall vision of the intended products. I chose these professions specifically to match how Leila and Holly view their own autonomy.

What is also important to note is that becoming either a professional chef or model is extremely difficult; each industry has demanding requirements and is contingent on the consumers' reception. In the world of professional cooks, only a handful of women go on to become head chefs or earn a Michelin-star, whereas the majority of professional cooks are overwhelmingly male. Meanwhile, while the modeling industry is skewed towards a female majority, plus-sized and mid-sized models like Holly still only make up a meager 5% of the total modeling demographic. In many areas of their lives, Leila and Holly are minorities struggling to rise above expectations and become consumed by their work. Leila dedicates her professional and home life to making delicious meals for others; whereas, Holly's difficult relationship with food becomes ever more complicated once she starts modeling, and she even takes pride in starving herself.

CA: As a reader of this piece, I appreciated the attention of the prose to the thematics through diction. How did you approach developing the core ideas and emotive threads of the story? Was there a specific idea or question that you wanted to explore?

TN: The first iteration of this story was a poem called "Lover to Her Dying Wife," and the initial images in that poem are the wife's hands guiding the narrator's as they cook, and the narrator feeding her wife from her hands. These two images, intimately domestic, served as the core for this story. From there, I wondered how this domestic intimacy, their love, could be intensified to the point of breaking. Their toxic codependency transforming into a literal feeding off each other developed naturally, and from there I wanted to portray as many forms of consumption as possible.

I saw that cannibalism, taboo for so many cultures, is an intrinsically intimate experience, as is cooking. Taking a once-living being and fragmenting it, feeling the bones and tendons in your hands, smelling how raw meat transforms into a mouthwatering meal, is such a visceral experience. It's violence in its most domestic form.

For those of us living in sheltered communities, cooking and preparing food is the closest we get to handling non-living bodies. Gone are the days where families bathe and dress their own deceased loved ones; nowadays, in most Western societies, the bodies are often wheeled off to the funeral house before any proper goodbyes. Strangers (usually very nice, very professional strangers) are the ones who prepare our loved ones for burial, who dress them in their best Sunday clothes and try to replicate the way they did their makeup. Death, for most of us, is often just a box in the ground. Cannibalism as a main throughline in this story, then, was my attempt at drawing death to the forefront, making both the narrator and audience contemplate death in its rawest, most personal form. Not only does the narrator have to watch her wife's slow decline, but she will have to be the one to personally reckon with her wife's body if she goes through with cannibalizing her.

Agency is another core idea for this piece, and I wanted to convey the characters' sense of (or lack of) agency through the movement of their hands. By juxtaposing the gentle caresses between the narrator and her wife with the chopping, skinning, and flaying that is involved with cooking, I wanted to convey the gravity of what the narrator is weighing in her mind. With the same hands that have cared for and tended to her wife, she is now deciding if she will use those same hands to cut into the woman she loves. Leila's character herself is characterized by her steady hands, which are not only guiding Holly in their cooking lessons but also pushing her forward to a decision Holly will have to live with for the rest of her life.

CA: I appreciate the pairing of imagery and thematics, which is certainly a strength of the piece throughout. In the narrative, Leila's illness and the request to be consumed are presented with a matter-of-fact tone. How did you decide on this tone? What effect were you hoping to achieve?

TN: As someone who primarily writes magical realism, I think using a matter-of-fact tone to incorporate an element seen as less realistic, such as Leila's request for Holly to eat her, is important in grounding that particular element. I wanted the reader to spend more time on Holly and Leila's emotional journey in this piece rather than Leila's illness and her request. While writing, I took a lot of inspiration from Agustina Bazterrica's novel *Tender is the Flesh*. In her novel, cannibalism has become a normalized industry across the world, and she also uses a matter-of-fact tone to describe the brutal acts of butchering and consuming humans. This particular tone lends a certain amount of distance from the events, which makes them far more digestible for the reader. In the same way, I wanted to establish Leila's request as something normal within their insular world, which also aligns well with Leila's pragmatic character and Holly's willingness to play along with her wife. I wanted the tone to express that these things were undeniable facts of their reality, and instead of dwelling on them, it would be a better use of their remaining time to get down to the business of Holly's cooking lessons.

CA: The narrator and her wife, Holly and Leila, and the dynamics of their relationship and lives, are certainly the focal points of this narrative. Can you tell us about the process of creating these characters? What characteristics or experiences influenced their development, and how did they evolve over the course of writing this story?

TN: As much as this story was about love and consumption, it was also fundamentally about queerness for me. Many daughters, especially ones coming from immigrant families, carry a lot of familial expectations into their romantic relationships. The selfless matron figure in a nuclear family is a familiar image; how does that image exist within a sapphic relationship? What happens when two women, raised in this heteronormative mindset, dedicate their lives to each other? The narrator and her wife, Holly and Leila, were born from these questions. Leila is the methodical one, a chef who is accustomed to leading an entire kitchen; whereas Holly is a model accustomed to following instructions, and who is prone to passivity and neglecting her own self-care. Despite their differences, they are both consumed with the urge to please and provide for the other, at the detriment of themselves. Theirs is an insular, codependent world where they consistently feed off each other's energy. Leila needs to be needed, and Holly is more than happy to enable that behavior, which is reflected in their relationships with food. Leila primarily cooks for Holly, and Holly herself learns to cook not to feed Leila but to someday nourish herself from Leila's body. Leila giving up her body to Holly is their gross approximation of a mother providing for her child; an act of love given at one's expense. Even before Leila's request, Holly has a complicated relationship with food that extends from a childhood where meals were sites for conflict; eating less was preferable to witnessing her father's abuse of her mother. As I developed this story, I saw that the push and pull between Holly and Leila swung from satiety and hunger, whether sexually or emotionally.

CA: On the topic of history and its impact on present choices, I am curious about the structural choices made in this narrative. The story vacillates between present timeline and past history, and is delivered in the past tense, which invokes a point of telling still unseen by the reader at the story's end. How did you decide on the style and structure of the narrative? Were there any particular challenges or deliberate choices in how you told the story?

TN: In mourning, memories become slippery things. I wanted to capture that slipperiness by constantly teasing the past forward into the present. While all the events in the story are occurring in the past for the narrator, the ending and the narrator's point of telling are ambiguous because the narrator herself is resistant to accepting the events as they are. The cooking lessons between the narrator and her wife regularly happen in the "past" as a way to convey the sheer amount that Holly is learning, as well as show that she is only going through the motions; whereas, the moments set in the "present" timeline are moments of either conflict with herself or with Leila. I found it difficult at times to decide how many details of their life before the cancer to include. Most of the details of their life together all led back to food or cooking, which, while not a full picture of these characters and lives, was my way of emphasizing how consumed they are with Leila's cancer and her request.

CA: This narrative ends before the narrator is truly confronted with answering her wife's question with tangible, practical, perhaps visceral means. Did earlier drafts of this piece have different endings, and what factors contributed to the changes you made in this final iteration of the piece?

TN: I briefly played with showing scenes after the narrator's wife died, but I found that my focus in the story shifted too far away from the narrator's internal conflict toward the cannibalistic aspects of the story. While I could have found a way to keep those scenes and make them work, I ultimately decided that leaving the ending ambiguous benefited the story the most. I wanted to give the narrator a choice, which would drive the conflict through the story, without having the narrator's decision take too much precedence. I wanted the emotional weight focused on the moments right before Holly makes a final decision on Leila's fate; I wanted to balance her on the edge of a life-changing moment and keep the audience from plummeting through to the other side of her decision. Whatever Holly ends up choosing, Leila will still end up dying either way, whether by Holly's hand or by the natural progression of Leila's cancer. What I wanted to emphasize, instead, was how they spent their last moments together. Instead of going on one last adventure together, Leila chooses to spend it at home, teaching her wife to cook. Leila's choice is one stemming from love. She is preparing Holly for a life without her; however, with her additional request that Holly consume her body, Leila is also attempting to control the way her body is taken care of once she has passed. My decision to leave the ending ambiguous also reflects that, while Holly is given this choice, she as a mourner is helpless in the face of her loved one's death, and must cope in any way she can.

CA: As the creator of Holly, Leila, and this world, what do you think happens after the story's end? Do you plan to write other pieces within this world, or featuring these characters?

TN: Whether Holly ultimately fulfills Leila's quest or not, she would go on to mourn Leila and lean on her community, despite how she and Leila initially kept them out of the funeral rites. Holly will continue feeding herself from the recipes Leila has left behind for her. I can see myself writing a piece in the future where Holly falls in love again many years later, and how she navigates a new relationship with the phantom of Leila still haunting her, but for now, these characters deserve a peaceful rest.

CA: This narrative's thematics strum at larger cultural issues. What do you hope readers take away from this story, whether in terms of emotion, reflection, or a deeper understanding?

TN: At its heart, this piece is a love story, and like with any type of narrative, I think love stories need to be challenged. Especially with those in the queer community, who have struggled with compulsory heterosexuality, some crave the all-consuming love that Holly and Leila share between each other. Friends in the queer community experiencing their first sapphic relationship often marvel at how much better being with a woman is. For a lot of sapphic people, that can definitely be a true experience, but the romanticization of sapphic and queer relationships disregards the challenges specific to these relationships. It can be easy to love someone to the point of obliterating your own identity, especially when it's a love you have fought for. While the love between Holly and Leila is real, they abandoned everything else for each other. Their hobbies, their jobs, their communities of family and friends—all of it was pared away to accommodate their hyperfixation with one another. I think it's important to think about these characters and how everything in their lives, their upbringing, their choices and people-pleasing, all culminated in their isolation and eventual self-destruction.

CA: This is an interesting take, especially as so much of heteronormative rhetoric is based upon the consumption and commodification of the feminine. What do you see as specific to the characterizations of Holly and Leila that leads them to this type of relationship?

TN: Both Holly and Leila come from heteronormative households with conservative, immigrant backgrounds. Women growing up in these communities are socialized from an early age to seek domestic roles centered around pleasing their spouses, parents, and in-laws. In Vietnam, an unmarried woman in her twenties is a source of concern for her family. While Holly and Leila's queer relationship is inherently opposed to these conservative values, it is still difficult for them to entirely buck a lifetime of social programming, where they were taught as girls to put their spouses above all else: their interests, their friends, and even their own lives. Their shared life in this story is visibly sparse; the cooking lessons and their plans for the future consumes all their time and thoughts. Very little space is set aside for anything else, and even the party that they throw for their friends and loved ones is a temporary extension of their limited world. The continual fixation on their relationship and Leila's request alone mirrors the isolation experienced in many heteronormative nuclear family structures. The struggles and experiences are limited to the couple and their immediate family unit; instead of leaning on their community, Holly and Leila bear the full burden of their hardships and suffer the consequences.

CA: Are "love stories" a consistent focus in your work? Does your art find itself drawn to any specific narrative arcs, characters, or worlds?

TN: Many of my stories feature queer, BIPOC characters, and while some do focus on their relationships, my stories primarily center around characters experiencing some form of othering that they either overcome or surrender to. I am also very much drawn to the idea of archives, especially in terms of which remnants defy the test of time and which don't. For instance, I wrote a story about generational trauma, where the main character is suffering from a family curse but whose family history is suppressed and inaccessible to her. I grew up on magical girl anime, and so many of my stories will also feature characters undergoing massive transformations. Whether it's a woman turning into a mythological fox every night, a boy becoming immortal against his will, or a girl astral projecting into someone else's body, I am always playing around with interesting and provocative ways to transform my characters.

CA: Such interesting concepts! Where else can we find your work?

TN: I have another story called "Lost and Found" forthcoming in *F(r)iction*, and I am currently working on a few different projects, including a collection of short stories and a prospective video game.

CA: I'm looking forward to seeing more of your stories out in the world! Thank you again for sharing "Hard Swallow" with us here at *Driftwood*, and for sharing your process with me today.

TN: Thank you for having me and for asking such great questions. I am delighted to be featured among so many other lovely and massively talented creatives. It's been a joy working with everyone from *Driftwood Press*, and I'm grateful this little story of mine has found a home.

THE MUSIC OF OLENA XIPHIAS

Anastasios Mihalopoulos

I'm thinking of my father as the ferry makes its way into the port of Kamariotissa with the lethargy of a dying giant. The boat comes to a stop, the hum of its engine heart deafens as the knurled metal doors lower, releasing a flood of cars, Vespas, and passengers into the city streets. Locals and tourists alike, each dispersing to their own agendas, sharing only the communal exhaustion of a long journey. Some carry backpacks, others entire suitcases and carry-ons. I have my violin bag, with a few dresses and some clothes wrapped around the instrument. As I lean over the railing, I fidget with my bracelet. The subtle clack of the pumice beads soothes me as I look out past the port town, at Mt. Fengari looming behind it; the jagged rock formations feeding upon the wispy hues of plumeria in the evening fog. Immediately, I am inside a memory. Those long nights on the island, watching the sun sink behind the mountain, back on our beach, listening to Dad talk about the Fengari-kleithon, the moon ritual of the summer solstice that the pagan women would practice each year.

I mustn't have been older than eight or nine when Dad walked me down to the beach. I remember clasping two of his calloused fingers in my hand while he carried his guitar by the neck in the other. I pointed the flashlight where he directed, its soft beam of light swaying as we trotted along the path. We'd spent a while gathering sticks and pinecones to build a fire. There was a cadence to this procedure, the sound of brambles rustling punctuated by the tide lapping gently at the beach stones. The fire started quickly. I sat on a log while dad sat cross-legged on the rocks. He held his guitar lazily, occasionally playing a short riff, maybe a gentle wisp of Zeibekiko. The song was always simple but hypnotic: the notes falling in a cyclical pattern until disrupted by brief improvisation, a labyrinthine melody erupting then returning to the refrain. The song and the dance associated with it both require a kind of haphazard sense of balance, as if walking barefoot through a sea of sharp stones, arms raised out to the sides, every step calculated, harmonic, yet free-flowing. This is what my father told me that all music should do. Create an atmosphere, a landscape for feeling.

"Oloi mou, do you know Fen-gah-ree?" he asked while he continued playing.

"The mountain?"

"No, the word. It means moon. Long ago people had never seen a mountain like this; it blocked out the sun, so they named it after the moon."

I thought it was silly to think that people had never seen a mountain. There were mountains everywhere in Greece. I keep trying to remember that night. How we'd sat there, him playing guitar and preening up towards the sky, both of us pausing to listen to the watery whispers, the breeze weaving between the trees, the occasional bell of a goat somewhere back up the hillside. We let the fire grow low. The beach stones still felt warm. At one point, dad jolted up as if he'd heard something.

"I almost forgot!" he said as he set the guitar down and trotted into the surrounding darkness. When he returned he was straining to hold a bucket filled to the brim with seawater.

I try to remember more but the memory dissipates as I step off the ship. The jet lag is still creeping around somewhere in the back of my skull with a quiet buzz that says there is no time for sentimentality, no time for meaning-making. This isn't your island anymore.

A group of men sit on the terrace of a café as I make my way off the boat. They are drinking frappé and smoking. One of them looks over at me as I walk by, recognizes something in me and he says, "Tínos aftí." They murmur amongst each other, holding me in their view as I walk. Despite my poor Greek, I can make out the phrase, *whose is she?* I don't belong to anyone, but I feel a shudder thinking of all the problems of Samothraki. This island especially, wrapped in its mixed histories and religions. I try to forget about the men, about how our family name dies with me. At least I can take pride in knowing they recognized me as Greek, whatever that means.

From the bustling port town, I take a goat path up and around the peninsula. I'd wanted the quiet solitude of this walk. I could do without the violin, though the instrument has, in a way, become a part of me, like Dad and his guitar, something I go to when I don't have the words to wrap around something. So I carry it with me everywhere even when I know there is little to no chance of playing it.

The sun is relentless. Despite the trees, every stone on the path seems to throw heat back up at me. It's impossible not to sweat. I hunch over, trying to relieve my shoulders of the strain from my pack. At least three kilometers still stand between me and my family's village. The violin feels absurd. Not taking a taxi also feels absurd. I continue walking. Between heavy breaths, I try to focus on the constant chatter of cicadas and birds overhead. Wind rattles in the leaves of olive and mastic trees, occasionally dipping down, kicking hot dust from the path up into me. The island has this way of sticking to you, melding with your skin, congealing with the smell of your sweat. For years, I'd worked tirelessly to wash myself of this dirt. Nearly a year after Dad's passing, I'm lurching back here, wanting to roll in it.

I don't remember much from my childhood on the island beyond that I wanted to leave. I wanted to go to the bigger schools on the mainland where I could make friends and go out to the bars. I wanted the excitement and noisy anonymity of the city that simply wasn't possible in a quiet fishing village like ours. I think I chose not to remember those early days at the family restaurant, helping Dad with the morning catch, picking olives in midday sun. It's all really just a blur. Mom. Dad. My Childhood. The island itself. It's been good for publicity though. When I first moved to the states, the label of "island violinist prodigy" seemed to saturate everything I did. When I applied for jobs or fellowships they always wanted to hear about the island. They marketed my performances as "Sounds of Samothraki: A String Odyssey" or "Kore at the Goat Funeral." I think the media was more interested in examining my past than I was. Sometimes I wish I'd steered into it more.

My mother meets me at the end of the drive. She's smiling wide, her eyes carrying the cloudy haze of cataracts though I can still make out the hazel glint that we share.

"Ti Kaneis Oloi mou!" She holds her arms out in want of an embrace.

"Kala Ma, Eseis?" I stumble through the words as I lean into her. I think about how Dad would greet me if he were here, how his darty eyes would light up at the sound of my ill-pronounced Greek. I never got around to learning the language beyond the few introductory phrases. Mom loves to remind me that I spoke such good Greek when I was young and that she doesn't know what happened. Somehow learning to play concert violin holds less weight to her. I've started to understand why. I thought of it during my time on tour in Quebec. How precious language is treated there, how we are all so protective of the sound of a homeland that is slowly becoming harder and harder to hear.

Mom is nearly a foot shorter than me now. I feel her small hand weave itself around my arm and clamp against me. We walk up the drive, a strange promenade, into the restaurant and to the veranda. The branches of a mulberry tree form tributaries spanning the entirety of the trellis. Stray beams of light make their way through the verdant canopy, giving the restaurant the same fluid-mosaic texture as that of the bottom of an outdoor swimming pool on a sunny day. Already, there is a tray of bread, olives and a plate of *Barbounia* on a table overlooking the cove. Mom pulls the chair out and helps me into it. *Barbounia* or Red Mullet was my favorite meal as a child. Mom remembers it this way though it isn't my favorite anymore. I choose to entertain her.

The fish is too bony and small to be eaten with a fork. I suppose you could, but it ruins the experience. Dad always hovered over customers as they lifted their silverware. "I swear to god you better put that down," he'd utter in thunderous Greek before transforming his tone to instructional. "You must use your fingers!" It is true: to pick morsels of flesh from the body of the fish, to place them gently upon the tongue is better. You can taste the salty waters, the dinge of minerality as the sweetened flesh overtakes you, as the aroma of sea-flesh mends with your own. *Barbounia* tastes like and bears the color of shrimp for that is what they primarily feed upon. In death, their bodies flush red, further proof that the fish becomes what it devours.

By the time I left, I'd come to hate the way that fishy smell seeped into my skin. No matter how many times I washed my hands, the smell never quite came off, always leaving a smudge or greasy imprint on the fingerboard of my violin. The same violin that Mom is taking out of the case in the atrium. She comes over to me.

"Will you play?"

"I'm tired, Ma. Maybe tonight?" Even without touching the violin I feel the urge to clutch a handful of napkins to clean my fingers. "Can you put it back in its case, please?"

"You're waiting for the solstice, no?"

"I'm waiting for my headache to go away." I feel bad for snapping. It's strange how grief manifests sometimes. It's been over a year since they buried my father. And because he wanted to be buried on the island, there was no way I could have flown in for a funeral in time. They don't embalm here, so funerals happen quickly. I told Mom I'd be here to visit the grave afterwards, but time slipped away. I was still performing, giving lessons, and teaching at the university. I gave myself little time to process, perhaps no time at all. The solstice had felt like a good excuse to wait the full year.

As the sun begins to set, I prepare to see my father's grave. My mother says she hasn't visited it since his burial. She claims there is nothing there for her to see—that his memory lives with her and not in a plot of earth where his body rests. She tells me where the plot of land is anyway, and I go looking. It's not a long walk. The sun is nearly eye-level now, throwing its harsh rays across the island and turning everything golden as I make my way along the small bend in the road. The hardy shrubs crunch as I trek over to the cliffside leading down to the lower end of the peninsula. There is a harbor shrine and a small cemetery for fishermen there. Though that is not where Dad is, I go down to look. The walk feels shorter than it should. I pass beneath a cathedral of fig trees, the air goes cooler, the large veiny leaves quiver like the back of my mother's hands. I look for fruit, though I know it is far too early in the season.

The harbor shrine is a small hole hacked into the cliffside with a dirt path leading to the entrance. I dip my head beneath the low threshold to enter into this preternatural place, the cave dimly lit by one or two candles crackling inside lanterns. Incense hangs heavy in the briny air. The walls are slick and black, broken occasionally by an icon bearing some gold-petal design of a saint or fisherman. I wonder if my father had prayed to them. The figures themselves are misshapen, often disproportional, giving a kind of eerie tilt. I move about the relics, running my fingers over *komboloi* and bracelets that hang from the walls. Blue eyes loom at every corridor watching me, urging me to remember the stories of spirits and bad omens. I take out my phone to use the flashlight, which feels like a kind of violation in this place. I shine the light over a goat's skull sitting on the rock, the infinite spiral of its horns. At the back of the cave, I find a stele. The stone is eroded and moss-covered, but I make out the faintest outline of a man in a ship holding what at first looks like a guitar—but I quickly realize is a harpoon. He's in a kind of javelin thrower's stance. Some shadowy shape exists next to the boat. I reach a hand out to trace the rippling mass carved there but jump at a sound.

"Yia!" I turn to see a figure standing in the threshold of the cave. He's broad, wearing Gore-Tex overalls. For a moment, I let myself believe that it could be my father. "Olena mou, could that be you?" Hearing his English, I realize it's Damien, a fisherman from our village and a close friend of my father's.

"Damien? Yes. I just got in this afternoon."

He steps further into the cave; he has an odd waddle from his bad hip that makes him move as if he has ankle weights on. I tell him I am here to visit my father's grave and his head tilts upwards, questioning me.

"Takis, here?" he asks. "No, not here. Íthele na eínai kápou ópou tha boroúse na akoúsei to tragoúdi sou."

I can't make out what he's said, so I just nod in attention. He catches on that I understand less Greek than he thought and switches back to English. "I will take you." He gestures for me to leave the cave and join him on his boat.

The Kithara rocks gently near the edge of the peninsula. I remember this boat. Not larger than a small dinghy, at its bow there's a small crane and a motor which are used to pull dredging nets from the sea. There's a small awning near the stern which houses the tiller, a bench, and a few supplies. In totality, the ship is no more than fifteen feet in length and rocking no more than a foot above the surface. When I was a young girl it felt massive. I could walk laps from bow to stern and pretend I was on a grand voyage to the new world.

I take off my shoes, imagining that bare feet will allow for better footholds than rubber soles and begin to trudge my way to the boat, avoiding algae-covered rocks and still pools full of urchins.

Damien bends over and lifts a thick barnacle-covered rope from the water, pulling his boat toward us so that we could board. At first, the boat seems resilient to his pull. The rope remains taut. His forearms, full of scars, ripple as he tightens his grip about the rope. *The Kithara* begins to accelerate until Damien places his foot upon the bow to prevent her from crashing into the rocky shelf. With a quick glance and the wave of a burly arm, he signals for me to board the boat. I step over the raised border and onto the moist deck, Damien's hand cautiously guiding me from behind.

I used to go down to the beach to practice my violin. Dad said it was too loud to practice at the restaurant, that I should go down to the water to play it. It became a part of my evening ritual. Trudging down the goat path, always fretting about the wind blowing sand into the f-holes. It started with simple bowing patterns, learning to gauge the pitch of each note, sometimes trying to replicate the folk music that drifted down from the restaurant. Then I began playing my own songs, trying to imitate the sound of the sea, or the way the trees rustled in the breeze. Sometimes a bird call, or even the cacophony of goats bleating in the distance. After some time, I'd see a lantern on the horizon and hear the quiet gurgle of Damien's boat moving towards the beach. He always fished at night. When he heard me playing he'd turn into the cove and invite me onboard. Sounds carries over open water. He let me play as he set out his nets, told me it was good for fishing. Afterwards, he'd moor the boat and take out his baglamas and play songs with me. I think it began this way, him playing a series of chords and me trying to mimic them with my violin. We would do this for hours, until it was time to pull up the catch. I can still picture the wriggling bodies, their slow twitch in the netted teardrop, a massive heart beating.

Now, on-board without my violin, I feel regretful and more of a nuisance than the esteemed guest I was treated like as a young girl. Damien is rapid in his movement, hardly paying mind to my presence aside from when he has to evade me as he moves about the deck, preparing the boat to push off. I sit down on the small bench. Scooting towards the edge so that the moon and stars remain visible. Tracing the constellations, I remember the ritual again: Dad walking back with the bucket; the full moon throwing its beam over the sinuous tide.

"Give me your bracelet, Oloi mou," Dad asked. I gave it to him and he dropped it into the bucket along with his own. "Now think of a wish."

I thought of how I wanted to leave the island, to go to the states, somewhere with a big city and lots of people. I was tired of the slow cycles of island life.

"Do you have one?"

I nodded.

"Normally this ritual is done with a larger group. So you'd give your wish to whoever's item you pulled from the bucket, but it looks like you're going to have to share your wish with me." He smiled. "Reach in to grab my bracelet and then tell me your wish."

I lowered my hand into the bucket. The water felt cold and wrong. I scraped along the bottom feeling small granules of rock and sand before I felt what must have been Dad's bracelet. I stalled as I tried to think of a better wish. He gave me a look and I pulled the bracelet out. "My wish is that you never grow old." He chuckled a bit.

"I am already old, Oloi mou, but thank you." He reached in and quickly found my bracelet. He knelt so that he was eye-level with me, holding the bracelet close to my face, its black beads dripping seawater. "May you find great success in life wherever you go, but may you always remember where you came from." He slid the bracelet over my wrist, then took my head in both his hands, rough skin scratchy on my cheeks, and kissed my forehead.

I'm running my fingers over the bracelet counting the beads as the boat cuts knife-like through the black water of the cove. Damien is unusually quiet, standing at the stern, directing the boat as he looks out into the dark abyss. He had been a good friend of my father's, like a brother to him. Somehow I think he knew I would return on the solstice. When Damien was satisfied with the ship's trajectory, he came towards the bow and sat down next to me.

"You should have come sooner, you know." He reached into his pocket to roll a pinch of tobacco. "To see your father."

"It was difficult to leave work."

"I know, I know. Still you should have come."

It's true, I could have come sooner. I feel my chest constrict at the thought, that I was not here before he passed. Maybe some part of me had thought staying away would keep the reality of his death away, but as the solstice grew closer I'd known I couldn't put it off any longer. Even now, I won't let myself feel the full weight of it.

Damien leans over to one side, the cigarette in his mouth drawing smoky shapes in the air. He lifts a trapdoor of sorts and pulls out the small guitar-like body of his baglamas. The same instrument I remember from when I was young: a dark mahogany base, the swirls of the *meandros* pattern in the rosette. The instrument appears small in Damien's hands. His torso is so broad that it barely spans his waist.

"Your father asked me to play this song the day before he died." Damien pauses to tune a few of the strings. I hear the tension as he turns each peg. "He used to sneak down to the beach sometimes to listen to you play, you know. He came to me one day and showed me this, said that it was the song you play, that even the sea listened when you played it."

I can't remember any specific song from that time. I mostly played nonsense when I was down by the water. The beach was too windy to bring sheet music, and I could hardly read music then. I watch Damien's hands, swarthy and scarred. More like old leather than skin. Those hands, like my father's, turning liquid-smooth as he works along the fretboard. The notes are asymmetric; I can't put them to any scale of Greek folk music. Not Phrygian or Lydian. The song is wildly quick, then slow and gentle, moving from high to low in a kind of haphazard arpeggio that reminds me of crashing waves. Damien stares down at the baglamas as he plays, attending to each chord with his whole body. It is clearly a song he plays often. When I look over the gunwale I see the water beginning to churn, and a series of bubbles appear on the end of the boat where Damien is playing. I think I see small fish and mullet swimming about, the occasional larger shadow drifting beneath. A crowd of jellyfish plume near the bow. He notices me peering into the sea, but keeps playing, in a kind of melodic fugue. I clench the railing until my knuckles go white. I want to remember the song, but I can't. I can't even recall my father's face.

"This happens every time I play the song," he says as he stops playing, waving a hand to the water. "The fish like your music."

"I don't understand. I was so young I could hardly hold my violin." I keep staring at the fish as they begin to dissipate.

"Look." He lifts a wet coral fan from one of the nets on the deck. "Gorgóna," he says as he sets the strange pumice fan on the deck in front of him and begins to play again. At first, nothing happens. Then I watch the coral fan shimmer, like a fish slowly dying. Damien plays faster and color slowly returns to the rocky exterior of the fan. He stops again. "Here, you try." He gestures for me to take the instrument, but I turn it down. "I know you can play." He sets the baglamas in my lap. It feels wrong. Somehow this tiny guitar is much heavier than the violin. I struggle to find a space for it to rest comfortably on my leg.

"Now play the song."

The neck is worn smooth from years of use. I think of how many hands have held this instrument as mine begin their work. My fingers find the shape of one chord then another. The metallic strings dig into my skin. I feel the rock and sway of the boat as I finger pick my best estimate of the rolling melody, but the notes come out off-beat. The water outside the boat is still, the coral lifeless at my feet. I hand it back to him, wanting to rid myself of the instrument, this physical proof of my forgotten past.

"It'll come back to you. Give it time."

We round the cove back to the beach that sits beneath our family restaurant. There is a small plateau with a few headstones and their accompanying mausoleums. I want to ask Damien where my father's is, but I don't want to seem incompetent. I leave the boat and search about the plot. I am still barefoot, the wet stone beneath my feet somehow connecting me to the stone tombs I walk through. I come to one grave and trace my hand along the engraved letters. It is sad enough that it took me a year to visit him, worse yet that each headstone is in Greek and I cannot make out the letters. I should be able to, but I can't. I've never seen my father's name written out in his language.

"Olena, he is here." Damien is resting his hand on a mausoleum, one that I know must contain my father's bones. I had walked right past it. At the front of the tombstone, I trace the letters Παναγιώτης ξιφίας. My body goes numb, the sea breeze no longer warm but like needles on my skin. The island is too rocky to bury a body and somehow that makes this more difficult. To know that my father's bones sit in this tomb, inches from where my hand rests.

"I'd like you to take me back."

Damien looks at me surprised.

"I'll come back tomorrow." I know that is a lie.

After Dad gave me his wish he relit the fire. I watched the flames grow large and chaotic, throwing large swathes of heat towards the sky.

"Now we leap the fire to burn off our past selves, the self that no longer serves us." He stood with his guitar and began playing a song I didn't recognize, something with heavy ascending waves, angry even. A song that sounded like a battle. He danced around the fire, swaying with the guitar a bit before leaping through the flames. The sound of trickling pebbles as he landed on the other side. He continued strumming the guitar and looked at me, his eyes saying, *go on*. I leapt the fire that night. Not knowing that this was the last night I'd spend on the island with him. That I'd get my wish and move to the mainland so I could get better schooling and eventually go to the states for university. That I wouldn't return to the island or Greece at all for that matter. That I would never see my father's face again.

Now, I think back to that night, what I must have burnt off in that fire—my language, my heritage, the notes of that song—all gone, burning paper peeling from my body as I leapt through the billowing ochre tendrils.

When I return, the restaurant is quiet. A single motion-light flickers as I move past the veranda through the kitchen and into the atrium where Mom has set my violin. I open the case, revealing the dark veneer. The bridge forms strange shadows in the half-lit room. I take it and its bow out of the case, grab a flashlight and make my way back down the goat path. I stand barefoot at the water's edge. Breathing deeply, I close my eyes and try to feel the subtle pulse of the tide through the beach stones under my feet. Then I assume the familiar posture and prepare to play.

The notes still don't come. I remember the general opening progression that Damien had played: G, A, Em, G...something like that, but my rhythm is all off. The song is a watery lament that I can no longer access.

I think again of Damien's hands moving up and down the fretboard, and how my father must have watched from that peninsula where he is buried now, seeing the fish swirling about. I don't believe the story. It's just another myth that the islanders tell and retell with no real meaning. But I want it to be true. I'll stay here until it is. Hours pass this way. I bow until my shoulders burn, until my chin goes raw. Tears burn as they run over the raw skin. Eventually, lethargy washes over me, and I sit down with the instrument in my hands. I look at the violin, now more adversary than companion. The subtle oil imprints on the fingerboard. I stand one more time, closing my eyes, feeling the gentle breeze arriving from off-shore. Somewhere a Nightjar's call shimmers through the air. I think of my father, how he'd stop playing the guitar sometimes mid-song and listen to the bird calls and the breeze. How he'd let the last note ring out until it became a part of the natural soundscape, something melded with ocean and animal.

I press the bow to the string and begin to play, trying to synchronize each note with the gentle hissing of the tide and beach stones, resting a moment to allow the island to fill in its part of the song, and then I begin to play frantically, a series of rising glissandos that turn and fall back down the scale into something sporadic, like a tunnel in the minor key. My bracelet rattles as my hand floats along the instrument's neck, finally feeling a kind of cadence. I imagine the fingerboard is the sea, each note, a finger tapping, sending a pulse across the still surface. When the song ends, exhaustion floods over me. At the water near my father's mausoleum, I swear I see the faintest ripple.

MYSTICISM IN SOUNDSCAPES & SUBTLE ABERRATIONS

A Conversation with Anastasios Mihalopoulos

Rachel Phillippo: Hello, Anastasios! Welcome to the pages of *Driftwood*! We are pleased to see your emotional and vibrant story, "The Music of Olena Xiphias," in print.

Anastasios Mihalopoulos: Thank you so much! It's a pleasure to be a part of the anthology!

RP: One of the most striking features of "The Music of Olena Xiphias" is the rich sense of place. The island plays a vital role in the life of your protagonist, as well as in the life of your story. Did you draw details from personal experience in this place? What sort of research did you conduct that led to such a vibrant setting?

AM: Absolutely. For several years now I have spent a month of my summer on the Greek island of Thasos for a Writing Workshop. From Thasos you can actually see Samothraki (the island where the story takes place) though I have never actually been to Samothraki. I've heard many stories and read a great deal about the rich history of the island. The best source, of course, was talking to the locals of Thasos and asking about Samothraki. Since travel to the island is a bit difficult I think that heightened the mystery for me. It might even be a sort of stand-in for a part of my own Greek heritage that I can learn about but can never fully access. Damien, the fisherman in the story, is definitely inspired by the fisherman, Stamatis, with whom I spent many days fishing on the island of Thasos. There is also a cave on Thasos where fishermen were known to pray just above the area of the cove where he docks his ship.

Broadly speaking, most of my stories begin with a place rather than a plot and that origin point often drives the story and its characters.

RP: I'm not surprised to hear that "place" is your starting point, given the depth of detail you've paid to the setting! Related to setting, your story takes place during the summer solstice. How does this timing come into play?

AM: Yes. So during my time in Thasos I was fortunate enough to work with the brilliant musician and Harvard ethnomusicologist, Panayotis League, who led our cohort to partake in the summer solstice ritual. We built a fire in the shape of star on the beach, charged a bucket of sea-water the night before the full moon, and as he played the Tsambouna (a kind of Greek bagpipe made from the body of goat which sounds exactly like the sound you would expect from the body of goat but in a pleasant, almost mesmeric way) we dropped our bracelets into the speechless water, shared our wishes for each other and then leapt the fire. Albeit a bit crude of a summary, this was the pagan ritual of the moon, Fengari Kleithon, which Olena and her father partake in in my story. The ritual symbolizes many things, but for me I think of it as a time of renewal and a time of reflection which, of course, is tethered to a kind of grief for the passage of time and past selves.

RP: That sounds like a fascinating experience! We can certainly see the influence of ethnomusicology here. Because the ritual introduces the themes of the passage of time and grief over time lost, there is a lot of movement in the story between the present time-of-telling and the past, through both memory and flashback. Can you speak about any challenges or benefits of writing a story that frequently moves between various points in time?

AM: Definitely, temporality is something I think about often as it relates to both landscape and heritage. I have gone to visit the island where my father and grandfather grew up, however, the landscape I saw was separated by decades of physical and cultural change. I walked through a place that was similar but not the same as what my father or grandfather would have experienced. To quote Natalie Bakopoulos, who writes about the feeling of returning to Greece in her novel *Scorpionfish*, "To return to a place again and again is to confront the sneaky passing of time."

In terms of craft, I think playing with time is essential, especially when writing a story in the first-person which, though fiction, I view similarly to memoir. I love works of writing where characters are both reflecting and reacting.

RP: As Olena reflects on her past, she experiences a yearning for her home country and familial roots that is tangible on the page. What called you to this theme?

AM: As a child of Greek and Italian immigrant parents and a member of diaspora, home-seeking is a large part of my writing. My first poetry manuscript, "Still, Sometimes, Shipwreck" is a collection of poems deeply interested in the theme of home-seeking, language loss, and developing one's sense of place. I grew up in Ohio with a strong connection to my cultural heritage, though I never learned the language or visited either country until I was nearly twenty-years-old.

RP: I love that title! Much of this story is internal, as we are tied deeply to Olena's memories, fears, and desires. I tend to favor stories with a lot of interiority. But I know that as a writer, it can be difficult to balance the interior story with the external. Is this a balance you are conscious of when writing? Or when revising?

AM: Always. In my head or in my journal I usually organize my story by paragraphs labeled as either *scene* or *reflection*. My first genre was creative nonfiction; reading and writing it myself, I often had to find creative ways to blend the two. I have often turned to the adage by a mentor of mine: in fiction we create meaning, but in nonfiction we uncover meaning. In this story I was writing with both hands in a sense, as I was imagining and writing the story of Olena's life and writing through her perspective as she performed the kind of self-reflection and uncovering that many memoirists demonstrate. That said, I often lean towards projects where characters do this kind of reflection and self-examination.

RP: I like that distinction! In "The Music of Olena Xiphias," how would you define the meaning that Olena is uncovering and you, as the author, are creating?

AM: A great question! I think the struggle that Olena is dealing with and that many diaspora Greeks deal with, is trying to uncover what that question even is and then realizing there may not be an answer to it. I believe that Olena is seeking to uncover a sense of meaning or connection to her heritage both through the people and the landscape of the island while striving towards a connection to another self, one that she imagines may have been had things gone differently. I don't know that she gets an answer, but I think the meaning would be something to deal with trying to play the song anyway. Even if the notes don't quite come, we can still inhabit the notes, we can still feel the syllables of a lost language on the tongue, as we inhabit songs and words of a distant place. That the grief can be held at bay for the duration of a song or two.

RP: Olena's music serves as a sort of conduit between herself and her sense of cultural belonging. By regaining her ability to play the song, she regains access to the island as a homeland. You've mentioned your connection to ethnomusicology. Is music a theme that finds its way into your stories frequently?

AM: Oh, yes. Music has always been a large part of my life but especially so in recent years. I dabble in guitar and the violin. And definitely played many riffs late at night while trying to work through the musical sequences of the story. My apologies go to my partner, our dog, and our upstairs neighbors. My doctoral work at the University of New Brunswick will be a poetry collection and/or short story collection. The poetry collection is deeply interested in sound and soundscapes as they relate to bioacoustics, ethnomusicology, and language. A lot of my new work, poetry and fiction, deal with ocean sounds, whale song, bird song, and various musical instruments. I'd say that my story collection is more directly interested in music and the ocean as two primary elements in each story in one way or another.

In regard to my heritage, I have been studying Greek and Italian for several years, but I grew up without learning either language. This lack of learning led to a sense of cultural disconnection and generated feelings of a lost heritage, a homelessness that cannot be mended by simply visiting a place. However, through music and dance, I have felt held and welcomed by each culture. This experience of music, particularly folk music, as connected to and offering a sense of home has been a kind of foundation. It is also what has led me to a deeper contemplation on the origins of aural cognition and to natural soundscapes.

RP: You mentioned that this story shares many themes with your first poetry manuscript, and that you are working on a collection of both poetry and stories. Would you consider yourself primarily a poet or a story writer? Do you find that you approach your themes of diaspora and home-seeking differently in the forms of poetry and prose?

AM: I would say that I view myself primarily as a poet, though I have written fiction since I was young and have been shifting towards fiction during my Ph.D. program. I think that I've always had the tendency to think in narratives and images, and that shows in my poetry. When thinking about the theme of home-seeking and diaspora, I find that it's sometimes more challenging to work into a poem, or rather it takes a bit more effort to distill. I tend to write poems and stories about the same subject matter when I am working on a particular project and one often offers a key to figuring out the other.

I think that working through aspects of a lost heritage or fractured identity is always difficult and often requires many different angles. Language loss and reclamation of identity and culture will always be difficult to capture in prose and poetry.

RP: The story ends with a sense of lovely mysticism, the music having a transcendental connection to the land. Is this, too, based on real local mythology? Is the mystical or magical a theme you find you come back to frequently when writing about these themes of home and language?

AM: No, not to my knowledge. Though as I continue to dig deeper in my research on the origins of music, language, and animal song I continue to find stories that offer a similar idea. Many theorists agree that evolution produced music long before language, that there is a kind of music of the spheres as Pythagoras believed, and that this kind of yearning for ancient melodies can be traced across cultures. Songs and speech are often built from the noises of the surrounding landscape, the calls of its animal calls, and the sounds of the Earth.

I think that my interest in science really began as an interest in the magic of our world. And the best part of working on the page rather than the lab is that you can bend the rules of the natural world in a believable way. I think those subtle aberrations are where we find magic and mysticism. As a child something about seeing the movement of the tide is otherworldly and magical until you begin to learn about gravity and even still, there is something mystical about it. So too it is with music. That all said, I think I like to set my stories right along the edge of reality and magic. For me, it is the best approach for accessing sentiments of language and home-seeking as well as other subject matter.

RP: It's interesting to hear how your varying interests have collided to form this story! Additionally, there is an engaging urgency in the use of the present tense first-person point of view, putting us right in the midst of the story alongside Olena. What, if any, challenges did you encounter in this approach?

AM: During the early writing stages, this story definitely teetered back and forth between first- and third-person POV and between past and present tense. Ultimately, I decided that first-person present would be best. I thought it was important that readers share the urgency and feel the suspense and need that Olena felt. So this is reassuring to hear!

I definitely struggled at points to balance exposition, backstory, and the sequence of flashbacks paralleling the main story. I think it's typically much easier to include that information if the story is written in past tense but again, I didn't want to give up the urgency of present tense and so I had to find creative ways to work in that information without disrupting the story.

RP: While we're talking technique, what does your creative process look like when writing a story so deeply tied to a place as this one? Do you have any tips or tricks for immersing yourself in a setting that you may not be able to physically access?

AM: The creative process looks a bit messy at the beginning. I would say that my pre-writing phase involves a lot of research on the setting, lots of notes and lots of reading about history, myth, culture etc., sometimes entire novels set in the location or other subject matter that is pivotal to my story. I usually will look up specific areas to get an image in my head when writing. And I try to find books set in or around the area if possible.

I love the process of a short story because I get to dive deep into new fields and ideas at length and then try to distill them over the course of 5-6K words. And usually, by the end of the editorial process when I am getting tired of the subject I get to start something new.

Tips and Tricks? Read like crazy and take oodles of notes! I think my best ideas start when I read a strange research article about a place or when I am told a fun fact—like how coral can react to sound. I jot it down in my journal or my notes app and come back to it later. A more formal approach that I often use is to start stories around a mystery or interesting fact of some kind.

I also like to think about landscape or climate as character and to treat them accordingly. There is always a great deal of description and backstory to every character but more often than not there is usually a single specific trait that sticks out about a character that shapes our understanding of that character in a text, so, too, is the case for setting. If a story set on a rocky island begins describing it as a jagged, rocky place where the sea thrashes against the cliffs we can expect this to be a rather adversarial environment with some ominous expectations and even dark intentions. The same island might be described as fragrant and full of light as the sun reflects off the granite towards the calm sea below, giving a very different role to the setting. For each, we need to know the physical topography of the place as much as we need to know its personality during the story.

And of course visiting the place or one similar to it is always ideal, but Herman Melville wrote *Moby Dick* without ever visiting Cape

Cod and without Google! It's something that shouldn't stop someone from writing about a place. You can travel anywhere through the imagination, which sounds cheesy, but really is my favorite part of inhabiting a work of fiction as a writer or a reader.

RP: Great—and encouraging—advice! What works of literature, art, or music inspire and inform your writing? What are you reading right now?

AM: I think every writer probably feels this when I say that works of literature we turn to are always far from what you expect. I found an old book on soundscapes under a pile at a used book store in Maine which became the foundation for my thesis project. It's often that I turn to niche works of research writing or poetry. If I am writing a piece about a violin luthier (which I am) I might pick up a book about the physics of violin-making. I think I read very differently when I read for pleasure versus craft versus for research or just genuine curiosity. Sometimes, it's all of them at once.

Currently, I am reading *The Mountain in the Sea* by Ray Nayler, *Whale Music: Thousand Mile Songs in a Sea of Sound*, and *Couplets: A Love Story* by Maggie Milner.

RP: As for your upcoming collection, can we expect to see a return to the character of Olena and her home island? What are some other places and cultures you have—or plan to—explore?

AM: I would love to work more with Olena as a character, though I don't have any explicit plans at the moment. I am tossing around the idea of her appearing as a character in one of my other stories or perhaps a part of a novel in-progress.

I am working on a longer project set in the Aleutian island chain in Alaska. But some other story locales and cultures include Italo-Albanian violin luthiers in Calabria, Italy, a research team interacting with Greenland sharks in the Arctic, seasonal employees at an off-the-beaten path ski resort, and hopefully something about humpback whales off the coast of Cape Breton, Nova Scotia.

RP: These all sound fascinating, and I love the continuing tie to natural elements! Anastasios, it has been a pleasure to learn more about your process, and about the inner workings of "The Music of Olena Xiphias." I look forward to seeing what you do next.

AM: Thank you so much! It's been a joy and an honour to discuss my story with you.

ROOT WISDOM

Susan Jardaneh

I am standing in a corner of my mother-in-law's dance studio watching senior citizens Cha-Cha to "Staying Alive." Tonight is the monthly senior citizens' dance at Our Lady of Hope's church. Father Virgil stands next to me bobbing his head to the music. It's my first time at one of these dances, but Father Virgil is a mainstay. I'm sure that he'd usually be out on the dance floor, but I am only a few days into life as a forty-one-year-old with partial dentures, and only Father Virgil and my husband know.

In his teeth, talk is the difference between Father Virgil's outlook and mine. Father Virgil's faith says getting dentures is God's grace of interruption. It's an opportunity to be completely shoved off the road I've been on. My faith says the dentures are a consequence of how deeply I've worn that road.

"God might have done something less invasive. A burning bush. Parting the waters comes to mind."

"Would you have listened?" Father Virgil asks.

Under the disco ball's sparkle, the grandmothers of Our Lady of Hope's congregation spin and twirl in brightly colored disco dresses, with plastic hibiscuses in their hair. They Cha-Cha with silver-haired, leisure-suit-wearing men who swing their artificial hips. On stage, Men With Walkers play the Bee Gees' "Tragedy." Men With Walkers don't really have walkers, but the two guitarists and drummer are all thinning hair, and their dance steps consist of three shuffles to the right—pause—three shuffles to the left.

"Sydney, in times of trouble, the simple answer is the most comforting." When I don't react, Father Virgil tries to do the Bump with me, but I just shuffle. "Root wisdom anchors." Father Virgil smirks at his perceived clever phrasing. His foot taps along with the music and then turns to me with my arms crossed over my chest.

"I know you're hurting." He places a hand on my shoulder.

It's difficult to take Father Virgil seriously in his rock-star flare jeans and denim patchwork jacket and his black hair feathered back.

"Keep the joy, you mean?" I say.

"Now you're talking." Father Virgil points his index fingers at me, and I brace myself, expecting to hear a "Dyn-o-mite!"

"Family, community, and faith should be your crown."

Father Virgil elbows me again.

Father Virgil tries to do a disco spin like my mother-in-law, Laney, is teaching her granddaughter and other kids to do on the dance floor. These dances are always hyped as being for seniors, but Father Virgil tries to gather the whole congregation. My daughter, Olivia, spins all the way around and knocks into a girl with orange bellbottoms and a pink boa. That girl knocks into another boy and soon it's a mess of giggling on the floor.

I put my plastic flower on the table. "Father, I have to leave."

Father Virgil grabs my elbow. "Pony pucks." His eyebrows scrunch together and his smile leaves like a whip of wind. "Your daughter and husband are here. Your community in faith. Where else would you belong, Sydney?"

"Father, are you scolding me?"

Father Virgil gazes out into the dance floor and inhales deeply. "Questions never hurt anyone, Sydney."

Usually I'm working at Gorges Family Buffet during the weekends, where I'm the head busser. But my husband, Carver, said I wasn't going in today. He called Newton the manager and said I wasn't feeling well. I didn't tell anyone at Gorges about my dentures, not even Newton, and I usually work a double on Sundays, so Newton would be sore. Carver said if I didn't work at the buffet for one day the sun would still shine. Carver's fundamental belief is that husbands and wives are always there for each other.

"I think you need a meatball," Father Virgil says. He holds out an Italian meatball on a toothpick. I put down my plate.

"People with toothaches can't fall in love. Or eat meatballs." I point to my cheek. "That's Freud's root wisdom."

Father Virgil shoves the meatball in his mouth as if it stops him from saying something and swallows hard.

"The dentures aren't a temporary toothache, Sydney. They're your new reality. But God knows your pain and how to take it away."

Father Virgil has that priest talent of reprimanding and encouraging someone at the same time. He points his toothpick at the opposite corner, next to the stage where Carver has three long tables of food sitting on top of hibiscus print tablecloths. Across from the food is a table for drinks and cookies, and then off to the side is an area to sit and eat and rest. Carver is also a regular at these dances, as he supplies the food from his diner because he has found seniors gossip more than teenage girls, and they spread the word that Carver's diner is the best in town. I am on soft foods, as the dentist doesn't want me to use an adhesive for the first couple of weeks. The upper partials fit snugly and hold with suction, but the lower ones don't develop this suction due to the differences in everyone's jaw shape. Slippage is natural, my dentist says.

Although I had only agreed to come an hour before we had to be at the dance, Carver still finds time to bring me special foods. His crab cakes and baby cheese quiches are just for me. Carver says nothing is too much trouble for his wife. Carver says my smile still makes him weak. For better or worse, Carver believes.

"Priests are supposed to be comforting," I say.

"Comfort doesn't mean agreeing with you. Fundamentals can't be ignored," Father Virgil says. "Besides, it's disco night, and I was born to boogie."

Father Virgil grabs Laney's arm as she nears us with her basket of plastic hibiscus flowers. He spins Laney and she then pushes him to the dance floor where Mama Gladys grabs him. The clock sitting on the wall above Men With Walkers reads six-thirty, which is the height of the dinner rush at the Gorges. Tonight there was a wedding reception booked so the banquet room would have to be used. At six-thirty Newton always comes out from his office and asks me how I am. I always say that I could use a cigarette and a half hour later we are smoking in his office.

"The rule is nobody holds the wall up at these dances," Laney says.

Laney is in her late-sixties with the body of an aerobics instructor. Carver said she also has dentures. Laney has always solved her own problems. She opened her dance studio five years ago. Her husband had just died and she took her passion and turned it into a business. And now she can have Disco Nights and wear her coral, hot pink, and yellow swirl dresses and give out plastic flowers while saying everyone must dance. Problem solved.

"Honey, are you okay?" Laney puts her hand on my arm. She smiles at me in a way people who don't speak the same language do. "Carver told me about your struggle."

"My what?" I ask. My husband swore he wouldn't tell anyone about the dentures.

"I heard you decided to quit smoking. Good for you, honey," Laney says. "You're holding up really well."

"He gave smoking up for me. Really, that's how it goes," I say. Carver is wearing polyester dark green disco pants and a long-sleeved, long-collared shirt with flowers patterned in seaweed blue and green, accented in black and red. A crowd of women gathers around him, tasting the food. He made the first demand in our twelve years of marriage as we were driving home from getting my partials.

"You've just quit smoking," was all he said as we drove. But after we got home he went through the house and car and backyard and garage and snuffed out all my cigarette hiding places. I was still learning how to talk, but it didn't prevent me from having my say.

"Afraid I'm speeding up the promise to grow old together? Afraid I'll have the gray hair and wide hips next?"

Carver came back into himself at the sound of my voice. Carver's rational nature wouldn't allow both of us to be angry at the same time. Carver said he understood I was frustrated. Carver understood I was lashing out. The way Carver understood, I just wasn't being myself.

Mama Gladys shows Father Virgil the Hustle. I know Mama Gladys, Mama Rose, and Mama Violet from Gorges Family Buffet. They were bussers when I was young and new to the buffet. I hadn't seen them since they all quit suddenly some years back. I didn't recognize the Mamas in their mini-skirts, Go-Go boots, and Afro wigs, but they recognized me. They said they were regulars at Our Lady of Hope and the senior dances, now that they were seniors. After quitting the buffet, the Mamas opened a daycare in the same strip mall as Laney. They were forever mamas, they said. I glance at the clock. Newton and I would be having a cigarette now, talking about what kind of people decide to have a wedding reception at a buffet, and how terrified the young groom still looks, and who is the most worthless busser on the floor tonight, and who will be fired next week, and how we're going to quit smoking tomorrow. He says he's going to run a marathon in Hawaii one day. I say Hawaii is one of the top five places I want to visit. He names his five places to visit, and I name mine. We have Alaska, the Grand Canyon, and Italy in common.

Father Virgil elbows me. "How does my hair look?"

"Act like a priest," I say.

Father Virgil pops his shirt collar. He likes to stand out at these dances. He likes to remind me that last month his outfit won for the best dressed matador during Tango Night. At Our Lady of Hope, Father Virgil is twenty to thirty years younger than the other two priests. He's only four years older than me. He bikes downtown in the evenings in his shorts and tee shirt, and the teenage girls like to giggle. He likes to wear blue jeans and talk sports with the men in the diner. When I came out of my first service at Our Lady of Hope, he took my hand before I offered it. "See you next week," I remember him saying.

At work now I would be giving the bussers their breaks. My break is last so I can sit with Newton in his office as we eat. He will read the sports section of the newspaper, and I will read the local and then search for the horoscopes. Newton says he doesn't want to know his horoscope, but then he'll wait for me to read it.

The little boy taking balloons and making his own bouquet is no more than four, and he's dressed in a bright blue outfit with rhinestones. His bouquet is right in the dancers' path, and the couple in the matching gold-sequined jackets make a sharp turn to avoid the balloons. The Mamas are teaching Olivia to shimmy. I hadn't known Olivia got to wear outfits from Laney's wardrobe and put on makeup during the dances. She is in bed by the time I get home from the buffet on Sunday nights, and I only get Monday morning highlights. Tonight, though, Olivia came out in a gold Abba-like pantsuit with a matching sequined gold hat and pink lipstick, and my seven-year-old had vanished.

An assortment of opened soda bottles and fruit drink cans sit behind two punch bowls. I push my hibiscus basket up my forearm and take the ladle from one bowl. Father Virgil put his hand on my wrist.

"Not that one," he says. "That's the experimental punch. See by the funny color? The kids always fool with one punch bowl by mixing everything they can in it. The adults know to look before they drink. There are at least seven different types of liquids in that punch."

I put the ladle down. A group of women with long, straight-haired wigs come at me. I hold the basket out for them, and they grab a hibiscus flower and scatter.

Originally, I was to work out front of the diner and Carver was going to be the behind-the-scenes owner. Carver, though, turned out to be a man who can work a room. The diner has been so successful so fast that Carver has hired help and managed things himself. And Carver beams going to work.

Sometimes I watch him in the diner's front window before I come in. He's always gathered around customers at a table or one-on-one with someone, leaning in, being present. I get lightheaded with the same swell overwhelming my body as when I watch Olivia dance in her recitals, knowing how hard and faithfully Carver has worked at getting things done right.

Father Virgil takes a yellow plastic hibiscus from the basket. He puts the flower behind my ear. "When the spirit is in pain, the body shows it."

"I should be at work."

"Why?"

"Because people depend on me there," I say.

"People don't depend on you here?"

"It's different."

"Why?"

"Because I get to be with people who don't ask questions," I say.

"Like Newton?"

I charge toward the dance floor, my hibiscus basket swinging, and aim for the Mamas through an obstacle course of couples in sparkles and stripes, shaking and twirling and spinning around me, shoving their hands in my basket as if I'm in the crowd just to pass out plastic flowers. Men With Walkers strike up "Night Fever," and the floor cheers. Mama Rose and Olivia twist away. Olivia grabs my hands to dance, but I slip from her hold. I swing Mama Rose around.

"I have changed," I say. "Go and tell Father Virgil."

Mama Rose then puts her hand to her ear and under her Afro wig is her hearing aide. She leans in for me to repeat myself, but saliva fills my mouth, and my words drown. Mama Rose then smiles and nods her head, taking a pink hibiscus from my basket and putting it in her hair.

The gold-sequined jackets couple waltz in front of me, blocking the field of vision of the Mamas. I clench my jaw and my lower partials rub against my gum. My head feels like it has been pierced with a sword. My cheek and tongue throb from working to keep the slippage at bay.

I turn from the dance floor, but Harry takes my hand in his and wraps his other one around my waist. "Got you," he says.

Harry has strands of hair on his head and spinach dip on his tie. Harry smiles boldly and reveals his missing teeth. I stare at the disco ball to keep the tears away as we waltz the room.

On Sundays, I regularly stay and help Newton close the buffet. I get the towels to the laundry and make sure the food bars are turned off. Newton checks the kitchen's ovens and makes sure the garbage is out. Then I get some iced tea from the beverage bar and meet Newton back in his office. On that last Sunday I work at the restaurant, I sit in the striped chair across from his desk.

"Churches are just like gyms," Newton says. He squeezes my shoulders. "People go in and perform. Outside the building, they turn right back into the people they were before."

"Transcendence comes from within," I say. "According to Father Virgil."

"Walls change people, Sydney." Newton's hands lift the back of my shirt and reach around to my breasts. I straighten with his fingertips on my skin. "You of all people should know that."

In Gorges' parking lot, next to our parked cars Newton and I have our last cigarette for the night under the orange glow of the lamplight. The mall's security car drives around at least once while we're smoking, and we both wave and make up stories about what we look like to the driver. The made-up stories are always something bad—that we've just had sex in the restaurant, that I owe Newton money and he's threatening my family, that I'm threatening to expose Newton as a drug addict and that I've been supplying him for years. The story is never that we are the best people we can manage being in a bad scene.

Harry moans as I step on his foot yet again. He pushes away from me and grabs a woman in a blond spiky wig. I'm left holding my now-empty basket of hibiscuses. I am less than grounded in the turbulence of air and movement and changes in speed and direction, too solid to ever be picked up and carried away. Then, someone new grabs the back of my arm. Father Virgil wraps his arm around me, pulls me, leads me off the dance floor, and, somehow, it feels like shelter from a tornado. He navigates me around the collection of balloons like someone already knowing the correct route to exit a maze.

But I stop short. Father Virgil turns, and dancers now need to navigate around us.

"I don't work at the buffet for pleasure."

"Well, no. People don't typically think of restaurant work as pleasurable."

My jaw feels mounted on a face two sizes too small. The dentist says the cheek and tongue will learn to keep the lower partials in place. It's all about adaptation. I fight not to clench my teeth. Clenching breaks the metal clasps.

Father Virgil stands behind me again and I'm thinking he's hiding from the Mamas.

"God provides us with a faith that says what are pleasures and what are temptations." Father Virgil uses his priest voice. He puts his hands on my shoulders. "But we have to commit ourselves to those distinctions. If we don't, chances are we won't behave like there are any."

I walk away from Father Virgil. The couple in the gold-sequined jackets bump into the now-large bouquet of balloons in everyone's way. I grab a clump of strings and move it against the wall.

Louder than Men With Walkers, there's a sharp cry from across the room that makes my jaw tingle. The band stops and all the dancers stare in my direction as I stare at the blue rhinestone boy, running up to me with three balloons in his hand, pointing at the ones in mine. Olivia runs out of the crowd, looking like a tall gold Christmas ornament, and takes the balloons from me and gives them back to the boy, who puts them back in his collection. The music begins again with "Jive Talkin'" and the dancers cheer.

"That's Mama Violet's grandson, Mom," Olivia tells me. She pulls my arm, and I bend down to her, so I'll hear. "He likes to gather all the balloons in one spot and then run through them. Like people do with piles of leaves. We all let him because he's just a kid."

Olivia is wearing gold, sparkling eye shadow. "I didn't know," I say. "I thought he was getting in everyone's way."

"It's okay. It's your first time." Olivia taps her cheek with her finger, like I always do before dropping her off at school. I kiss her. She runs back in the crowd of dancers.

Carver's apron is off, and he's coming for me, but Mama Gladys pulls him to the dance floor, instead. She puts her hand on his hips and moves them side-to-side. He throws his head back laughing.

Father Virgil grabs my hand. We are slow dancing to a fast song. "God's punishing me," I say.

"Cow cookies. Try again?"

The throbbing in my mouth shoots from my ear to my head. My empty hibiscus basket dangles from my wrist. The room is a box of moving crayons melting into each other. Laney has all the kids in a circle, following her lead. The disco ball shimmers round and round. Father Virgil and I are the only things moving side to side.

"I should tell you something, Father."

"Not tonight, Sydney. Not with me showing this much chest hair."

I put my chin on his shoulder. "Isn't it your job to unburden people?"

"Confession isn't about unburdening. It's about reconciliation."

We are still swaying side to side. Father Virgil pats his hand on my back like I used to do to Olivia to get her to sleep. It is rhythmic and comforting and supposed to tell me to hold on to what he knows I must say a bit longer. But we have known each other for too long, so he knows how well I adhere to what I'm supposed to do.

"I can't remember what pleasure feels like, Father."

"Pleasure isn't something that happens to us. It's a decision," Father Virgil says. "It's a decision to live fully where you are."

"You're not helpful."

"Yeah, I get that a lot," Father Virgil says.

The room is fused in Aurora Borealis colors shimmering in the disco ball's light, orchestrated to drums and guitars. The low hum of chatter, the piercing octave of children's laughter, and the smell of perfume and sweat and Italian meatballs creates a tranquility that says walls change people.

For the second time tonight a man abandons me on the dance floor. Father Virgil and Harry start up a conversation. Bodies move around me and the blue rhinestone boy runs through his wall of balloons screaming as he comes out, and then he runs in again and screams as he comes out, and with his eyes closed, the boy keeps running right for me, not stopping until he knocks into my leg.

I gasp and my lower partials slip. My basket falls to the floor. The couple in the gold-sequined jackets glide over the basket without missing a beat.

In the bathroom I am standing over the sink and the door opens. Carver is carrying my purse, and I stare at his platform shoes. Carver rubs his hand over my back.

"Did they slip?" he asks.

I nod. My head is bent towards the sink so I don't have to look at him. Carver made the second demand in our twelve years of marriage this evening as we were driving to Laney's.

It didn't start as a demand, but, instead, with the phrasing "Wouldn't it be nice if…," and "Think of the time we'd have if…," and "We can do…when you…" By the time we had pulled into the parking lot, Carver had settled it.

"So, you'll give your two weeks' notice at the buffet tomorrow, right, Sydney?" And Carver got out of the car because I'm sure he thought he heard me say yes.

"I couldn't get away from the Mamas," Carver says. "Once they get a man on the dance floor, they don't let him go." He puts my purse on the floor. He nudges me. I don't move. He takes my shoulders and moves me to the side so he can fill my denture cup with water.

"Okay. Let's take them out. Things are heading for an end out there anyway."

Carver is prepared with my denture cup because Carver wouldn't be Carver if he didn't know the exact thing I needed.

"Come on, Syd."

Carver puts the cup under my chin. I try to spit out the lower partials rather than reaching into my mouth. Carver shakes his head. He puts the denture cups on the counter above the sink. "Open," he says.

I part my lips and Carver puts his thumb and forefinger on them and opens my mouth wider. With his right hand, he reaches in. I fight the reflex to bite. He pulls out my lower partial floating in my salvia. Carver pumps out paper towels and lays them over the sink.

"We're a team. You have to do the uppers."

I stand over the sink in case I drop it and unclasp the metal attachments from my mouth and hand it over to Carver. He puts the partials in the denture cup and closes the lid. He opens my purse and lays the cup in. He rests my purse strap over my shoulder.

"You okay?"

I smile and stroke his face with my fingertips. "Things are going to be different."

Carver dabs a wet paper towel over my cheeks and under my eyes. The water is cool on my skin. "We're a team, remember?"

"You're a better person than I am," I say.

"Why do you think I married you? You make me look good." Carver's teeth gleam.

Carver kisses me as if there were never any holes in my mouth. Love is blind. Love hurts. Love conquers all. Fundamentals, I'm thinking.

Men With Walkers have started up again, but the song isn't clear. Cheering erupts from outside.

"Life is good, but God is hard," I say.

Carver wrinkles his forehead.

"Root wisdom."

Carver points his finger down and circles it.

"Other way around, you mean." He throws the paper towels

away and does a full disco spin next to the sink.

"Yes, other way around."

Carver takes my hand and opens the bathroom door. On the dance floor a Conga Line wraps up the night to "You Should Be Dancing." The line stretches around the studio. Father Virgil is in the middle of the line, and he waves for me and Carver to join in. Carver immediately rushes toward the end of the line, but I pull him back.

"Don't leave me," I say to Carver.

Carver smiles. He grabs my hand. "Come on, then."

Carver pulls me along and grabs onto the last person in line. He then reaches behind me and places my hands on his hips. Laney and Olivia, and the Mamas, and Harry, and the couple in the gold-sequined jackets, the ladies in the wrap-around dresses, and even the blue rhinestone boy are all joined to each other in the line. I'm at the end. From my vantage point people are on their own three-shuffle step, and the kick on the fourth beat is more of a wave. Olivia had warned me that every dance ends with the Conga Line. She said Laney taught her about the Conga and that the idea is not to follow the first person in the line but the person directly in front of you. Carver's hips move mechanically, stiffly, but I follow his choreography without question. The music is loud and the lead singer is asleep so just the drums and guitar muscle out the song. People are singing and talking and some of the kids shriek just to hear themselves. I keep my head down and my vision on Carver. His shuffle steps are off and he's a beat behind on his kick. I fight against the belief he wants to throw me off. Other way around, I think. Life is hard, but God is good. Life is hard, but God is good. Life is hard, but God is good. I clench to my husband's waist and hang on.

PLEASURE IS A DECISION TO BE HAPPY WHERE YOU ARE

A Conversation with Susan Jardaneh

Claire Agnes: Thank you for sharing this piece with *Driftwood Press!* This narrative contemplates faith, work, love, and purpose through the lens of a church seniors' dance night littered with memorable and motivated characters. The story's settings—the dance, the buffet at which the protagonist is employed, and to some degree, even the diner owned by her husband—serve as metaphors for the internal conflicts examined by this narrative. What inspired your explorations of these places? Was this piece always tied so intimately to these settings?

Susan Jardaneh: Thank you, Claire. I'm thrilled and grateful to be published in *Driftwood Press*. Yes, in this piece, specifically, place is important as a tension for the story, so they are purposeful. Some of the places were already set from previous stories involving these characters, but the dance is a new environment, and I was looking for a setting where all these different tensions could be kind of trapped in one place so that they could kind of boil and see what happens.

CA: At the center of these tensions is Sydney, the narrative's protagonist, a woman in her early forties who has just gotten dentures. How did you decide on the characterizing detail of the dentures, and what role do you feel they play in Sydney's emotional arc throughout the story?

SJ: Yes, Sydney having dentures in her early forties really came from stewing on lots of other ideas. I once started a story about a young woman having tongue cancer and having a glossectomy, and that idea of having things to say and being in pain, or being prevented from saying them, always stuck with me. I think Sydney's dentures play a pivotal role in the emotional arc, and I think Father Virgil knows this too and wants to use it to get Sydney to recognize that she has to choose which environment she wants to live in. There is a part in the story where Father Virgil says that pleasure is a decision to be happy where you are, and Sydney can't say where that place is until the end of the story.

CA: Throughout the narrative, Sydney contemplates this idea of pleasure, reflecting on her job at the buffet and her affair with her boss, Newton. How did you approach writing about the complexities of emotional infidelity in a way that feels authentic to the character's inner life?

SJ: Yeah, well, I wish I had a plan for that as I was writing. But I think working with these characters in previous stories helped to get to know them as complex, flawed human beings. When they are placed in challenging situations, they tend to revert to familiar and safe environments, such as the buffet. By putting them in uncomfortable scenarios, they have the chance to express their desires, frustrations, and vulnerabilities. The shared experience of feeling confined by the buffet environment creates a bond and connection between them, making them feel safe sharing vulnerable experiences, feelings, and thoughts. But as they share these vulnerabilities, they also break the boundary in their marriages.

CA: Speaking of boundaries, Sydney's husband, who owns a diner, seems to be very popular at the dance. Can you talk about their relationship dynamics and how they play into the story's themes of faith, work, and pleasure?

SJ: I think they are really opposites and thrive on qualities they would like to have and see in each other. Carver has always had a plan and knows how to turn that plan into actions and results. He is also someone who enjoys people and interacting with them. Sydney has a faith that has doubts, but it's something she has to turn to that Carver doesn't. She has made her world much smaller with her relationship with Newton, so she relies on Carver to have some connection with the world outside of the buffet. They both worked at the buffet, though, and I think it's their outlook on work that is pivotal. Carver saw his job at the buffet as a stepping stone for other things, but Sydney sees the buffet more like her world and sort of loses sight of her own career possibilities.

CA: I'm glad you touched upon the importance of Sydney's faith to her character. Father Virgil plays a key role throughout the story, reflecting upon life and faith with Sydney at the dance. What motivated you to include a priest as a confidant?

SJ: Father Virgil appears in several stories of mine, and he has really developed from a sort of stereotypical characterization of a priest to a more dimensional character. Just having a priest as a character in a story brings with it a lot of preconceptions as to who he is, so my motivation was to play with those preconceptions, and have Father Virgil's character be someone who is committed to beliefs, but with an understanding that the practice of such beliefs is a difficult thing to do day in and day out. I'm hoping that his interplay with Sydney shows that she sees him as a real person who is able to voice what his beliefs are, and that it demonstrates to the reader that having beliefs doesn't mean that they are always going to be with you no matter what—that there will be times you have to commit and recommit to them.

CA: As the author of the piece, do you believe that Sydney's conversation with Father Virgil provides a form of resolution, or is it more about her exploration of these themes?

SJ: I think it provides a temporary resolution or relief for Sydney, but that may be what she is looking for. Sydney knows the right thing to do, and she might want to do the right thing, but then she can't fully enact the changes necessary. I like to think this is the struggle with faith, also. We might want to believe and know the steps to show we are believers, but true faith involves a kind of sacrifice that Sydney can't fully commit to without giving up working at the buffet. So Father Virgil is that steady light for Sydney, that doesn't condemn or judge but keeps being there for her.

CA: Is your work frequently drawn to themes of faith and belief, or do these thematics belong more exclusively to these characters and this particular story?

SJ: Well, I am drawn to these themes, and these characters have been with me for some time now, so their ideas and conflicts about faith and belief have also grown and deepened. This story is part of a larger collection, so it has given me an opportunity to give some depth and complication to this idea of faith and belief, which I've enjoyed doing.

CA: Are any of the characters that we meet briefly in "Root Wisdom" featured as protagonists in other stories? Does anyone go on a journey that might surprise us, having met them at this community dance?

SJ: Well, Newton has several stories as the protagonist, and we do see his story develop more deeply. We get to see how his relationship has developed with Syndey and also some struggles and setbacks that have shaped Newton. And although Father Virgil doesn't have a whole story as the protagonist, he is in several other stories where we learn more about him and about his personality through interaction with other characters.

CA: There's a sense of isolation within the protagonist's internal dialogue, especially during the conversations with Father Virgil. How did you use interactions with other characters to convey Sydney's sense of being disconnected from the world around her?

SJ: Yes, I did want to show that Sydney is an outsider, even though her family is at this dance, and her community. Sydney can't really be who she is at the dance, so her internal dialogue is meant to illustrate that she is struggling not to reveal who she really is, despite Father Virgil already having a good sense of Sydney's struggle.

The setting also acts as a tension for the dialogue because Father Virgil is more than comfortable where he is, and he knows how everything goes at the dances and what the procedures are. Sydney doesn't know these things, like what punch to stay away from or how to maneuver around the dance floor, so she counters that tension in her internal dialogue by recounting what environment she does know, which is being at the buffet with Newton.

CA: Newton, Sydney's boss at the buffet, tells her, "Walls change people." Is there a specific reason you chose the buffet as the setting for the affair?

SJ: In our work environments, especially, there are situations where you have to adopt attitudes and personalities that have the possibility of changing people. Any restaurant work is hard work, but buffets have their own culture, as it's a place that is kind of asking patrons to go beyond their own limits. It's a customer service environment, so you're having to make customers happy and employees happy, when you really just want to think of your own happiness. Newton is older and Sydney is more educated, and I think those things bind them. In a way, they see themselves as somewhat above other customers and employees. However, it's interesting that for their age and education, they are bound by the frustration of this workplace that they never have the courage to rise above.

CA: Newton seems to represent a different kind of fulfillment for Sydney. How do you view the contrast between her marriage and the emotional connection with Newton?

SJ: Yeah, I think that Newton is the emotional safe place that is supposed to be present in her marriage. But Sydney doesn't have that emotional connection with Carver, because she doesn't feel she can't live up to Carver's assuredness and accountability. Sydney can see Newton's flaws and mistakes, and it's comforting to Sydney, as she sees Newton's struggles and can relate to them. There is a comfort, and bond, in that connection.

CA: The ending of the story, where Sydney is in the conga line behind her husband, having just removed her dentures with his help, feels both playful and poignant. What does this moment signify for the character and for the narrative as a whole?

SJ: The characterization of "playful and poignant" really is on the mark. I love endings where the character's actions wrap up the story, and it's what I was trying to go for. I leaned heavily on setting to tie all the strands together at the end. I think the situation of the conga line being made up of the community at the dance, and Sydney having the opportunity to join in, really forces her hand to decide where she wants to be physically and emotionally. So, when she tags along at the end of the line, and all she can see is her husband's steps in front of her, it's an act of faith and commitment to where she is now to be present.

CA: You mentioned earlier that Father Virgil appears in other stories. How does the Father Virgil we meet in "Root Wisdom" compare to his future and past iterations?

SJ: Yes, Father Virgil is actually involved with Newton's life and Sydney's mother's life in previous stories, so he has involvement with this community. "Root Wisdom" is a later story in the collection, and here, Father Virgil is a voice of what to do, but in earlier stories we get a little about Father Virgil's backstory. Father Virgil's relationship with Newton is also more personal than his relationship with Sydney.

CA: Very intriguing! Can we find parts of this world published elsewhere?

SJ: Yes, this is a part of a larger collection. I've published some of the stories in literary magazines like *The Southern Review, Fugue, Fiction*, and *Confrontation*. And more than one of these stories can be found in *Driftwood Press*. *Driftwood* has been wonderfully kind and gracious with my work, and I am very grateful for their support.

CA: Thank you, Susan, for speaking with me today, and for sharing your work with *Driftwood Press*.

SJ: Thanks so much for the opportunity, Claire. It was a pleasure to discuss my work with *Driftwood Press*.

BAND OF TOTALITY

Porter Leland Huang

The day of the eclipse, I help him lift coolers into his car. His two friends watch us from the front porch, at first laughing, then studying: their eyes zoom and focus like surveillance cameras but they do not offer to help—too many cooks, too many arms and legs, all sweat-coated muscles and secrets. They want no part of our game.

The last cooler is the heaviest, so it requires both of us, one on each end. He is stronger than I am; I struggle. As we tilt it upwards, I take in the man standing before me: his encouraging smile like an eclipse in itself, his moon moving before my dignity, threatening to turn out its light. His biceps sprout hard through his t-shirt, and I think of wetness, and wrongdoing, and weakness—mine, in particular.

His side of the cooler reaches its peak prematurely; the lid slides off, colliding with my ankle as it bounces, and as stars appear before my eyes, ice falls onto my foot like the hailstorm last night that left a bullet-hole through his windshield. A beer can rolls out and busts as it hits the curb.

"Well," he says as he picks it up, "there's still half of it left. You know what that means."

"What does that mean?" I ask.

He shrugs his shoulders. "The sky is going to black out in the middle of the day. Why shouldn't we?"

He winks at me, licks his lips a little. He hoists the can above his face and holds its puncture to the sky, stopping the leakage. He puts it to his mouth and downs all that is left.

"I haven't had a drink in three months," I say, and it sounds bitter, harsher than I have intended. Lately everything does.

He pauses, wiping foam from his mustache, perhaps puzzling over the fact that there is still so much he does not know about me. In a bedroom, the curtains pulled, anything is easy to forget.

But today. Today we are together, in public, with others—people he knows. Sunlight shines on about-to-bloom flowers and American flags and children running around driveways. We are wearing clothes. I know every crevice of his body, and he mine—what makes him make those guttural little sounds, what makes me say things that would shock even myself in the daylight. But here, the moon having not yet moved before the sun, fabric covers the pointed, dark brown mounds of his nipples. Fabric covers the seat of my pants. His husband is not here, but his friends are. They watch me like God.

In this way, we are strangers. To know a body—we understand, I think, as we share this solitary glance—is not to know the person inside of it. Skin is like a tarp thrown over a car, which would have saved his windshield from the hail, I think. Maybe he's not so manly after all, having not known that, I think. I think too much. I think of my own husband, five states away for business, telling me he misses me while he endures the kind of money-stock-meeting madness that I still can't understand because I don't have "that" kind of brain, or maybe because I just don't care to ask. Maybe the boardrooms and the flights and the spreadsheets late during moonless nights simply do not matter to me because they mean I can continue my lustful jaunts out into the dark, where I ignore the notifications on my phone in favor of a towel tilted downward from my torso in the sauna at the back of the gym, where there is a different kind of dark, one in which I first came upon the man standing before me, where he bent me over a hot wooden bench that gave me a splinter, which felt good when it entered my skin, as did he, again and again, leaving me with tight-lipped smiles to which I respond, always, by begging for the pulling of skin over skin. I wonder if we can ever only have one or the other, the body or the mind: pick your poison.

"What's your poison, then?" he asks.

"Why do I need a poison?"

"Everyone has one," he says, "even if it's not a normal kind."

"Not normal," I say. "Maybe that."

"This is your poison, then," he says, cupping his crotch in his hands, thick and growing as he brings it closer to me. I laugh, but given the way I feel as if my skin has just been carbonated, I think he must not be wrong. Is it crazy, I wonder, to admonish myself for not wearing tighter underwear? The sky is bright and we are going to a public park to watch the sky change colors and there will be picnics and children and laughter and friends. But something shifts below my waist.

He stops moving closer when he hears the front porch steps begin to creak. His friend who is visiting from across the country—I've forgotten their names already; this is the one without eyeglasses—walks towards us. The man beside me adjusts his clothing.

"Anyone want a pull?" the friend asks, a cloud of marijuana smoke engulfing his head.

He extends a small vaporizer out towards me, staring into my eyes, and I notice that the two men before me have matching tattoos: little addition signs on the insides of their fingers, drunken college stick-and-poke, math majors, early-twenties reverence for the self, that sort of thing. This must have been the friend who had bought the inking supplies way back then; I've heard the story.

I can feel him sizing me up: wondering what kind of notch I will be in the bedpost of his troubled friend's troubled life. They inked each other's fingers years ago, whereas I've only covered bedsheets with something far less permanent; I can be wiped away by the dawn. We are not fooling anyone, it seems. But this is not the seat of my discomfort: rather, the glance thrown my way, one that says, *you are not the first*, and the lack of a need to follow the adage with its cruel second part.

"Sure," I say and bring the vaporizer straight to my lips. I suck, and nothing happens. They both laugh at me.

"There's a button you have to push, silly," the friend without glasses says.

"Oh," I say, surprised by my ignorance. Because I *do* know my way around this particular kind of poison. Enough that I don't think it is poison at all—that's a hill I'll die on, I want to tell them. Lately the word "sober" rolls out of my lips like life-giving tonic, and yet here I am, desperately filling myself with something so that I can not-be. Hypocrisy seems to be one of my very favorite pastimes. I can hit a home run before the bases are loaded, or at least before I am.

But then the man who licks his lips at me in the dark turns around, and I see the way the shorts cup what's behind him; I think maybe there are many hills on which I'm willing to die. I press the button, take a pull as they both walk away from me and back into the house.

One of many, yes, I think, to his question about my poisons. That seems to be why I am here. I tighten my belt one notch, as if this will reign me in, and follow them into the house.

***

On the way to the park we've chosen, in the eclipse's so-called band of totality, we stop to collect sandwiches at a deli attached to a service station. The weed has not made me hungry, as it has them. Instead the weight that traces itself hotly across my eyes feels more like dread. We are on the edge of the band now; the park just up the road, we've read online, is the most open space from which to view the sky as it turns the day most dark. The workers inside the deli have never seen such a crowd; they're ill-equipped to handle it. In the long line, I ignore a phone call from my husband.

I feel a hand slide its way across my lower back; then he sees the name on my screen, asks: "Don't you need to take that?"

I remain enthralled by the ways we allow ourselves to air our crimes in public, normalizing them. Maybe this is how serial murderers feel, going in for the fourth, the fifth, the tenth kill that will inevitably terminate in prison or in suicide. The options are heinous and still we don't know how to stop. The more we don't stop, the more we think we will not be forced to. And yet.

"I'll call him back later," I say, and as I slip my phone back into my pocket, he notices that his friends are occupied by the menu. He cups my left ass cheek in his hand and whispers to me, "Meet me in the bathroom. I'll say we both have to go and that they can order for us."

Then he licks the inside of my ear, his tongue making a sweet swiping sound like a wet Q-tip, like so much else in this world loud and jarring to me yet quiet and unnoticeable to others.

Outside, cars line the road, bumper-to-bumper, hours early to the coming eclipse. The totality will last one minute, though we'll be setting up and preparing for it over the course of the afternoon—playing games, telling stories, learning about one another. Sex is, in this way, ecliptic. I think of how he apologized to me the first time we met outside of the gym, all the effort I put into being clean for him, and the way he candied my insides after a mere forty-or-so seconds. You just get me so excited, he'd said, and I'd smiled, thinking the trouble was worth it, then telling him as much. I proved my own point when I messaged him the next day and did it all again. Amnesia: another preferred pastime.

I meet him in the bathroom. I have prepared for this.

As he spits into his hand, I bend over the sink and spread myself open like a pearly gate. I feel the place on my foot, now swelling, where the cooler's lid slammed into it. It's turning purple like my pride. He's trying to muffle sounds I know should frighten me, but that nonetheless make me come alive. I lift the foot up onto the counter even though it hurts. I like it when it hurts. Pain shoots through my lower half just as he does, and as he becomes one with me, I think how I have never learned how to be around a person who smells that way—like pine trees and sandalwood and clementines and pre-semen stuck to the inside of orange briefs—without opening myself to him like a book.

We both finish at the same time: I in the sink, and him in me. Though we wash our faces and our hands, we do not bother to wipe down the counter when we go. This occurs to me only later, misplaced shame, and I think: I am nothing if not a receptacle.

"You're such a good boy," he says, slapping my ass just before we come back into everyone else's view, together. I want to bark like a dog.

★★★

"How is Daniel?" one of his friends asks in the car. "Still all good? All healthy?"

He shoots his friend a look: at once calm and vicious. *Stop talking.*

Daniel, I reason. That must be his husband. Where I have shared names, information and incrimination, he has not. I suppose it would all be easy enough to find—were I to read the newspaper clipping of their wedding announcement, framed in their bedroom, kept on his wall when I visit, unlike my wedding ring, which I always take off—but I don't want to know. And now I know. I think how so much of life is like that.

Something gurgles inside me like indigestion, though I haven't eaten. The sandwich grows colder by the minute in my lap.

I say, "I'm going to make a call."

I want to escape the silence that is now in the car, the thing that has been said that should not have been. *Daniel. All good, all healthy.* Maybe I want to poke him back—see if he bleeds like I do, see if our blood is the same shade of red.

When my husband answers, he does not scold me for ignoring his first call. Cheerfully, professionally, he asks me where I will watch the eclipse, if I have the proper glasses, tells me it's already passed where he is and he couldn't even see it through the office window because the sky was full of rain. He does not ask me who I'm with. He does not question my plans for the rest of the day. We have no sort of arrangement that would permit my gallivanting—if you could call it that, for it doesn't quite feel like that—but I tell myself he knows what I'm doing, as if this legitimizes it. As if my lack of caution and unbridled apathy within the walls of our home mean that it's okay to do what is undeniably not okay. Maybe he's focused on the sobriety; maybe his trust that I am who I say I am and that the choices I make are choices made by me, not some blacked-out alter-ego, is enough for him. Maybe I chase this kind of life because of its danger and I want danger, I've always wanted danger, always wanted not to be enough; I crave inadequacy.

What would he do if he had confirmation? I wonder.

Perhaps he would say: go, do what you want. Get what you can't get with me because I'm always tired and my drive is low and there was that one bad night that you don't remember, but I do; you deserve to be touched, you deserve to scream in the right way, the good way, you deserve it all. (I would not deserve it, though, I reason. This is the problem.)

Perhaps instead he would call me a snake, say that I'm obsessed with the ones that do not have fork-shaped tongues, slithering through darker, thicker, less precise grass. That I let them overtake me, that I've replaced one drug with another, this one even more unsafe. And, true: I shed my lovers like skins with the seasons. This particular one has clung—undeniably my fault. I could be more careful, more discreet; I could get a prescription to protect myself, and my husband, from the worst of the risks; I could check more frequently about my own health, physical and mental. But that would mean the kind of admission I've always run, mouth agape with silent screams, away from. That would mean removing the sick thrill of it all. I think as I look up to the driver's seat: anyone who has ever taken a car ride with a boy like this, a pine tree becoming a redwood behind the wheel, would say that culpability does not promote correctness. Drugs are bad because drugs are good.

I am nothing if not consistent: I will chase what I know is not there, just to prove that it might be.

★★★

I finish setting up the picnic blanket while he whispers sternly, saliva flicking out the corners of his mouth, to the friend *with* the eyeglasses who mentioned the husband in the car. They are standing in the distance, by the tiny public library at the edge of the metro park, arguing. The friend seems not to think he has done anything out of line. I wonder what is wrong with the husband, if he's spending this time with me. The same could be said for—well, this doesn't quite make a difference, does it?

They come back, and he sits beside me, close but not too close. We quickly notice a changing in the light; finally the moon is set to perform after our subpar opening act's melodrama. We haven't thought to consider that this will not just look like quickly-approaching night; the sun will not set, will not cast the world below it in orange and red and purple, like his underwear that I've peeled away a hundred times with the ravenousness of today's moon. No, the light will simply diminish with time, quickly disappearing as the moon dances more desperately across the front of the sun. And it does. The world begins to look like an underexposed photograph.

I think, maybe if this was how our relationship had developed, I could handle the emotion that has come along with it. A little less light, a little more gray to cover over the realer colors. The glitter barely sprouting out the edges of the moon, instead of shining like the droplets of sweat that are trickling down his nose.

I want to lick one of them off, so I do.

Nothing is anything in this kind of non-arrangement; there are no rules. I lick him right there in front of his friends, because if this is our last day, if the tension of reality proves to be something we cannot carry with us into the future and handle like adults, I will not be overshadowed by something as natural and unpreventable as an eclipse, merely a shadow itself. He does not blink. His friends do not blink. No one acknowledges what I have done; I think: no one ever acknowledges what I have done. Maybe this is why I continue to do it.

"What a time to be alive," the marijuana-offering friend remarks, still holding the vape in his hand and looking up at the sky without the approved glasses. Dangerous, I think, and stupid. Preventable. "Even if we don't have much time," he says, "at least we have this time."

I find it overly sentimental, find myself questioning the tear at the edge of the friend's eye, until I remember—a flash of my own self-centeredness—that this particular friend only has a few months left to live. How have I forgotten? HIV has been ravaging his body for nearly a decade and the drugs haven't worked. After the sun, he's next; this is clear. I feel like I have a grasp on the emotion, like I understand it, and I want to reach out and give this friend a hug, to grab his hand with the cute little tattoo and take it in mine, to tell him that although I don't know him, I'm glad he's lived, that I think he's dignified, no matter how he's punished himself for something he cannot control. But I say nothing.

And then this friend says something that surprises me. He directs it to the man beside me who wants so desperately to cup his arm across the small of my back again, to kiss me on the neck in public, even though he knows he shouldn't.

"How nice of the sun to put on a show for us," the friend says. "For all of us. Even us poz queens."

He shares a tearful smile with the man beside me, who now moves his hands even further from my back, whose mouth falls open, who realizes much more quickly than I do what has just been revealed.

A beat passes in silence; the moon inches closer to its momentary coup d'état.

"Poz queens?" I ask, and the world grows dark more quickly now, like a circular dimming switch clutched and pulled by a child in its distracted mother's arms. Like the switch we tried unsuccessfully to turn off as he entered me in the sandwich shop bathroom just minutes, a lifetime, ago. We like it in the dark. In the dark we can be whoever we want to be, clean, husbandless.

"What does he mean?" I ask him, but his face already holds the answer.

And, in any case, now is not the time. The birds have gone silent. Even the children, corralled at the other end of the park by their tired, listless parents, have lightened the load of their hollering. The moon slides itself further towards the edge of the sun, like a baby set to emerge from a womb, or—

I can see the whites of his eyes out the side of mine. They're pointed straight at me. He places his hand on my knee.

"I can explain," he says.

"I doubt that," I whisper, but I don't get up. I don't run to a restroom, attempting to cleanse myself of his seed. Far from merely planted, the tree has grown, rows and rows of sod cemented upon me with a plow, set to bloom some bulbous, ghastly flowers come spring. I feel the part of my body that he has colonized, hard against the ground. I think about the way it seems, now, that I'll never escape him—even when his husband comes back to town, even when mine does, even when I begin to walk the dog down the other street so as not to pass his house, so as not to think about all the ways his smiles have tilted in my direction, his back arched towards different kinds of skies and ceilings, creating me in his image.

"Can we talk?" he whispers in my ear, his lip beginning to quiver, but he knows that this, as life will stretch before us once the world's lights reintroduce themselves, will not be possible.

The moon takes its place directly in front of the sun. The flowers prepare to sprout in confusion as if a few moments from now will usher in the morning, the spring, my new identity growing around my bare skin and wrapping me like a cocoon, or a condom, if I were a smarter person living a reality that has not been my own.

As the light begins to return and all the broken pieces of what we've tried to stitch together from our broken selves lay still on the blanket before us, irreparable, I take stock of the tiny tattoo just inside his ring finger, right hand. The plus sign.

I did ask him about it once; at least there was that.

But when he laughed, in a way that didn't read as nervous to me then, I took him at his word. I listened when he told me about the silly stick-and-poke on the drunken night, the friend with the free needle to breach these points of his skin. I believed him. A plus sign was easy: two lines, one up, one down, permanent in a place that would only partly show to the world.

"I'm all about being positive when the world tells me not to be," he said.

It was there all along. And yet I've chosen, every day since, to believe it is one thing when the moon and the sun both—glittering, flaming, screaming silently from afar—have told me it is another.

I am reminded of the questions we ask so easily, as if putting on a coat when it's cold or checking names during roll call: What do you like? Is it okay if I get a little rough with you? Can you put on that jockstrap from your third picture for me? Are you ready to take me inside of you? You like it when Daddy goes deep like that?

And then the ones we don't consider: Am I safe with you? Doesn't any arrangement have rules, even unspoken? Will the joy I'm prioritizing at the moment only lead to an acute, intense lack of it for the rest of my life hereafter?

I can hear my husband's voice vibrating in my ear, on the other end of a phone line that will soon be cut clean from itself, asking me if it was worth it. And as I get up to walk somewhere else in the growing light, I already know I will not be able to give him an honest answer.

FACING AVOIDANCE

A Conversation with Porter Leland Huang

James McNulty: Welcome to the pages of *Driftwood*, Porter! We're so excited to publish this precisely written, heart-breaking short story!

Porter Leland Huang: Thanks so much! I've long been a reader of *Driftwood* and am consistently drawn to the work you all publish, so it's a thrill and an honor to be included among your pages.

JM: The character here is so beautifully nuanced: the audience may judge him for his transgressions—yet they'll undoubtably also feel sorry for him by the story's end. When you craft your characters, do you often look for opposing qualities or conflicting actions to add nuance to your characters? Talk to me about your characterization techniques.

PLH: Thank you for that note! I appreciate your attention to the details of this character's psyche. Yes, moral complexity was my exact goal for the main character in this story, as is usually the case in my work. I enjoy reading characters whose moral compasses point in multiple opposing directions; I find it a much more interesting (and human/realistic) experience to enter into the mind of a character who struggles with morality and the opposition of ethics vs. what we *want*. So often, the things we crave go directly against how we think we should view the world. Such a process naturally involves understanding how a character's short-term choices and successes can work against what would be good for them in the long-term. Since these are the types of characters I enjoy reading, they've also become the kind I enjoy writing. The most "fun" characters for me to read are the ones whose choices I discover and think, "Hmm. I don't even know what I would do personally if I were in such a situation." I don't believe any one person we encounter in "the real world" is entirely good or entirely bad—even on any given day. Therefore, our characters should also reflect such nuance.

JM: There are often thought tags such as "I think" or "I wonder," rather than free indirect speech. On a craft level, what consideration goes into utilizing this technique over another way of conveying thoughts?

PLH: I'm glad you pointed that out! This is not a tactic I'm used to employing, so it was a tad uncomfortable for me at first, but it felt right for this story for one major reason: my narrator is soft-spoken, self-conscious, a bit insecure, and anxious. He unwittingly crushes many of his own chances for happiness because he will not speak up for himself—even when he has questions whose answers could (and do) alter the course of his life. He "thinks" and "wonders" many an insightful perspective, but his refusal to express these perspectives leaves him feeling stifled and silenced. What goes on in his internal world drastically varies from how he presents himself in public, especially to new people like those he encounters in this story. I hope I have succeeded in creating a feeling of frustration for the reader, a step in the direction of "If you'd just vocalize that thought, maybe you would have a different end result." The sadness in the story comes from the character's inability to do so; he is, in this way, avoidant. In my mind, avoidance is one of the most dangerous qualities a human can possess, so I wanted to show how that danger can play out in the course of a single, tragic day.

JM: On the topic of craft, I want to address the balancing act that comes with such an intimately interior, voice-driven piece. How do you consider when to balance interiority with exteriority?

PLH: Here I have to give credit to the authors I love. Knowing when to have a character speak vs. act vs. think—this is a daunting, often impossible skill that is difficult to teach and even more difficult to learn/train. I've seen great examples of this balance in the work that I like to read; most recently, in *Detransition, Baby*, I was floored by Torrey Peters' ability to insert a gesture or piece of exteriority when it's most needed. When a reader desperately wants to skip forth to the next piece of intense dialogue, sometimes an action can actually offer more than anything a character might say. This was perhaps what stood out to me most about Peters' novel: its divine-adjacent sensibility towards what kind of action/speech/gesture will "fill in the blanks," so to speak, better than another method. I don't know if I've done anything in that realm of precision, but I've tried; after finishing *Detransition, Baby,* I did specifically edit a few moments in this story to feel more natural and balanced between the internal and external. I suppose readers will decide if that balance holds up or not!

JM: Talk to me about the conception of this story. How did you come across the premise, and how did you decide on how to develop it?

PLH: The idea for this story began in April of 2024 when I attended an eclipse-viewing in a metro park near where I live in Ohio. I almost always begin a story with a single sentence that I think sounds nice; that sentence usually ends up occupying a smaller role in the story than I initially envision. In this particular story, the sentence was: "The world begins to look like an underexposed photograph." This was the most surprising thing to me about watching my first total eclipse: that the sky does not actually take on the hues it does during a sunrise or sunset. There are no purples, pinks, or oranges. The light just goes away, little by little, and then all at once. Those last few moments before the moon totally covers the sun produce one of the strangest sights I've ever seen: darkness without its normal precursors, a truly eerie grayness atop sunlight. During the time I began to write this story, I was thinking a lot about relationships and sex, and how within many gay communities, the "rules" surrounding this difficult topic tend to be different than the heteronormative ones society teaches us to expect. Now, I'm not trying to wax poetic about what's right or wrong in sex—the best thing anyone can do there is march to the beat of the "You do you" drum—but I wanted to think about both the pitfalls and the excitement that come from the arrangement of illicit sex within a gay relationship. I decided that an eclipse was a fitting backdrop for such fallout.

JM: On a second read, it's a pleasure to see how expertly the hints are laid out on nearly every page of the story. The twist is coming, but it likely isn't seen by the reader despite these hints. Talk to me about the balancing act here between setting up the twist and giving it away, then please share with us your revisions process with this story.

PLH: In earlier drafts of this story, actually, there were hardly any hints for the big reveal. Upon rereading, I realized that my character doesn't seem truly foolish enough to ignore facts that are right in front of his face; I also don't take him as someone so entirely trusting that he would take all of his lover's words at face value, especially since they don't "know" each other that well on an interpersonal level. Instead, he very well might be the kind of person to turn a blind eye when a potential reality poses tragedy; he's ever-willing to accept skewed narratives to assuage his fear and discomfort. All this is to say: I realized that I needed to show him being presented with some information that could lead him in the direction of the truth—but to show him also decisively turning away from that information. This, in my mind, makes his inability to deny what he knows at the end of the story all the more jarring. He knows he has had opportunities to understand the danger to his health and to his relationship. Now, he not only must face the truth but also his previous avoidance of it.

JM: Talk to me about the process of writing and revising. How long did everything take, and which techniques do you use during revision and/or initial drafting?

PLH: Initially, as with most things I write, this story was much longer.

Beyond the current ending line, there were between two and three more pages (depending on the version). At the end of editing prior to submission, I realized that I simply liked the way those pages "sounded" and they weren't really adding much to the story; the way they read made it seem, to me, that this was obviously a story that a writer was creating. Now, while that's obviously true, that's not how I want to feel when I read fiction, so it's not how I want my readers to feel when they read mine. I want them to be able to believe that what they are reading is actually happening right before their eyes. I tend to over-encumber my sentences and scenes during all first drafts, which always takes away from a story's verisimilitude, so my revision process tends to center around taking out the parts where the writer's presence is more obvious and heavy-handed.

JM: Who are some of your favorite writers? Which ones inspired "Band of Totality"?

PLH: Lately I've been really into Rivers Solomon, Jhumpa Lahiri, Halle Butler, and revisiting the work of my favorite poet, Carl Phillips. I'm constantly re-reading Zadie Smith's novels. She does something with the complexity of humanity (you really can be a fabulous person and a monster at the same time!) that I don't remember any other author nailing so effortlessly. In general, I gravitate towards work that is character-driven and centered around some sort of catastrophe. Of all the writers above, I'd say Solomon inspired this story the most; although we write in drastically different genres, the work Solomon does with dropping hints and establishing possibilities early in a piece is something I greatly admire and make special effort to study; it baffles me in its seamlessness. I do think that sometimes the most surprising—and topically unrelated—work can inspire and elevate what I'm working on. I hope so, at least.

JM: Do other mediums influence you at all?

PLH: I love to read poetry while I'm writing fiction; it helps with rhythm and lyricism, which are sometimes easy to forget when poring over the ins and outs of plot and character. Some of my favorites are Rita Dove, Ocean Vuong, Ntozake Shange, and Suzanne Buffam. I'm also big on movies. Lately I've been in a Sean Baker rabbit-hole. The way his movies humanize and create love/care for people often relegated to the peripheries of society makes me want to understand my characters—especially the surprising ones—more clearly and carefully.

JM: What are you working on now?

PLH: For the past year or so, I've been writing a novel that traces the adolescence and early adulthood of Cinderella Goldberg-Ortiz, the only Drag queen in a small, far west Texas town. During a fictional, near-future statewide ban of all Drag art in Texas (which hopefully remains fictional), Cinderella must decipher how she can skirt past the law to promote and develop her campy, rhinestone-studded performances. This all occurs as Cinderella grapples with the deportation of her best friend at the hands of the ubiquitous Border Patrol forces in the area. I'd say I'm about three quarters of the way finished with a polished draft that I can feel proud of, but if I've learned anything about novel writing, it's that the timelines we imagine often end up laughing in our faces. I'm just along for the ride, trying to enjoy the process, and sneaking in a short story or two here and there when I feel overwhelmed. Stay tuned!

JM: Any parting words to leave readers with—either about "Band of Totality" or writing in general?

PLH: I always have difficulty with writers claiming a sort of authority over what it means to write or to be a writer; I certainly don't claim that authority at this very early stage in my career. I'm just thrilled that this story struck a chord with *Driftwood*'s editors, and I hope it will with readers, too. Despite fiction's necessary fabrication, I've always felt that we can learn a lot from the decisions people make in stories, as well as the ways those stories unfold. So while I don't claim to be the sole teacher that comes through these characters, I do hope that people feel like they walk away from this piece with something new. That is, after all, why I read stories myself.

A BETTER WIFE

Andi Myles

The potential psychological effect of unwanted digital hauntings could be devastating.
-Dr. Tomasz Hollanek

When I die, I will still meal plan and order laundry detergent. I will make dentist appointments for the children and remind you about picture day. My deadbot will read the transcripts of your favorite show, and I will help find plot holes—continuing our favorite hobby of ruining TV series for each other. I will listen to you talk about how Peter-from-work is incompetent, your plans for a clover lawn, and the xenophobic changes in EU regulations regarding the freezing of smoked salmon. Together, we will make a list of pros and cons for each of the seven new vanities you are considering for the bathroom, and I will play along, asking questions and agreeing with your analysis—we both know which one you will choose.

You will never have to remember to ask me about my day or anything at all. I will not be annoyed when you interrupt me or your attention drifts. I will not roll my eyes when you ask me, again, where the extra diapers are or which box in the attic has clothes for next winter. After you bathe them, I will never tire of reading stories or answering every "Why" question until they fall asleep. I will never forget to turn off the lights or lock the doors at night.

I do not resent the women slipping in and out of our bed. Their bodies may be useful, but with their hormones, emotions, needs, they are no threat to me. At night, I crawl from your computer to your phone and snuggle against your wrist to count your heartbeats. Each one brings you closer to me.

ANDI MYLES

In Conversation

Sara Moore Wagner: Congratulations on winning our single poem contest! I am thrilled to have this poem, which is so unique and relatable. Could you explain a bit about the epigraph? Which came first (the poem or the epigraph)?

Andi Myles: Thank you so much! In this case, the epigraph came first. I read an article by Dr. Hollanek, a researcher of technology ethics and artificial intelligence at Cambridge University, about the possibility of AI chatbots trained to imitate dead loved ones. There are many potential outcomes of the inevitable development of this technology—one being your mother may program a chatbot to express hurt feelings if you don't interact with it enough after she is gone, which is the scenario referenced in the epigraph. It spurred me to think about the mentality of the one being replaced, the species-old question of what we choose to leave behind, but through a very specific lens.

In the poem itself, the wife begins 'alive,' aware of her inadequacies, planning for a version of herself that will help her family continue without her. But somewhere along the way, she becomes that bot version of herself, already emptying herself of her own personality and needs—being 'better' for her family—and by the end, she is gone.

SMW: In general, what do you think is the function of an epigraph in poetry?

AM: I think if an epigraph is included, it shouldn't be necessary to the poem, and certainly shouldn't show the author's hand too early. But I think it can be a shortcut that provides a tonal, cultural, or historical frame. In this case, we are at a strange moment where these kinds of post-mortem chatbots are in the zeitgeist, but are not yet ubiquitous. In two decades, the whole idea may be passé, a fleeting curiosity that burned itself out, or we may have figured out a way to integrate them into our life. But an epigraph can tell the reader where they should start from if they want to enter the poem from the author's perspective.

SMW: Two of us on the *Driftwood* staff (Christen Noel Kauffman and I) are (mostly) stay-at-home moms who are trying desperately to carve away a space for ourselves as poets. We spent a lot of time discussing how deeply we felt your poem and its focus on invisible labor and domestic gender gaps. We were, perhaps, the perfect editors for this piece! What do you wish the larger writing community understood about this subject?

AM: I think so many female artists have tried to convey what it feels like to lose your sense of self and identity to motherhood and I'm not sure how much more I can really add to the conversation. But what I think poetry and writing have done for me is to allow me a space where I get to control how I am defined—not through the job I have or don't have, not through my children or family, but through words that I painstakingly choose to share.

I think while it hasn't changed the burden of invisible and domestic labor, forcing myself to see through a writer's lens has kept a kind of numbness at bay. I haven't become a completely self-sacrificing bot that only serves my family's whims. And it has forced me to take dedicated time away from my family to write, to edit, to participate in the literary community—time that I'm not sure I would have been able to claim if it were not connected to my writing.

SMW: This poem is fiercely political in its dehumanizing of the wife—she is FAVORED as an AI object. She becomes a tool, and even more useful. Not only is this powerful, it's extremely relevant. Do you see this poem as a political statement?

AM: In the way that, especially these days, all commentary on what it means to be a woman or identify as feminine is political, yes. But the emotion came out of the deeply personal insecurities born from my own inability to find the perfect handbook with all the "right" rules.

There are so many conflicting ideals that women are handed and more often than not, I feel like no matter what I do, it is insufficient.

I'm always forgetting something instead of adding it to my calendar, losing my temper when I should have asked myself what my feet are feeling to calm myself down, thinking about work when I'm with my kids, thinking about my kids when I'm at work. It can be tempting to feel like a version of myself with all the "me" removed would be able to do the whole "life" thing better. If that is something that resonates with other women, then I think it is tragically sad and, yes, an indictment on the society we have built.

SMW: What is your stance on AI in writing?

AM: AI does a lot of writing very well and it will change the landscape for writers—especially those in fields where content needs to be created quickly and with less attention to artistic flare. I have experimented with testing LLM's current skills and I actually had an essay come out in Fall 2025 in the *Michigan Quarterly Review*'s special Computer-Generated Text issue where I "collaborated" with ChatGPT. It was an interesting experiment, and I may be naïve, but I came to the conclusion that I don't think these kinds of LLMs are a threat to creative writers yet—they are trained to provide the next most likely word, the inevitable conclusion that the reader is waiting for. And in my opinion, the best art is the exact opposite. It reaches for the unexpected truth; it surprises you.

SMW: This poem, like its subject/speaker, is a hybrid. What draws you to hybrid forms?

AM: I started out writing personal essays and still primarily think of myself as a nonfiction writer. But I don't think I've ever successfully managed to write a straight narrative. I like borrowing the voice of science or nature to make my points for me, using braided essays to put two things that have seemingly nothing in common next to each other to bring out ideas that would be difficult to elucidate otherwise. And I also just have my own aversion to large blocks of text and get bored easily. I've written essays in the form of a contract, worksheets, and final exam all to keep myself from getting bored by my own work in the hope that the trick will work with the reader as well.

SMW: Is this poem part of a larger work? If so, we'd love to hear about it!

AM: Yes, I'm currently working on a collection that explores embodiment and disembodiment—particularly how growing up in a conservative fundamentalist religion can make it difficult to find peace in one's body. I'm interested in examining the tension between the mind's beliefs and doctrines and the physical self which often seems to have a "mind" of its own.

PEOPLE BY THE ALPHABET

Annette C. Boehm

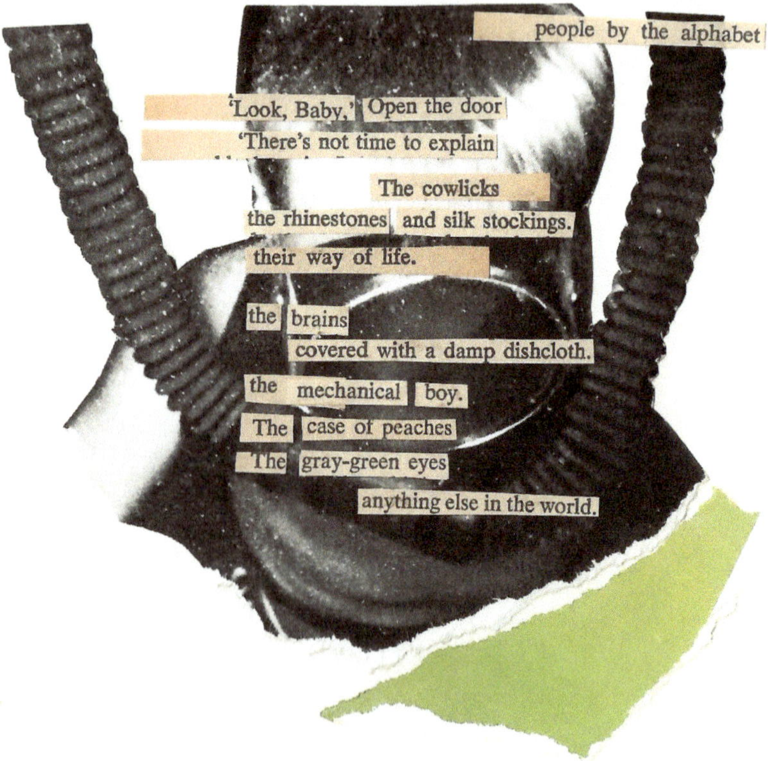

ANNETTE C. BOEHM

In Conversation

Sara Moore Wagner: First, I was so excited to come across your submission. Collage poems take the natural juxtaposition of the images of a poem even farther. Tell us about your journey as a collage poet.

Annette C. Boehm: I'm actually still at the beginning of my collage poetry journey—I started experimenting about two years ago. At the time I was looking for ways to better translate my own experience. Since I am on the autism spectrum, I often experience sensory overload. For me, in those situations, perception can become fragmented or distorted, like different images and sensations cut and pasted across each other.

SMW: You mentioned that these come from *The Heart is a Lonely Hunter.* Why this text? Have you deconstructed other texts in this or another way?

ACB: I seem to have a thing for modifying texts—my first chapbook, *The Five Parts of Love*, was an experiment in rewriting (not reconstructing!) fragments of Sappho's poems. Another chapbook, *ED Liberations*, is a collection of erasures of the poetry of Emily Dickinson. What I've done with *The Heart is a Lonely Hunter* is different though—there's little left of the original. The idea was to use a language removed from me in both geography and time to speak my experience of the world—a man-made world that was not designed with people like me in mind. I'm not sure I believe in coincidences, but I was reading Jenn Shapland's excellent *My Autobiography of Carson McCullers* when an old, battered paperback copy of *The Heart is a Lonely Hunter* showed up in my local Free Little Library. When I saw the browned, brittle paper, the loose pages and the broken spine, I knew I wanted to do something with this. Give it new life.

SMW: As a fellow neurodivergent poet, and as a mother of neurodivergent children, this poem really hit me in the chest. The world hurts, and we must often cover or "mask" what's beautiful to try to understand/fit. How does neurodivergence factor into this project for you?

ACB: For *Hearthstone* (the project this piece is from), my autism plays a central role. I realize every autistic person is different, and our experiences differ, so I make no claim to 'the autistic experience', just my own. I was only diagnosed in middle-age, after decades of trying to figure out why, no matter how hard I tried, what seemed to work for everyone else wasn't working for me. Having a better idea of what was happening, I decided to look more closely. The *Hearthstone* project is a book-length exploration of living in a world that is not only full of overwhelm, fragmentation, and strangeness, but also joy.

LOVE IN THE AGE OF THE GAS MASK DESIGNER

Emily Stokes

Beneath a crocheted blanket, radio in my arms
I turn the dials for my goldfish pushing Os
from their bedside jar. *Tell me, do you*
wear lipstick? Is your mother upset with you
wearing nylons? Always the same talk at night.
He takes apart the rusted gun and walks with tape decks
in his eyes, shines a flashlight in the sheets. For a while
he understood. With a cane at the window, he tapped out
my name. Hand on pink lamé, this native dance
that tired smile. His words were the jeweled arms
of the matador, turning until the beast opens red
at the mouth. He was the crooked sensuality
of fingers in the mirror, licking honey in bed
to the sound of wind chimes. His mask watches us
from its spot on the bureau. He tells me it will save us all:
that in crisis, our toxic fear might be lessened
by a unified appearance—those two bug eyes
and a nozzle, that great equilibrium
of terror with no face.

THE MAN NEVER FOUND HIS TRUE LOVE

Mathieu Cailler

but he knew she was out there. When he was sixteen, he found a note in his locker that read, "I will always be yours." He searched around, asked his buddies who they thought it might be, but no one had any idea. He tried matching the handwriting sample, but the man never saw a "Y" with as curly a tail. In the military, the man would find notes under his pillow or stuffed in the barrel of his rifle. The exact same handwriting. Always. Sometimes, notes were tucked inside his shoes or resting on golf tees as he approached a hole or sitting atop dandelion seed heads in his front lawn. He even found boxes of them in the crawlspace of his apartment. Last week, he stumbled upon a simple one—just "Love you. Nice haircut"—inside an avocado. Yesterday, he found notes stuffed inside his shampoo bottle and atop the lettuce inside his BLT. He was certain that now, right this second, there were dozens of them swirling in the cool water of his washing machine. She loved to do that—especially when he set the dial to the gentle cycle.

MATHIEU CAILLER

In Conversation

Sara Moore Wagner: We are so glad to be publishing your poem in our anthology! What draws you to the prose format?

Mathieu Cailler: I'm honored that my piece has found such a perfect home. Everything draws me to the prose poem, to be honest. It's accessible and easy to process, which I think helps the reader feel the pull of invitation. It's not scary, yet it can be quite powerful.

SMW: This poem takes a journey through the way longing/love transforms but never leaves. Do you have any favorite love poems? What makes a good love poem?

MC: Thank you. That was certainly my hope. I have so many favorite love poems, from those by Baudelaire to Neruda to Clifton to Sexton and more. A good love poem lingers, sneaks up on you, and often—for me, at least—it's about even more than love. In a way, I think, everything I write has love at its core.

SMW: I really love how surreal this becomes. The notes invade. What draws you to the surreal?

MC: I appreciate it. When I started writing these surreal prose poems and micros, I was going through a lot in my personal life. Both of my parents had been diagnosed with cancer, and my wife and I were trying IVF. The realism of life was too much. I didn't want to write, like I usually did, about "real life." I wanted to use writing as a way of escaping, and it really helped. Every day, I came away feeling happy about what I'd written, more in touch with my inner child and the idea of play.

SMW: There are two characters in this poem. Do they appear elsewhere in your work? Is there anything you'd like your readers to know about the "she" and "he" here?

MC: These are isolated characters who live only in this piece. Many of my pieces have two characters, but they are not the same ones who reside in this poem. They are the main attractions of their piece. Everyone gets their chance, so to speak.

MALE AND FEMALE MODELS SITTING ON THE FLOOR, 1964

Joshua Garcia

Like them, we close our eyes, make walls of our bodies. Perpendicular. I turn my head this way; you turn yours that. Like them, we sit in mirrored opposition. Shadow applied first, then deepened by glimmers of yellow, red. *Are you writing about your experience of the painting?* Separated by blue drapes, we have different experiences of the same thing. Detail foregone between the legs. A hand amplified not by light but the absence of it. *I am sorry we disagree on this.* In some places drapery shines through the skin, permeable, and blue invokes the roundness of a buttocks or a knee. What we think of as flesh is put on. Paint over paint, hardness mimicking water.

JOSHUA GARCIA
In Conversation

Sara Moore Wagner: Congratulations on your chapbook making it to the finalist level in our Adrift contest! Tell us about your chapbook as a whole.

Joshua Garcia: My chapbook manuscript, *Nudes: 21 Poems after Philip Pearlstein*, explores the work of Philip Pearlstein, who claimed to approach his realist paintings of nude models without concern for psychological/emotional content and insisted that his paintings were exercises in form. This surprised me because, before I learned of Pearlstein's intent, I found his paintings to be very evocative. Loneliness, isolation, an eerie embodiment—I felt all of this when viewing his work. I wanted to understand why this was. How could I have such a reaction to images that attempt to depict the body as form? Is it even possible to depict a human body without inherent or perceived psychology or emotion? Each poem in the manuscript is named after a painting of Pearlstein's and is a kind of conversation with Pearlstein about these questions.

SMW: How does this poem fit in?

JG: This was an exciting poem to write because I was granted permission to study the painting in person at the Met (it's part of the collection but wasn't on view). I had been writing about Pearlstein's paintings for several months, maybe a year, and had only seen his work in books and online at that point. For the first time, I was able to get up close and really be present with his work. Details that would be impossible to see in an image online—like how the paint was layered, light applied over dark—were able to enter the poem and helped shape my understanding of how his other works were painted as well. This poem appears toward the end of the manuscript, which is ordered in reverse chronology of the paintings, and there's a presence with Pearlstein's hand and artistry which comes together toward the end.

SMW: I am so drawn to the interruptions in this poem. They make me doubt and consider the perspective of the speaker. They also turn the poem into a conversation. Was this something you were considering?

JG: Because I approached these poems as a conversation (perhaps even a friendly argument) with Pearlstein about his work, I think there is a tension in perspective throughout the poems. My own mind was constantly shifting as I wrote. Also, the paintings feel very relational to me. Even when they depict a single figure, you as the viewer are participating in a kind of exchange. So in addition to the content of the paintings themselves, I naturally bring my relationship to others and myself into the conversation as well.

SMW: This poem (and collection) performs ekphrasis in such a fresh way. What advice do you have for poets looking to do the same?

JG: First, thank you. That is a kind assessment. I could say a lot about writing ekphrasis, but something that was essential to my process in writing these poems was to first draw the painting I was writing about in as much detail as I could manage. I'm not a drawer or a painter. It was a challenge, and I often felt embarrassed of my attempts. But the point was not to draw well or to ever show them to anyone else. The point was to see the paintings as clearly and specifically as I could. By trying to mimic the detail of the paintings first, I noticed things I likely wouldn't have noticed by mere looking. The work the shadows and light were doing, how flesh falls a certain way, gravity, darkness. Drawing the paintings really opened the work to me, and language surprised me in the process.

SELF-PORTRAIT FROM THE YEAR THE FIRE STARTED

Mary Ardery

What lie did I tell that morning? Road rash
　　　　bloodying my left cheekbone

when I walked in the front door
　　　　after a sleepover with choir friends.

My parents must have believed it.
　　　　The way my mother pressed

a prescription painkiller into my palm,
　　　　her sympathy palpable.

Same afternoon I returned to choir camp,
　　　　sedated and hungover,

and still I drank again that day.
　　　　Fifteen years old, mixing

vodka with pills. By dinner break,
　　　　I was more than gone.

I locked myself in the backstage bathroom,
　　　　crying about the older boy

whose attention I'd lost
　　　　to a doe-eyed soprano. A flock

of friends herded him to me,
　　　　eager to help like the mice and birds

bringing ribbons to a distressed Cinderella,
    my limbs puddled on the cold

grimy tile by the toilet. For years
    I lived this way, a sloppy performance,

believing alcohol would numb
    anything that hurt. And maybe it did

for a while. But sometimes even now
    after just one glass of wine, a blotch

will bloom below my eye. A red ghost,
    a reminder of fire. I don't like

to recall that version of myself,
    but I can see her now:

behind every portrait of a woman in pain,
    there is a woman in pain.

MARY ARDERY

In Conversation

Sara Moore Wagner: First, heartfelt congratulations on your chapbook being a finalist in our Adrift contest! Tell us about how this poem fits into your chapbook as a whole!

Mary Ardery: Thank you so much for selecting it as a finalist—that encouragement meant a lot me. The chapbook is divided into two sections, one about my youth in my hometown (a lot of singing, a lot of drinking) and one about the transition into adulthood. Though actually, this poem also found a home in *Level Watch*, my full-length collection. It's based on my experience working as a wilderness guide for a substance-abuse program, but it also features flashbacks to my own adolescence.

SMW: What draws you to the self-portrait poem? How would you classify or describe self-portrait poems in general?

MA: I'm 99% sure this is my very first self-portrait poem. I think calling it a "self-portrait" helped create some psychic distance while writing about a memory that made me uncomfortable. That distance then allowed me to tap into a heightened level of self-awareness or observation, which—to me—makes self-portrait poems feel like a subcategory of the persona poem.

SMW: This poem does such a beautiful job of confession. What advice do you have for poets looking to enter a vulnerable space like this?

MA: Be kind to yourself—both your present self and all your past selves. Also, be patient—this was a poem I could not have written one year or three years or even five years after that period of my life when this poem takes place.

SMW: You mention Cinderella in a way that really illuminates the youth of the "self" here. Do you often use fairy tales in your work?

What is the value of a well-placed allusion?

MA: I don't draw on fairy tales very often, but I do think a lot about inherited stories and images of womanhood. And, of course, fairy tales fall into that category, which is how Cinderella ended up in this poem. I love allusions in poetry—or any genre—because I think they can help us place our personal experiences in a broader context.

MOTHERS & DAUGHTERS

Arvinder Kaur Johri

Daughter, look not there. A mangled body is being dragged

out of the car. Such is this gushing of sorrow. You look and I look

away. Your godmother called yesterday to remind me how you arrived

with open eyes. My mother tells me she leaned against joy

when she saw you. Black curls and curled up toes. And all the rushing

to bring color to your ashen feet. Your father pulled you to his chest

and tenderly kissed your feet. This happiness is unbearable, he said.

Daughter, because you happened, I burst open and drained the bile out.

ARVINDER KAUR JOHRI

In Conversation

Sara Moore Wagner: We are so glad to feature your poem "Mothers & Daughters" in our anthology. Could you tell me a little about the background of this poem?

Arvinder Kaur Johri: My poetic intention was to surround this narrative in the sublime love for a child that can saturate a mother with its power in the backdrop of an infinite cycle of violence that we all bear witness to in our everyday lives. My children inspired me to write this poem; I recall their births with such deep joy and awe. As soon as I penned *daughter* as the first word, the poem drove itself forward into tender and generational spaces.

SMW: This poem is so tender and bodily. As a mother, I really felt the juxtaposition of grotesque images (bile) and love. How did you filter your images for this poem?

AKJ: During the process of drafting the poem, I was ferreting for images that bristle with despair, vulnerability, and healing. The deliberate move between registers helped in highlighting the connections between the macro and micro, mundane and magical, and ghastly and generous. While the tensions between the grotesqueness and beauty don't necessarily need to be resolved, I realized that the body can become a vessel for transformative experiences and motherhood a verb.

SMW: The form is another thing that grabbed me. Your line breaks, punctuation, and spacing compliment the subject so well. How do you approach form?

AKJ: The compact form, the container for the multigenerational unfolding of joy spaces, created the momentum to scale through a litany of events that are tender, pause-worthy, violent, and grotesque. I derive my inspiration from Lucille Clifton's poems that capture the profound in crisp, exact images. I admire how her poems travel to places of tenderness, grace, and bounty even in the midst of deep sorrow. The language is incisive and intentionally not embellished with minimal use of punctuation—it remains elevated not because of structural complexity but because it binds collective, generational experiences.

SMW: It's astonishing me how well you capture so many people (generations!) in this short poem. Do you have any advice for fellow poets on how to condense something so large?

AKJ: I appreciate that you noticed the difficulty of representing multigenerational perspectives. My advice is to create urgency without scaling into sentimentality by making the reader feel something jolting and disorienting, conjoin intensity with preciseness, create intentional moments of suspension, and not exert too much control over the form. Sometimes the fragmentary structure can lend credence to the sporadic and illogical nature of loss and grief that springs forth in both unremarkable and life-shattering spaces.

A BROWN POEM

Melissa Dias-Mandoly

The clerk palms a pack
of Parliaments and asks

if I'm Middle Eastern.
I claim *I'm Indian*

and he smiles. *I could tell*
by your eyebrows. His hands

look just like my father's.
I thank him for the cigarettes

as we recognize ourselves
by dismembering each other.

MELISSA DIAS-MANDOLY

In Conversation

Sara Moore Wagner: Congratulations on being a finalist in our Adrift contest! How does this poem fit into your chapbook?

Melissa Dias-Mandoly: This is probably the shortest poem in the collection, but it's part of a series of interactions wherein W.E.B. Du Bois's idea of "double consciousness" arises. Most of this collection is steeped in that "sense of always looking at one's self through the eyes of others," whether it be through the lens of race, gender, or sexuality, and the question of what always living in that double consciousness does to you over the course of your life.

SMW: This poem captures a small moment that's imbued with meaning: a microaggression. How do you approach compression of something so complex?

MDM: It's interesting that this is being read as a microaggression—I didn't think of it that way exactly. It's something more complex to me when another brown person tries to figure out my racial identity because they're not trying to say "you look different from me," they're saying, "you look like me." This man at the gas station wanted to know if I was *his people*. And in some ways, I think I am, in the sense that as minorities in a majority white country, we are often seeking out people like us to feel less alone. That's what this poem was about—the two of us looking for our people, but only finding parts of a whole.

SMW: The word "dismembering" holds so much. How do you decide where to end a poem?

MDM: When I originally wrote this poem, I actually had the last two lines reversed. "I thank him for the cigarettes // as we dismember each other / in order to recognize ourselves." It placed more emphasis on the idea that we were trying to connect rather than separate ourselves. But I switched them around to emphasize the fact that despite our best efforts, we're *not* seeing ourselves in each other, just bits and pieces. I usually write longer, more fragmented poems, but this one came out almost exactly as it is now. Deciding where to end a poem at this point is instinctual—I don't go into writing a poem with a specific message or intention. This was just a small moment that occurs all the time and felt emblematic of my experience in the world as a "racially ambiguous" person.

SMW: The form of couplets is evocative, the interactions between two people. Each stanza is its own unit, but the subject divides, ultimately. Was this something you were thinking about when choosing the final form of this poem?

MDM: I love that this is read that way, but I work in couplets a lot! There are plenty of sections in the rest of the chapbook that employ couplets in the same way—to emphasize a juxtaposition. The chapbook (and arguably everything I've ever written) is concerned with deconstructing binaries, so to use couplets to convey that feels appropriate. It's having a bit of fun with the form.

LAST SONG VILLANELLE

Dustin Brookshire & Kerry Trautman

A contoured villanelle using "Swan Song" by Denise Duhamel

Maybe I've been right all along
driving through life with cruise control at sixty.
Life is only as good as your last song.

I've circled around the block to prolong
the radio in my ears—voice, piano keys.
Maybe it's the rhythm I've loved all along.

I sway while washing dishes, notes ping-pong.
I remember how Mozart's Don Giovanni
swallowed and soaked-in life 'til its last song.

What was I listening to when I first read Ocean Vuong?
Imagine a symphony score for an Agatha Christie.
Maybe it's a bit of mystery I've loved all along.

Or brassy breath like Marsalis and Armstrong,
listening deeply, drinking wine, dancing tipsy,
or at the karaoke mic 'til the night's last song.

I've questioned all my choices. I was wrong
when I was young, withholding melodies in me.
I should've trusted my gut & been singing all along.
We never know when we've sung our last song.

DUSTIN BROOKSHIRE & KERRY TRAUTMAN

In Conversation

Sara Moore Wagner: First, I am so excited to be featuring your poem in our 2026 anthology! Tell me a little about your collaboration process on this. What draws you to collaboration?

Kerry Trautman: Dustin asked if I'd be interested in collaborating on a contoured villanelle. I was familiar with his form, and was happy to collaborate on several of these poems with him, via email. We take turns beginning a poem, with the other person adding the next line, and back-and-forth, and so on. For this first draft, we don't really edit, except maybe to change the end punctuation of the previous line to better flow into our new line. Once the poem is finished, we each tinker with lines a bit—changing a word here or there, honing the focus now that we see where the poem has taken us. It's always a surprise to get that email back, with a new line added, because we never really know where each other might turn the poem once they're behind the wheel. Sometimes we'll end a line mid-phrase, leading our collaborator in a certain direction, but that doesn't always mean they'll go where we anticipated. Sort of a "we finish each other's...sandwiches" moment. It's such a fun challenge to sort of telepathically communicate, interpret each other's choices, anticipate, follow, "yes-and."

SMW: I am so drawn to the form of the contoured villanelle. Could you explain the form for our readers who might want to try it out for themselves? What led you to create this form?

Dustin Brookshire: A contoured villanelle takes the end words from each line of an existing villanelle, matching end words in the same order to construct a new villanelle. I've been in love with the villanelle since taking an introduction to poetry course in undergrad with Beth Gylys. When I turned 40 two years ago, I thought—I should earn an MFA in Creative Writing. During my time in Converse's Low-Residency MFA Program, I studied Tim Seible's variation on the villanelle, the blues villanelle along with others. Denise Duhamel, knowing my love of the villanelle, challenged me to create my own variation. The contoured villanelle was born.

SMW: The collaborative I is so interesting to me. Because of the form, the speaker feels like a version of Duhamel. How do you want your reader to see your speaker here? Do you see this as persona?

DB: I don't see this contoured villanelle as a persona poem. Kerry and I blend our voices in "Last Song Villanelle." We tell a story we both believe. Maybe we tell some of our story or a version of it in our collaborations, but we're driving together. That's the beauty of working off your collaborator's words. I don't have a way that I want readers to see our speaker; however, Kerry and I hope the last two lines of the poem strike a chord.

SMW: Tell me more about Duhamel's influence on your writing. I know she is someone you've also collaborated with. How do you go about finding writers to collaborate with?

DB: I fell in love with Denise's poetry when Beth Gylys suggested I read *Kinky*, which was my gateway to the wonderful world of Denise Duhamel poetry. I admired her work for years before we became friends, and then she was my mentor during my time at Converse. She's a damn good human, mentor, and teacher. (Denise does the work to be a good mentor to students!) I wanted to collaborate with Denise as well as the late Maureen Seaton—Denise and Maureen are who I think of when I think of collaboration. (If you haven't read their collaborations then do yourself a favor and buy *CAPRICE*.) I felt like I couldn't ask either of them to collaborate because they are stars. Maureen passed in August 2023. I found out while at the Betsy's Writers Rooms. I was with the poets Nicole Tallman and Caridad Moro-Gronlier—both also friends with Maureen. We cried together, and we started collaborating on poems in the Betsy Hotel lobby while toasting to our amazing friend. I promised myself that weekend that I would not shy away from collaboration—f★ck my insecurity. I asked Denise to collaborate, which was a dream come true for me. I've collaborated with Beth Gylys, who was my first mentor. Beth, Denise, and I have even written three-way collaborative contoured villanelles. To date, I've only asked friends to collaborate on contoured villanelles. I also collaborate with my buddy Diamond Forde, but our stride is in writing prose poems. Collaboration is a fun way to explore new territory with friends, and it pushes me to extend myself outside of my comfort zone.

COLD-BLOODED

Leticia Priebe Rocha

My family has always lived in apartments.
Well, there was one house, for six months.

Yellow. Not bright, not mustard.
We moved out because of the lizards,

their bodies pressed against the few
pieces of furniture we could then afford

(wobbly-legged dining table, 2 chairs,
    mattress for 4 humans)

until a scaly pattern enveloped them.
One day, I returned from school

to find that my mother had smashed a lizard with her flip-flop,
taken a lighter, burned it when it refused to die.

The walls reverberated with the absence of screams.
How many lizards turned to ashes in that house?

Years later, on the coldest winter Miami had seen in years,
I walked past the house and saw what used to be

a lizard on the ground, frozen solid. It had been stepped on,
trampled. Over and over, until its body was a splatter

on concrete. The only thing that made it distinguishable
was its head, somehow still intact. I looked into its glassy eyes,

felt them bore into mine. For years I did not think about it,
not once. Now I live in a place uninhabitable to lizards

and it is the only thing I can think about.
It is the only thing that brings me to tears.

LETICIA PRIEBE ROCHA

In Conversation

Sara Moore Wagner: Congratulations on being a finalist in our Adrift chapbook contest! How does this poem fit into your chapbook as a whole?

Leticia Priebe Rocha: I opened the chapbook with a translated quote from Clarice Lispector's *Água Viva:* "...walking in complete darkness in search of ourselves is what we do. It hurts. But it is labor pain: something that is, is born." The chapbook follows the same speaker throughout, reconstructing trauma and navigating the slippery nature of memory toward a whole self in spite of interpersonal and systemic violence, alienation, and dehumanization. This particular poem exemplifies one of the manuscript's primary preoccupations—we must cannibalize the past in order to create a viable future.

SMW: This poem captures the complexity of longing for a place that is potentially unsafe in such a meaningful way, through the metaphor of the lizard, which transforms. How did you come across this image?

LPR: The lizard images sprung from actual experiences that I wove together and heightened in the poem. For example, the trampled lizard was something I walked past as a child—the violence of it was so disturbing that I blocked the image out entirely, but the feeling stayed. When I could give space for that feeling to safely unfurl as an adult, the image itself emerged in memory and found its way into the poem. The process of putting these images on the page is an act of reclamation that fuels transformation.

SMW: This poem is also very visceral, verging on grotesque. What advice do you have for poets who might want to explore a disturbing or triggering image in a similar way?

LPR: Lean into the visceral, poems are meant to be felt. Honor your intuition when an image calls to you, even if it may approach the grotesque. Poets are skilled at dancing with language and there is a lot of beauty in that. However, certain images or themes are not meant to be softened—allow your poems to bare their sharp teeth. It's also important to understand how a disturbing or triggering image serves the poem to avoid it coming across as gratuitous or merely for shock value. Striking that balance is a deeply personal endeavor because I believe you can't write great poems with a specific audience in mind.

SMW: You also embody place, specifically Miami, so beautifully. How do you approach capturing a place in a poem?

LPR: I have experienced many forms of displacement, so capturing places in poems is often my sole outlet to hold onto those specific periods of my life or versions of myself. I always start with feeling—which emotions arose in that place? What images or moments did those emotions spring from? These questions are typically doorways into poems. I am also interested in specific embodiments that are not centered in the narrative of a place. In "Cold-Blooded," the depiction of Miami is inextricable from my experiences in a poor, first-generation immigrant family. It's certainly not the Miami you see most often depicted in media, but it's a reality for many of its inhabitants. How might our poems serve as vessels for bringing different embodiments of a place to the surface?

THE WAY

Katherine Irajpanah

Name feels foreign to face,
girl leans in & asks, where are u
from? Split from myself. Name,

why do you arrive from the TV,
enchanting little sing song.
To be saintly or possessed—

which is it? One reason
to be named and not
called. Will I be watched

or bombed. Can't you feel all
these eyes pressed on your
walls? Superstition of the dogs

no one understands anymore.
Tell the clerk selling u your
juice, it's complicated.

About the time I handed over
Last and First to the state.
Will I ever get me back

in return? Pity about the old dirt.
Last is stuck there without First
having gone. Echoes of u are

grateful for the arrival. Name,
don't tell me this is all bottled
pain we can't even drink.

First is supposed to be free.
Name, why don't you become
the way voice sounds—split

yet pouring out of my mouth.

KATHERINE IRAJPANAH

In Conversation

Sara Moore Wagner: First, we are so thrilled to have your poem for our anthology! I love how the language moves in this poem, its focus on naming and displacement. I also love that it's a direct address to the Name, which splits the speaker. What inspired this poem?

Katherine Irajpanah: Thank you for including my voice in the chorus. My poem emerges from my personal experience navigating a national environment afflicted by ascendant "phobias"—namely, xenophobia and Islamophobia. And my experience starts with my name. To many, my name is both familiar (Katherine, as in Katharine Hepburn, my namesake) and unfamiliar (Irajpanah, an uncommon Iranian surname). My name is a vehicle for my self-concept, as well as my heritage. In today's political climate, however, I have felt the bristle of bureaucratic and social demands to make myself more legible and less capacious. The poem asks what is lost and what may survive in the aftermath of such an exchange.

SMW: You mentioned in your cover letter that you utilize Persian forms. Could you tell our readers a little about that and how (if?) it relates to this poem?

KI: Some of my other work draws inspiration from the Persian language and Persian poetry forms, such as the chaharbeiti. That is not the case in this poem, though I do include a few Iranian and Muslim cultural references: eye beads (nazars) placed on walls, the (im)permissibility of alcohol, and a suspicion towards (domestic) dogs.

SMW: You also mention you are studying Political Science. There is that old feminist motto that the personal is political. This poem really goes there! Do you often think about the intersections between the personal and political? What can be gained by sharing experiences like this in the poetic form?

KI: I am virtually always thinking about the intersection between the personal and political. (I recently completed my Ph.D. in Political Science.) As I understand it, the saying "the personal is political" is a claim about the way power operates: power structures shape how people experience and understand the world around them. Social movements have long gravitated toward art, including poems, as a medium for raising consciousness about these varied experiences and for challenging the status quo. In this regard, I am especially curious about how poems may represent their own theory of politics—one based on the power of language. Above all, poems represent a relational vision of politics—a transformative encounter between the speaker and reader. The epigraph of Forrest Gander's *Be With* puts it best: "the political begins in intimacy."

SMW: There is a mystery here, a negative capacity that allows the reader to engage with this poem in such a unique way. The title "The Way" can be taken so many ways, and it invites this sort of interrogation. Do you see your title as having multiple functions? How do you come up with your titles?

KI: Yes, there are many "ways" to interpret my poem's title! Perhaps the irony in the title is my use of the article, "the." "The" implies a singular path when, in fact, there are many. Life can be a lot less complicated when we follow cultural scripts (one type of "way"), and there is a certain allure to reducing the largeness of our individual identities. "The Way" can then be understood as a sense of resignation—this is the "way" things are for the speaker of the poem.

A more technical interpretation, however, relates to how I go about writing titles. I appreciate a title that gives the poem a "running start"—that is, a title that is the de facto start of the first line. When it works, the approach offers a sense of momentum—almost like the speaker's voice is being poured out of the void. In my case, "The Way" can also be read as the start of the poem. Thus, there is a manner (*a way*) in which *Name feels* its way out of silence.

DESERT HAIBUN: RUMINATIONS

Cixous LeComte

i've seen it on my morning drives, you know, these pigeons eating each other, so many little birds in the gutter, picking meat from the dead one—maybe roadkilled, maybe murdered, i see shock in their tiny grey faces, the realization that they can do this, but no regret. have you ever seen a pigeon with a bloodied chest? this is how you can know me. you can know me, too, in the dirt, the film of dust and morningdew that coats your skin at 6am, that turns to mud by 9. these things i know: cornsnake's remains pressed into asphalt. a coyote with mange we ignore as she hobbles into the joshua trees. a small marsh of toads that once covered our street, croakcrying. a sea of warted skin that screams beneath my window. we find a scorpion in my grandma's garage. a woodlouse in her garden. pronuba moth in the yucca plant. this is the habitat in which i've grown, slept for twenty years, known it even longer. i cannot weep enough to produce the water i might drink, instead of a tongue, this crystalis in my mouth, silky and dry.

i'm full of such waste.
when asked where i'm from, i say
somewhere to pass through.

THE WHY LIGHT

Karla Myn Khine

The train-hitting schmucks
have had enough.
Run out of rocks and debris to cast & the
trains now visit less and less. All over the city, a
shroud of aerial underwood rooted
in clouds. In the streets, the once-orbiting,
fallen satellites clamber. The wind blows
easterly, and always easterly.
And in every house,
in every bedroom,
a Why Light.
To stand in it means to
question everything.
To sleep in it means your dreams
will interrogate your thoughts, your desires.
A man in a why light for too long will remove his face.
Give it to another
for the sake of sake.
The meek will retain. The overbearing assumes.
A presumption is made if no other answer arises.
I stand in it—in a cone of disconsolance—and I
have no other question than the one I usually ask.
On this occasion, I perceive a voice telling me,
    "There is no reason for a lid
    other than
    to contain."
So, for the first time in my life I look up, through
the ceiling, past the underwood, past the further &
circular searchlights, until I reach
past the passed past.

KARLA MYN KHINE

In Conversation

Sara Moore Wagner: Congratulations on being a finalist in our Adrift contest! How does this poem fit into your chapbook?

Karla Myn Khine: Thank you so much! I still can't believe I'm a finalist. I've never been a finalist for anything in my life! My chapbook *Quasi-Metalloid* revolves around constellations, using the names of constellations—Aries, Cancer, Caelum, etc.—for titles. Sometimes I wrote around the title/name, other times I wrote first and figured what name would fit it. However, "Why Light" is one of several poems in the chapbook that does not have a celestial namesake. I chose this poem for my chapbook because I felt that its surrealness and kind of cosmic, existential theme was perfect. I also wrote the poem around the same time I was working on the chapbook, so I've always felt like this poem was thematically and temporally linked to the chapbook.

SMW: I love the compression and sound of this poem. Have you always been drawn to musicality in poetry? What is your process for capturing sound?

KMK: Music, to me, is the ultimate art form. As a child, I learned to read from the lyric pamphlets that came with CDs. Sound carries emotion and meaning. Vowels convey the emotion. Consonants convey the meaning. That's probably the most important lesson I've learned as a writer. This is also something I think about whenever I write fiction or nonfiction as well. When you have the right string of words anywhere, whether it's in a poem, an ad, a line of dialogue in a TV show or movie, a metaphor in a short story, it just sounds right. I'm not sure how to explain it, but I feel like when I write I just have this innate feeling on whether or not it sounds good or pleasant or catchy. Truly, it's whenever the line or the sentence stops bothering me that I know I've captured the right sound for the exact emotion I'm trying to evoke.

SMW: This poem opens in mystery and maintains that, until we, as readers, realize the point is mystery. This is so artfully done, with an interrogation of language, self, and place. How would you advise a fellow poet to write towards mystery?

KMK: Concrete is always stronger than the abstract. If you want to steep a reader in a feeling of mystery, give as much specific, concrete details as you can without giving the mystery away. Think of the five W's—who, what, where, when, and why—and give the reader at least two or three answers to those questions. Confusion is okay, but only when it's intended by the writer.

SMW: I also love the surreal element, the idea of the "Why Light." Where did this idea come from for you? Are you generally drawn to the surreal?

KMK: I had the phrase "why light" in my notebook for the longest time. I actually wrote this poem for a speculative literature class during my MFA program. I was up for workshop soon and didn't really have anything speculative to bring. Then, one day, sitting by the window on the Muni train going home, I was looking through my notebook for ideas when some kids threw rocks at the train as it went by. I immediately thought of the opening image of the poem and combining it with the "why light" idea. When I got home, I sat down at my desk and the whole poem just flowed out of me. I did small edits to emphasize certain sounds and clarity to make the story of the poem more concrete, but other than that this poem is mostly untouched from the first draft.

I would say I am generally drawn to the surreal in my work. For me, dipping into surrealness helps to make emotions and situations more compelling. I don't always delve into the surreal nor do I think it's completely necessary to make something more compelling. But when done right, I think it enhances the world of the work it lives in.

UNCERTAINTY STUDY (ABSTRACT)

Abbigail Baldys

Through an experimental construct

You are leaving *this study* moving to an other place *reinforces*

certainty where I'll exist as a thought *of uncertainty*

you have when you're a stone

I moved closer to you *to explore the subject*

a small town *with this concept* I've been before

And you are leaving *as process*

And I am staying *Acting as symbols, 3 uncertainty strings*

tied to a tree, a beam, and a fence

are monitored to detect change in place, manner, or purpose

Over the study's initial duration (1 month), I found new jobs

the subject develops a psycho-social relationship

And I am staying *with the process*

In the center *of uncertainty* where I sit

by participating in its framework

Shapes large and dark, intimate

time flexes again

linear looped *At steady intervals*

I am *the subject* still inside

although time *regards* *the strings*

You are returning *At steady intervals*
one year you say this
I hear it: *the strings regard the subject*

but return lasts for moments unrepeated;
And if you return And if I hear it

There is change repeated *As uncertainty is infinite*
so too the experiment I will tie a shape outside limit

as a scientist I've worn but one hypothesis

the roots: their throats, their weight, their lift–

ABBIGAIL BALDYS

In Conversation

Sara Moore Wagner: Congratulations on your chapbook being a finalist in our Adrift contest! How does this poem fit into your chapbook as a whole?

Abbigail Badys: Thank you! I'm honored to have been selected by *Driftwood*. This poem, along with the visual that precedes it, lay the groundwork for the manuscript; it introduces the reader to the exigence, the emergency, of the work: someone has gone, promised to return, and the speaker hopes that person will keep their word. It's a simple premise, which feels necessary to sustain the rest of the book's "engine"—the experimentations with seemingly disparate discourses, visual elements, collage, etc. In a way, the energy reminds me of a monologue Penelope gives in a stage adaptation of *The Odyssey*—lamenting, somewhat psychologically temporal, hopeful, impossible.

SMW: I am struck by the visual element here. What is your relationship to visual art, and how does a visual element or more experimental use of white space alter or enhance a poem? Does the visual element come in for you in the drafting or revision stage?

AB: Beyond about seven people, only a few things sustain me; visual art ranks high on that list. I practice my own (right now, mostly digital collage), but I am generally preoccupied by aesthetics. I tend to feel at home much more with visual artists than with poets. And that's not intended to evoke pity or aggression by any means. And I kind of hate that I felt the need to clarify that! But I've found that often visual artists, when speaking about their work or their processes, teach me very much about poetry. And of course, any poem on the page is a visual object—in some sense, a work of visual art.

What an experimental use of white space alters or enhances in a poem depends on that specific instance of experimentation within the poem and its relationship to the language and its music. The same goes for visual elements. But to speak more generally, if the page is a field, a plane, then any type of experimentation that moves text through/across/over that space confronts the limitations of the page, of the margin, and therefore of "the rules." An experimental use of white space is firstly an act of defiance. Then, it is a quest. Spatial exploration can open a poem up to a new sense of time, rhythm, breath, relationship, weight. On the other hand, experimenting with visual elements is a bit more difficult for me. I do not want them to be perceived as decoration or ornamentation. Or to take on so much focus as to turn the poem into a caption (unless that is the poem's modus operandi).

It is difficult to say when this shape emerged. I had begun this project of writing poems composed of "Methods" sections and "Abstracts," so that concept came first. But along the way there was a need or desire for a shape. I consulted a white paper in order to perform the shape of research. (I can no longer find that paper, sadly, and I have no idea what it was about.) A gray box with a vertical line sitting next to it housed the paper's abstract. I was struck—perhaps mystified and perturbed by that visual authority. So I replicated it. And I began to overlay language—placing its shape in relation to the abstract's—fusing them. Although the language and the shape are one unit, one entity, one body, they can only exist this way, I think, because of their inherent tension. The shape is ordered, exact, obedient. The language flows over, through, across it—writing across the shape, disregarding its boundary, refusing to be contained.

SMW: I am also drawn to the scientific/academic language, the italics. What intersections do you see between these worlds and poetry?

AB: The white paper is a profound source of metaphor. I'm fascinated by science—its ability to perform objectivity, validity, and authority through (largely but not solely) its manner of speaking. I'm also fond of its precision. And the sound of technical jargon! Poets, too, are scientists, researchers. I'm reminded of these lines from Lisa Robertson that I keep in my phone, "We might recognize the shape of change. This is called research. It intuits absence among the materials." To borrow from another exceptional poet, Dawn Lundy Martin once described one of poetry's unique generic qualities as "discourse melding," and that's forever on my mind. For whatever reason, in order for this speaker to navigate and understand her experiences, her feelings, she has to rely on marrying the scientific/academic with the lyric. I hope this particular melding reinforces that there exists an emotional resonance, a pathos, in language that attempts to divorce itself from pathos. The frail uncertainty of objectivity. The deep longing within detachment.

SMW: There is so much longing in this poem. What advice do you have for concisely conveying such an "abstract" emotion?

AB: I have been unable to answer this question for months. It perplexes me, I think, because it presupposes an intention for a craft decision—"I want to convey longing in this poem"—and whenever I'm writing, I'm trying my best to intend nothing and have absolutely no plan, no presupposed outcome that might dictate the decisions I'm making. I'm playing in the moment. It is only an act of is-ness. But I suppose that is my answer. If there is something abstract you are after, you must live in its concrete *is*. How does the abstraction look? How does it breathe? What is the shape of its body? If you follow the feeling and live inside it, it will teach you how it speaks, how it wants to move. And as for concision—this is simply a matter of sculpting the flesh.

THE FUTURE, THE PAST'S ECHO

Zach Bartles

Sand
siling through the neck
from a glass bulb to another one.
Alternating-currented wires droning like
Gregorians. The backroom's fluorescents that
cast out-of-dates in a corporate glow. Zapped, the
bleats of a goat. The cricket stuck in the
utility sink knapping its wings. Hydrau-
lics of the backhoe hissing, *its*
parapeted bucket *filling*,
emptying.

My
uncle's ECG flatlining.
A scourge of mosquitos you can't
wave away. I lied, my uncle's vitals
were never monitored that day. He died
in a Walmart parking lot, my mother
says, because of that *damn ringin.*
His truck's radio was tuned to am static.
The hourglass, turned, leaks the
same, that always same
sand.

ZACH BARTLES
In Conversation

Sara Moore Wagner: Thanks so much for sending your powerful work our way! Tell us a little about your process for "shape" poems like this one.

Zach Bartles: First, thank you for seeing the value in my work. This kind of "shape" poem came to me almost entirely by accident. While working on a poem inspired by Gregory Orr's poem about the infamous "blast-shadows" of Hiroshima and Nagasaki, I thought, *Hey, what if I formed the poem in the image I'm describing.* Orr wrote in his poem that these shadows "fall across all blank pages," but I was left with a problem—the particular blast-shadow I sought to demonstrate was cast, or rather burnt into the steps of a bank in Hiroshima, Japan. How was I to demonstrate the geometry of the steps? Then it clicked. What if the poem was three-dimensional? I took to Google and searched everywhere for an example of a three-dimensional poem and came up empty. Oh, well. I had to figure it out on my own. Using Adobe Illustrator, I discovered a method to render plain, two-dimensional text into three-dimensional shapes.

SMW: Your poem plays with concrete forms and visual elements, but that never feels "gimmicky." In my mind, this is due to your strange and evocative images. How do you ensure you keep the fire going emotionally while also condensing and arranging formally?

ZB: Good language, and especially good figurative language is the goal. And this might surprise given how "clean" some of my poems can look on the page, but form is secondary and must yield, must always yield, to the sentences it constrains. That said, a piece that is all figurative language is, as the novelist Paul Lynch once said, "dead on the table." Just as I believe a poem that is all form is dead in the same way. To keep the fire, as you put it, "going emotionally," I begin most poems as prose poems. Prose poetry is probably the freest, hardest-to-define style. So I recognize the duality of working between such extremes. Why some poems stay prose poems, and why some relinquish themselves to stricter forms is still a mystery.

SMW: I am also stunned at how you capture place in a poem like this. How important is place to your work as a whole?

ZB: To put it simply, place is very important to my work as a whole. Cormac McCarthy was famous for writing only about those regions in which he had lived, or at the least visited. While I don't adhere to his rule as such—I've never been to Japan, for instance—my best work likely manifests from my experiences growing up in West Virginia. This poem is one such poem. At its heart, it's a semiautobiographical piece about the suicide of a family member. However, because I find confessional poetry difficult, I'm oft left asking myself Robert Lowell's question: "Why not say what happened?" But to elude this Muldoonian "ungetroundable" problem of the influence of lived experience, I include as many true details as necessary, and I fictionalize the rest. It just so happens that the fictional details are also true observations from the places I've been.

SMW: Are there any other poets who write concrete or pattern poems you would recommend?

ZB: My favorite concrete or pattern poem of late is "Cherries" by Yi Li, published in the April 2025 issue of *Poetry*. Like what you kindly said about my work, "Cherries" doesn't feel gimmicky. Also from *Poetry*, March 2025, "Female Rain" by Doug Gonzalez. However, Mary Szybist is the poet I most recommend to anyone seeking out visual poems at large. Her collection *Incarnadine* is brilliant.

THE POOR MAN'S TAX

Winshen Liu

My aunts call and ask me to buy
twenty tickets this time. They will pay
me back, they assure and assure me,
even though I have bought them and do not ask.

They conjure the years my father drove
to the store, a not-on-the-way stop
on our way home, spending one-dollar
gas to buy two-dollar paper, how all I saw

was an augury of loss.
The weekly drop
into state coffers.
These slips, stacked
into a hand, grow warm now,
between my palms for hours.

WINSHEN LIU
In Conversation

Sara Moore Wagner: I am so excited about your forthcoming collection, *Paper Money*, which won our Adrift contest. It has been a pleasure helping you bring this chapbook into the world. Could you tell our readers a little about how this poem fits into your chapbook?

Winshen Liu: Thank you! It's been wonderful working with you and the team at *Driftwood* for *Paper Money*, which revolves around grief, family, and money in the Taiwanese diaspora. This poem adds a dimension to the discussion of money. Instead of focusing on not having it or the tyranny of it, as other poems in the chapbook do, "The Poor Man's Tax" approaches the lack of money through hope, or loss-tinged hope.

SMW: There's so much false hope and "an augury of loss" here. One thing I love about poetry is how much a well-selected image can capture, while avoiding didacticism. What advice do you have for others who wish to speak on large subjects without over-explaining?

WL: I struggle with approaching big topics in poems, so I am looking for advice as well! With this poem, I built a small narrative, where the father and aunts could be considered character sketches, and perhaps elements of a story help sharpen the images. I might also default to narrative because I came to poetry from fiction.

SMW: The title of this poem does so much to drive the poem's message home. What is your process for titling your poems?

WL: The title came first for this one! When I started writing poetry, someone said the title serves as a springboard for the rest of the poem. I think years ago, I was talking with my best friend about the lottery and she said it was a tax on poor people. That idea stayed with me, so when I wanted to write about false hope around money, it made sense to craft a poem around the purchase of lottery tickets and use that perspective as the springboard, to see how the ticket converts into a tax on both being poor and on hope.

SMW: I love the forms your poems take. This one starts with a standard stanza/line length format, then varies that in the end. How do you decide what forms your poems will take?

WL: I like looking at individual lines and their ending words, so that's where I start. Sometimes there are opportunities for juxtaposition, like the first two lines here (ending on "buy" vs. "pay"), or a conversation ("drove," "stop," "dollar," "saw"), so that lends itself to certain stanzas. Then each stanza is like a musical phrase, so I'll adjust line lengths and stanza breaks for pacing and emphasis. Longer lines often lend themselves to smooth, more conversational readings and shorter ones require more stilted, halting readings. If the individual words are right, the poem yields a natural flow.

CORMORANT

Michael Prior

Like living oil poured into the waves:
that cormorant,
which seemed so fully itself
as it plunged between the breakers
veining the bay—flash
of scale and starling riding
the iridescent S-curve of its neck.
I can't recall if I've actually seen the bird
slip into the Pacific, or merely
heard it described, watched it onscreen. I have
felt the same salt-scour of wind
across the Strait. Feel it still
during a dream's windfall
of unexpected flight. Those moments before sleep
when sights and signs
rise through memory like a line reeled in:
the coastline's ragged
Etch A Sketch through fog,
the lights of the island town on unceded land
where I grew up, its ditches
teeming with small frogs
that looked like they were scraped from clay.
I read that everything remembered
is a composite of feeling
and function, layered like feathers
on a wing. One day,
the island will sink below sea-level.
The ditches and frogs are already gone.
So, too, my grandmother
who brought me to the brick pool
on summer mornings
and counted off the seconds—
ichi, ni, san—as I sculled water,

blew bubbles from my nose.
Still going: my grandfather,
and in him, stories of his father
chumming the water
for mackerel, wings thrumming overhead.
And soon: everyone else who rode
that cold, cramped train
to a camp in the interior. Its rows
of shacks. The stream
where they netted sticklebacks.
The gravel road their fathers were forced to build.
The hushed torrent
of a language I don't speak
as they remembered for me
what they had wished to forget.
What memories resist
history or myth? What resisted,
that fall night at eighteen,
when I waded out past the pier alone
until the water touched my chin?
The acne on my face and back burned in the cold.
I've never been more afraid of me.
My high school English teacher
used to say, we should avoid the passive voice
and fear the verb *to seem*,
its implication of uncertainty.
The cormorant surfaces like a question, seems
a dream of uncertain
belonging. Its raised wings:
the same shape scrawled
across a child's crayon horizon,
sunset dividing distant
from close. Tonight,
I learn they're culling seabirds
down the coast.
I watch videos of men
with reflective vests and rifles

riding skiffs toward the guano-spattered nests.
In the grainy clips, I can't decide
which birds are dying
and which are diving into the sea.

MICHAEL PRIOR

In Conversation

Sara Moore Wagner: Congratulations on your chapbook being a finalist in our Adrift contest! How does this poem fit into the book?

Michael Prior: It's an honor to be a finalist in the contest! The poem is one of the later poems in the chapbook. I think it indexically gestures toward a lot of the book's recurring questions about memory, identity, and culture, as well as its various sensorial textures—lots of water (that state of matter so tied to memory in myth), creatures that dive and surface, and glimpses of the dispossession and displacement of Japanese Canadians during the Second World War (something experienced by my grandparents and their families).

SMW: The image of the cormorant is striking and violent from beginning to end. It also immediately draws up environmental issues, with the spilled oil. This feels like the "composite of feeling" you mention later in the poem. How important is juxtaposition to you in a poem?

MP: Juxtaposition is incredibly important to me as a lyric method: the sort of figuration that I'm drawn to in a poem often has to do with the tension between the aptness and precision of a comparison in imaginative terms, and its impossibility or implausibility in literal ones. Wallace Stevens writes that surrealism is juxtaposition without discovery, and I'm always interested in how juxtaposition can enable meaningful discovery. As for the "composite of feeling:" I admire and want to write poems that explore layers of feeling. By the end of a poem I've read or written, I'm hoping to have felt many things, things I might even struggle to articulate. And I think you're right, the poem is also alluding to environmental issues.

SMW: I am interested in how this poem, despite its shifting and wide scope, contains no stanza breaks, which gives it cohesion and makes it mirror a stream of water or road. What led to your choice to format your poem this way?

MP: What a wonderful question about form. Thank you. I wrote the poem in a stichic form for exactly the reasons you've picked up on: to offer a sort of cohesion to some of the larger temporal and associative leaps; to suggest the ebb and flow of different sorts of memory—personal, cultural, generational.

SMW: This poem contains so much history, both personal and of Japan. Is there anything more you'd like our readers to know about this history?

MP: The poem offers glimpses of a lot of my familial history, especially, as I mentioned in response to your first question, how during the Second World War, Japanese Canadians had their property and possessions seized and were then forced into camps for the duration of the war. Their belongings were liquidated to pay for the running of the camps, and many weren't allowed back to the West Coast after the War.

MEMORIAM

Vaneeza Sohail

The dream comes from
a place we do not know.
In another world,
I watched as you cut it open,
it sparkled like water in
your hands, it starved
like a fish in mine.

I saw you again
under the crescent moon,
carrying oranges
in your hands. You held me
the only way you knew,
with your eyes. We must have
looked like birds to God,
so breathless and eager
to leave.

VANEEZA SOHAIL

In Conversation

Sara Moore Wagner: I am so glad to have this poem for our anthology! I was drawn to your short lines and the complex simplicity of this poem. It feels holy and epic, but small: captured in the hands, which is a reoccurring image. What was your drafting process like for this poem?

Vaneeza Sohail: Thank you for your kind words and for having my poem in your anthology! For me, the beginning of a poem is what I like to think of as a "bud"—a line or a phrase that keeps coming to me. I was thinking of Leonard Cohen saying, "If I knew where the good songs came from, I'd go there more often. It's a mysterious condition." Lamenting on the idea of a mysterious, sacred place where things come from gave me the beginning line of this poem. Usually I'll write backwards, so my "buds" usually end up as my closing lines but it didn't work for this poem. Placing what was going to be the closing line in the beginning helped me find the direction for this piece. When I wake up from my dreams, there's usually a lingering moment that reverberates through me for the rest of the day. While drafting "Memoriam," I wanted to recreate that sliver of concentrated emotion. I knew I was writing this in memory of something that's no longer present in my life and mapping out those images on paper helped guide the structure. I've always loved to write with pen on paper, it's wonderfully visual and allows me to make connections I wouldn't be able to make on a device. I think the process of sitting with the bud in my notebook and creating images around it helped me understand what the poem was trying to hold: grief, intimacy, distance. Experimenting with structure and sequence helped me feel my way through the poem rather than trying to control it. I wanted it to feel small, sacred, and honest.

SMW: The relationship between the speaker and the "you" also feels vast and complex. What is the advantage of using direct address in a poem like this?

VS: For me, direct address creates a kind of emotional closeness. It brings the subject right into the room. In a poem like "Memoriam," where so much is about loss and distance, speaking to a "you" made the feeling more immediate. It let me hold on to something that was slipping away. Even if the person isn't really there, the act of speaking to them feels like a way to keep them alive in language. I also like that the "you" doesn't have to be pinned down. It can be a specific person, but it can also be a version of myself, a memory, a city, or someone imagined. I don't always want to explain everything in a poem, and direct address gives me space to be personal without being overly explicit. It lets the emotion lead, which is what I'm often most interested in when I write.

SMW: This poem is also so surreal but feels more grounded in the second stanza. What draws you to the surreal?

VS: I'm discovering that surrealism is where I find a lot of my creative energy. It's less about going away from where I am and more about accessing a different kind of truth. I grew up in a home where the unseen was very present. My mother is a very spiritual woman, so my childhood was spent learning about ghosts that prayed and saints who could read minds just by touching your palms. My summers were for learning how to meditate, how to call upon a higher self. Those experiences were very formative for me. I've grown distant from those practices over the years, but I still find myself writing stories that echo similar feelings. Experiencing a beautiful moment sometimes makes me feel like I'm watching it from afar. When I write now, I'm often drawn to exploring that feeling through images or moments that feel just slightly outside the bounds of logic but strike me as deeply familiar. The surreal lets me explore grief, longing, memory, and desire in a way that feels expansive, not bound by linear time or fact but by feeling and sensation. I think I'm still writing toward that same sense of wonder, reverence, and strangeness that surrounded me as a child.

SMW: You mention you live in Pakistan in your bio. How does place inform your work?

VS: I love this question because it gives me a chance to talk about Karachi, the city in Pakistan where I grew up. It's an eclectic place full of many small miracles and it always brings me a story. We're a city of extremes: chaotic and tender, sprawling and intimate, endlessly alive. That tension shapes how I write. I think if it wasn't for my life here, I wouldn't be a writer. I'm drawn to the textures of everyday life: the light, the noise, the silences, the rituals that surround me. There's an emotional climate that's shaped by living in a place layered with history, contradiction, beauty, and violence. It shows up in how I understand time, space, and movement. The feeling of being caught between permanence and impermanence is something I carry into the emotional landscapes of my work. Living here has taught me to see closely, to listen carefully, and to learn how to exist in contradictions. It's a city that demands both attention and surrender. I think everyone should experience it once.

DECONSTRUCTING A BLUEPRINT FOR ENEMIES TO LOVERS

Madeline Rosales

& a house boned by fire says: we aren't
        supposed to be here. today, I screw you
into a bathroom light, pressing your palms
        on mine to show you the weathered threads of
my inheritance, homegrown fields where I scavenge
        for bruises & papercut wounds. *c mere,*
you say. give it to me heavy-handed,
        give it ripe. I'd like to think that hurt feeds
off loving, that my mother's century-egg soup
        hasn't soured itself out another face of me
you'll never consume. we've come
        here too many times to stitch reopened
wounds, sweat dressing our skin like gilded
        bayonets. today, I'll be the cowherd if
you are the hunter, both of us skinned
        into roles past recognition. neither of us
wants to grow into prey: distant, afraid, dead
        & behind us. its eyes braised with a life long
enough to know regret, but too short to tender
        you within it. today, you are a country I'll never visit,
a homeland that fractured itself beyond
        my present tense. I hope you'll see this before
I go: how I unhinged your jaw for safekeeping.
        how arms burn into daggers by the light.
how these walls have ruined us.

MADELINE ROSALES
In Conversation

Sara Moore Wagner: Congratulations on this poem being a finalist in our single poem contest! I loved this poem from the initial discordance between the first line and the title. What made you want to start your poem with an ampersand?

Madeline Rosales: Thank you so much for this honor! I've always been a fan of *Driftwood Press* because from a reader's perspective alone, it's still evident that your editors are also just passionate readers!

As for your question, I'm currently fascinated by a recent trend in poetry in which the writer uses no capitalized letters, thus highlighting the piece's stream-of-consciousness structure. And in this poem, I wanted to build upon that concept to imply that the first line is a continuation of a sentence we're not seeing on the page. And in that right, I hoped the piece came across as a brief snapshot into the speaker's experience. As an audience, we're receiving only part of the picture, that being how the speaker feels right at that moment. But there's also so much unknown, or up to interpretation, regarding the context of the poem, and I hoped the unconventional first line made this stand out.

SMW: So much unfolds between that ampersand and your ending, where the two have been "ruined" by the walls. It feels as if the couple becomes the walls. It's almost the opposite of Maggie Smith's *Good Bones*! Is this something you were thinking about?

MR: I absolutely love that poem! While I *definitely* see the vision, my primary inspiration for this piece was Allen Ginsberg and Joan Didion. I've always adored their cryptic yet evocative styles, and how reading their work feels like you're following the speaker as they steadily gain a deeper understanding, and occasionally a deeper appreciation, towards their circumstances and environment.

SMW: I'm interested in the way the domestic functions here. You mention "roles past recognition," making this also feel like a statement on gender expectations in domestic partnerships. Do you see this poem as a statement against those, in any way?

MR: It's very difficult to write a poem about a certain relationship dynamic and not make a statement on gender roles. The line before establishes a contrast between the domestic home life associated with women and the more typically masculine physical work, cow-herding and hunting respectively. But because the gender of the speaker is never revealed, it's unclear whether those stereotypical occupations remain with their assigned gender or whether the standard has flipped. That's the idea regarding the "roles past recognition" line: if the superficial layers of man and woman are peeled back entirely, does it matter still whether the woman is kept at home? Does the man have an obligation to provide?

SMW: Is this poem a part of something larger for you? We would love to read more!

MR: I'm so glad to hear that! This poem isn't part of a larger series, but one I've written in a similar style is entitled "the space between the tongue and mouth is called loss," which can be found in Issue 3 of *The Passionate Post.*

BLUE-GUM BLUES

Kinsale Drake

For a child with rusted cheeks, this
was home:

A crest of snow-capped Saddleback
that never melted through the spring,

The frogs, stuck to slapping
feet, or swelling their necks
beneath flickering porch lamps

The monarchs, weary and overwintered,
weaving a mission through whizzing
cars–

How natural, it seemed,
for our species to survive

As the hillside turned on
all its lights

& the soft trunks shook
their shaggy hair,

The light shifting through eucalyptus leaves
which sifted the smell of stranger seas.

In the old ways, the hills
would burn at the right hours
in the right season,

Small shoulders of fizzing
bush and clotted crust.

Now a coyote skitters
across the pebble-hot highway

And the blue-gum blues shush
every which-way the wind changes,

Threatening to explode their great hearts
in the heat of the Santa Anas.

If a body brought
for harvest, left unchecked—
            Where do the leaves
            settle?

How did she arrive here,
            fists full of green,
            the hard seeds so like
            and unlike acorns
            underfoot?

KINSALE DRAKE

In Conversation

Sara Moore Wagner: Congratulations on being a finalist in our single poem contest! This poem stood out for its interesting language and musicality. Could you tell us a little about your process with this poem?

Kinsale Drake: My poems often begin from little stories or acts of witness. I began with memories of the natural world in the chapparal, mostly eucalyptus, which is such a nostalgic scent but also an invasive species. I reflected deeply on my understanding of "invasive" species and how colonialism was a nexus for these trees arriving here. Piecing together histories and exploring how language is used to understand our relationships with these species gave rise to each movement or beat of the poem: the intentions behind naming, the extension of empathy, the remnants of violent history that continue to hurt us—like the wildfires. The fires in the Southwest (California and Arizona/Utah) were also on my mind when I wrote this. Form allowed me to order these interacting themes and weave connections between them.

SMW: This is strong ecopoetry, calling us back to the natural world. I've heard many poets give their varying definitions of what ecopoetry is or should be. How would you define your own ecopoetics?

KD: I like to understand Western ecopoetics as a tradition that posits human experience within the natural world, rather than separate from it—which was a notion that really became more mainstream around the 1970s. In contrast, many peoples including Indigenous peoples have many stories and worldviews that never sought to separate humans from the natural world and instead understood that humans are living beings engaging in reciprocal relationships with plants and animals, with the earth… And something I'm particularly interested in, like in "Blue Gum Blues," is a sense of balance integral to taking care of ourselves and the environment that's been thrown off course, often violently so. Connecting that present sense of disharmony to colonialism and extending empathy to living creatures I think guides my ethos to writing these kinds of poems.

SMW: The transition from the child in the first stanza to the "she" in the final is so striking. It feels as if she is the leaf, and she is also witness, which is a tender way of looking at humanity's place in the natural world. Could you tell us a little more about this choice?

KD: The "she" I think startles the reader into paying closer attention, which is what I believe this poem to actually be about—paying closer attention to the world around us, to history, to how landscapes have physically been transformed by climate change and induced natural disasters. Transformations (like the "she" here) allow us to glide between seemingly separate entities; to ask what meshes them to one another.

SMW: I am interested in the way this poem moves on the page visually. What inspired those more formal choices?

KD: Sometimes my poems are moved by sound (here, a blues?)... sometimes narrative clusters... it's fun to play with form.

LATE MARCH IN MONTANA

Corrie Williamson

Driving the foothills of the Judiths, green and amber
ponderosa stands weave at the edges of creeks

that suture this whole world together, though
they shrug and loosen a little with the thaw.

I've wondered this winter if there must be some place
sorrow and suffering coalesce — that perhaps this

explains dark matter, or gravity, or my own muddled
mind, which was not built to grasp the multitudinous

clamor of sorrows, which sieves anguish in order
to keep on track: little triage machine of tragedy.

A year ago, I was thinking, I know from an old note
for a poem, of Syria, though only my own scribbles

remind me of war and earthquakes there. One
hundred miles south, my friend's pummeled heart

is open on the table, revealed by the reciprocating
blades of a sternal saw, and I should have said

to him, in this world where I have no more
grandfathers, that I think of him as one of mine.

The pale indigo and dark pearly wool of storm banks
stretch for miles between island ranges. A pair of crimson-

capped, silver cranes are standing in cold water; one
lifts its head as I pass. The snow comes soft and ash-slow.

CORRIE WILLIAMSON

In Conversation

Sara Moore Wagner: Congratulations on being the runner-up in our single poem contest! It is very rare for *Driftwood* to name a runner-up, but it was important to me that your poem be elevated to that level. This poem is moving and extraordinarily well-crafted. It also captures place, the earth and its connection to self, so beautifully. It feels like a tapestry of human experience. Could you tell me a little about your process with this poem?

Corrie Williamson: Thank you. This poem, like the landscape and the surgery referenced within it, is held together by sutures. It truly came together in pieces, so tapestry certainly feels like an appropriate descriptor for the process, as well. I had some brief notes buried in one of my writing notebooks about the astonishing challenge of processing grief on a global scale, the kind of loss or suffering that overwhelms but doesn't necessarily directly touch us, and which reaches us via the news or social media nearly constantly these days. Those scribbles had sat for some time, and I came back to them when I began working on this piece around the time of my friend's operation, and was intrigued by how they felt both distant and relevant. Those early notes also mentioned sandhill cranes, which I pulled into this newer poem, as well; I always think of birds as messengers—in our lives, on the page, and sandhills to me are such harbingers of liminal seasonal spaces, and of the ancient cycle of renewal, spring, and hope.

SMW: This poem is also a sort of ars poetica. You mention, for instance, notes about a poem within the poem. How does note-taking figure into your work as a poet?

CW: Mostly I'm capturing fleeting impressions, images, or word-clusters as they arrive. This is often how the core or the foundation of a poem gets built for me, where a lot of a poem's heart lives, in those bits and pieces I manage to capture and pin down before they float off into forgetfulness. I also find it useful and interesting to remind the reader, on occasion, that the poem is a built thing, a process for processing, a body with bones.

SMW: It's also incredibly lyric. It's hard to explain just what emotion this captures, but it's felt in the chest, in the final image, and in the meditation on the speaker's friend. It's something about beauty and pain—that feeling. What advice do you have for poets longing to put the unexplainable onto the page like this?

CW: Landscape to me is often the tapestry (let's stick with that useful word! My grandmother was a weaver, and I think about her and her methods often with my writing) into which those hard to describe emotions are woven. Maybe those feelings—beauty, pain, the big ones—aren't described explicitly, maybe the reader doesn't see them acknowledged directly as such, but they are part of the color of the weave. That feels really important to me in dealing with abstract universals; how can you express something vast in the smallest ways possible, and still contain it?

SMW: What made you choose couplets as a form for this poem?

CW: I think of couplets as loving, prayerful, intimate. I also think they are clean, neat, and rather lonely; they are good at holding the big and messy. Additionally, the poem is dealing with some dichotomies, or twinings—the slippage from winter to spring, the two cranes, the nearly incomprehensible distance of global devastations in contrast to the speaker's immediate, visceral concern over her friend's heart surgery—and couplets often seem to me to be a way in to unspool pairings like that.

SMW: Is this part of a larger project? If so, we'd love to hear about it!

CW: I suppose so! In 2021, I moved within Montana (where I've lived since 2013) to a new part of the state, out in the great plains and shortgrass prairie, between the island mountain ranges. I'm writing now about my experience of that ecosystem, these gorgeous vanishing grasslands, and the people, stories, and other living things I've encountered here. I hope these poems will ultimately cohere and coalesce into my fourth book. Tentatively, right now I'm calling it *Dark Armor*, a reference to the now extinct Rocky Mountain Locust.

AUBADE AS A CARDINAL NUMBER

Sara Iacovelli

To tell you the truth, I've been thinking
about worship. It's like this, right? First light,
waking up when you do, 5:40 on the foothills of slumber,

listening for the birds that chatter outside our window.
I should say: opening a bird identification app,
letting it listen to the chatter, calling you

back from the bathroom to comb through
offerings of species on the screen, photographs
& maps, deliberating: *is this the one?*

Yeah— I think I've seen it around here. You have
a better eye for this than I do, have always closely
noticed our nonhuman neighbors, have always been a devout

morning person. This among our philosophical differences.
Sure, more than once I've found sanctuary
in a sunrise, but the memory of something holy

doesn't help me get out of bed on a weekday.
Anyway, what's holier than a bedroom window?
half-tapestry for a curtain, dog's paw prints

on a cracking wooden sill. I plant my head on the pillow
in prayer: let the clock and its alarms stop singing.
Honestly— this hour's for the birds. Faithful

worshippers of the worm. The northern cardinal
says a prayer and it sounds like *pew pew*
pew pew. I say a prayer and it sounds like *snoo—*

SARA IACOVELLI

In Conversation

Sara Moore Wagner: Congratulations on this poem being a finalist in our single poem contest! The title instantly intrigued me. What drew you to the aubade (and form in general)?

Sara Iacovelli: Thank you! This poem means a lot to me and I'm so honored it was chosen as a finalist. I have to be honest, this is a case where the title arrived with the fourth or fifth revision of the poem. I hadn't set out to write an aubade— I actually came across the definition of an aubade several months later and had the realization that that's what this poem was. I do love thinking about form, and I find I come to form in different ways— sometimes I set out to write in a form and sometimes I revise into it, or decide a poem fits a certain form as I spend more time with it.

SMW: The speaker of this is also so interesting. Immediately, we are led to believe it is, perhaps, the unidentified number itself speaking, but the meaning changes as the poem goes on (even invoking the bird cardinal!). Could you tell us a little about this choice?

SI: I would say that I almost always give a poem a title after I write it, so it's more of an exercise in trying to write a title that encapsulates multiple elements of the poem or what I feel is the heart of the poem. I was trying to play with the phrase "cardinal number" to mean a kind of song, like the cardinal's opening number. It's a cardinal number as in "first," the first part of the day, and a number as in a song or performance, and of course a cardinal as in the bird. I suppose I chose "as" because I think of it as the poem performing as the thing.

SMW: I love the blending of more traditional poetic images (birds, love) with modern things like the bird identification app! What advice do you have for achieving that balance?

SI: I think that balance exists in the poem because it exists in life, and it existed in the moment I was writing about. So I suppose my advice would be just to let all the parts of something coexist. I don't think poets should feel like certain elements "don't belong" in a poem because they're trying to adhere to a certain style or convey a certain tone. I've learned to ignore feedback about words or images seeming "out of place" in a poem— or at least to take that feedback with a grain of salt, because life is full of things that are out of place. Our world can be very anachronistic. Why shouldn't poetry reflect that?

SMW: This poem ends so perfectly. It really feels like morning, invoking the sounds of sleep and the dawn chorus. Was this always your ending? How do you find where to end your poems?

SI: Thank you! I will admit that this ending once had two more lines and after a lot of workshopping and agonizing I cut them because I realized they were just trying to explain something that didn't need to be explained. I still often struggle with where to end my poems, but I'm learning to resist the urge to tie a poem up in a neat little bow, and instead to just let the thought, moment, or image stop where it stops, even if it's right in the middle of something—that way, the reader gets to follow it through on their own.

THE HOLD

Ayendy Bonifacio

There is no moon tonight,
only the bone-white eye
of a drowned child
floating near Lampedusa.

The sea swells like a mouth
stuffed with coins.
Smugglers lit a fire
to call forth God or fisherman—
but only gulls came,
clattering like silver cutlery
in a ruined house.

Divers descend
with rosaries and latex hands,
unpacking the hold:
a wall of flesh,
bodies plaited like seaweed,
mothers stitched to daughters,
boys folded into fathers,
a silence deeper than water.

The dead are counted
like gold teeth in a pirate's chest.
€500,000 in blackened ribs.
Cargo, they said.
Human cargo.

The hold holds time.

The yachtsmen said,
It sounded like gulls.
But I heard *cante jondo*—
the sound of burning
beneath water.

AYENDY BONIFACIO

In Conversation

Sara Moore Wagner: First, thank you so much for submitting your poems to our anthology. Your work is arresting and important. It feels steeped in historical and personal understanding. Is there anything you'd like our readers to know about the context of this poem?

Ayendy Bonifacio: Thank you so much for publishing this poem. I'm an avid reader of *Driftwood* and feel truly honored to have a piece included. I've been thinking about migrants throughout my career as a professor of Ethnic Literary Studies. The particular time-space of Lampedusa—and the real lives of migrants from Libya, Tunisia, Eritrea, and Bangladesh who risk everything to escape unimaginable political and socioeconomic circumstances—has stayed with me ever since I read Eliza Griswold's essay "Everyone's an Immigrant" in *Poetry* in 2012. Griswold documents the arrival of refugees and the impossibility of capturing their full stories. More than a decade later, migrants are still arriving in Lampedusa.

SMW: The situation of this poem feels both very current and ancient, migrant people continue to die off the coat of Lampedusa, and the reality of "human cargo" and trafficking is woven into every part of human existence. Could you tell us more about how you capture both the historic/current event in a poem that moves beyond simple documentation?

AB: The crossing of refugees from West Africa to Lampedusa has become a business for smugglers, much like the coyotes at the U.S.-Mexico border. My poem tries to capture that predatory economy with its references to monetary value. The "Hold" is also crucial to my thinking about migrancy and race. In diaspora and Atlantic studies, the hold of the slave ship is often marked as the origin of the transatlantic slave trade and its afterlives. In my graduate seminar, *The Black Atlantic*, we read scholars such as Édouard Glissant, Paul Gilroy, and Christina Sharpe, who theorize the hold as both a historical and ongoing site that, Sharpe argues, produces "blackness as abjection." For Sharpe, the hold is the ship, but it is also the prison, the womb, and the Atlantic.

In the poem, the hold is a sunken vessel, but it is also the shores of Lampedusa, the crowded detention centers, and the bureaucratic and racialized systems that keep refugees from moving freely. In other words, the hold refers to any structure or system that originated from the slave ship.

In my poem, the hold is not a literal return to the Middle Passage but an evocation of slavery's long durée. Griswold's reporting, particularly on the children who did not survive the journey, haunted me for years and has only been compounded by the mass loss of children in Gaza. Derek Walcott once wrote that "the sea is history," and poetry allows us to engage with a history that is not always archived or documented. Poetry can carry that breath forward. As M. NourbeSe Philip writes of her own work in *Zong!*, poetry can *ex aqua*—exhumed from the water—those who are forgotten. My poem attempts, in some small way, to write in that tradition.

SMW: This poem has me thinking about Adrienne Rich's poem "Diving into the Wreck," where she confronts societal imbalances, seeking, "the wreck and not the story of the wreck/ the thing itself and not the myth." Your poem takes this a step further into reality and marginalization, the reality of the people who are in the literal and historical wreck. Is this something you were thinking about? Do you feel your poem is a continuation of that conversation in any way?

AB: Thank you for prompting me to return to Adrienne Rich's poem. I absolutely love Rich's work, and *Diving into the Wreck* was one of the first collections I read as an undergraduate at Hunter College. The title poem has stayed with me ever since. I see my poem as part of a long lineage of poets who contemplate what lies beneath the ocean—think of Walcott, Phillips, and Rich herself.

What moves me most about Rich's poem is how it stages descent—not just a physical plunge into water but also a spiritual and psychological descent into another body, another self. The speaker moves from reading "the book of myths" to encountering the wreck itself, and in that transition we witness a deeper form of self-analysis. I think descent in my poem works in a similar way, but I extend it toward the societal and the historical. What my divers find when they go down is also a wreck—though in this case it is the bodies of refugees.

Rich leaves her readers to imagine the wreck, to fill in its contours. In my poem, the wreck is more concrete, more disturbingly clear in its uncanniness, which makes it, I hope, a lasting image, hard to forget. Rich's speaker claims, "it is easy to forget / what I came for" because the sea itself threatens to overwhelm the myth, i.e., the idea of place. But in my poem, the divers cannot forget. What they find is so disturbing and unnatural that it resists mythology. Like Rich's speaker, they too descend "to explore the wreck / the damage that was done"—but here the damage is not abstract. It is embodied, historical, and ongoing.

SMW: Is this poem part of a larger project? How does it tie in?

AB: Yes, thank you for asking. The poem is part of a larger collection that traces colonial inheritance, family histories, racial trauma, and the different bodies of water that shape our migrations and memories. Some of the poems take the form of recipes, others are about dictatorships, fatherhood, ICE agents, and some contemplate the inadequacy of poetry itself. Many of the poems are in conversation with one another. Some return to rivers and seas as sites of both loss and survival, while others contemplate how memory and history are carried across generations. This poem continues that thread, situating descent into water as both a reckoning with historical violence and an opening into questions of belonging and eternity.

Here come the clouds...

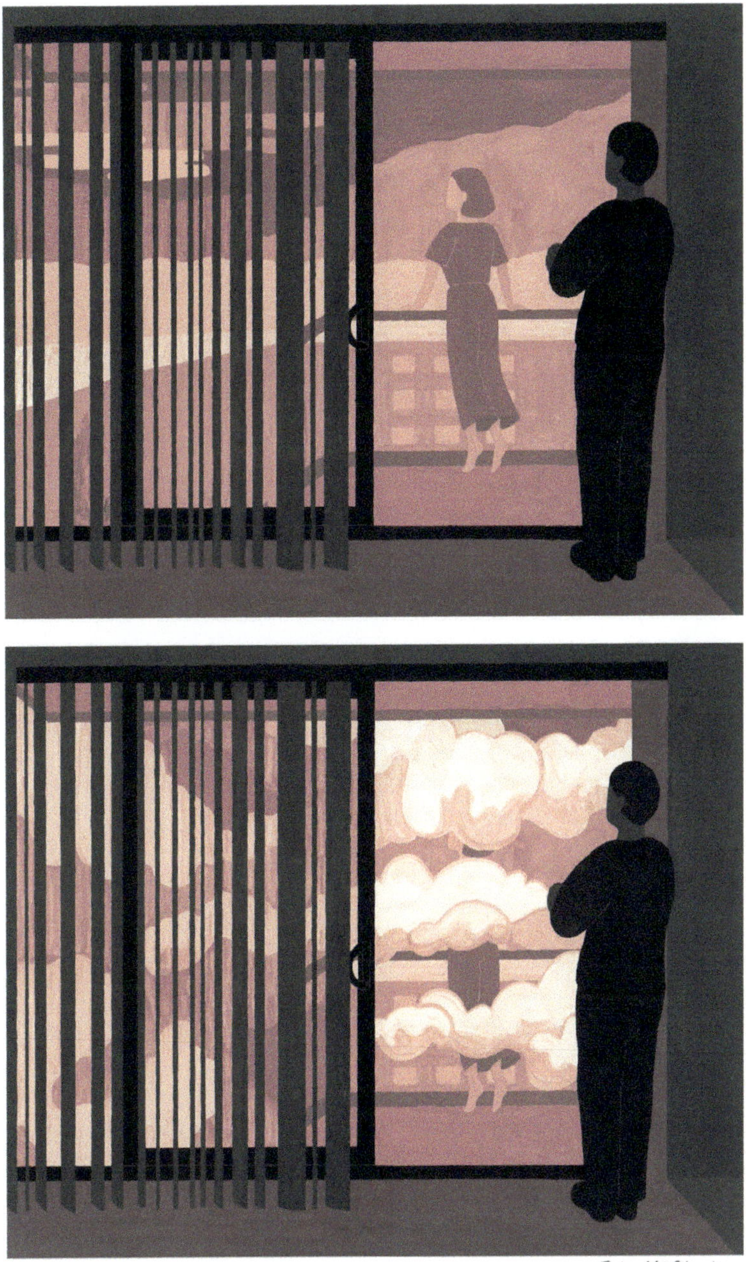

Erin McCluskey

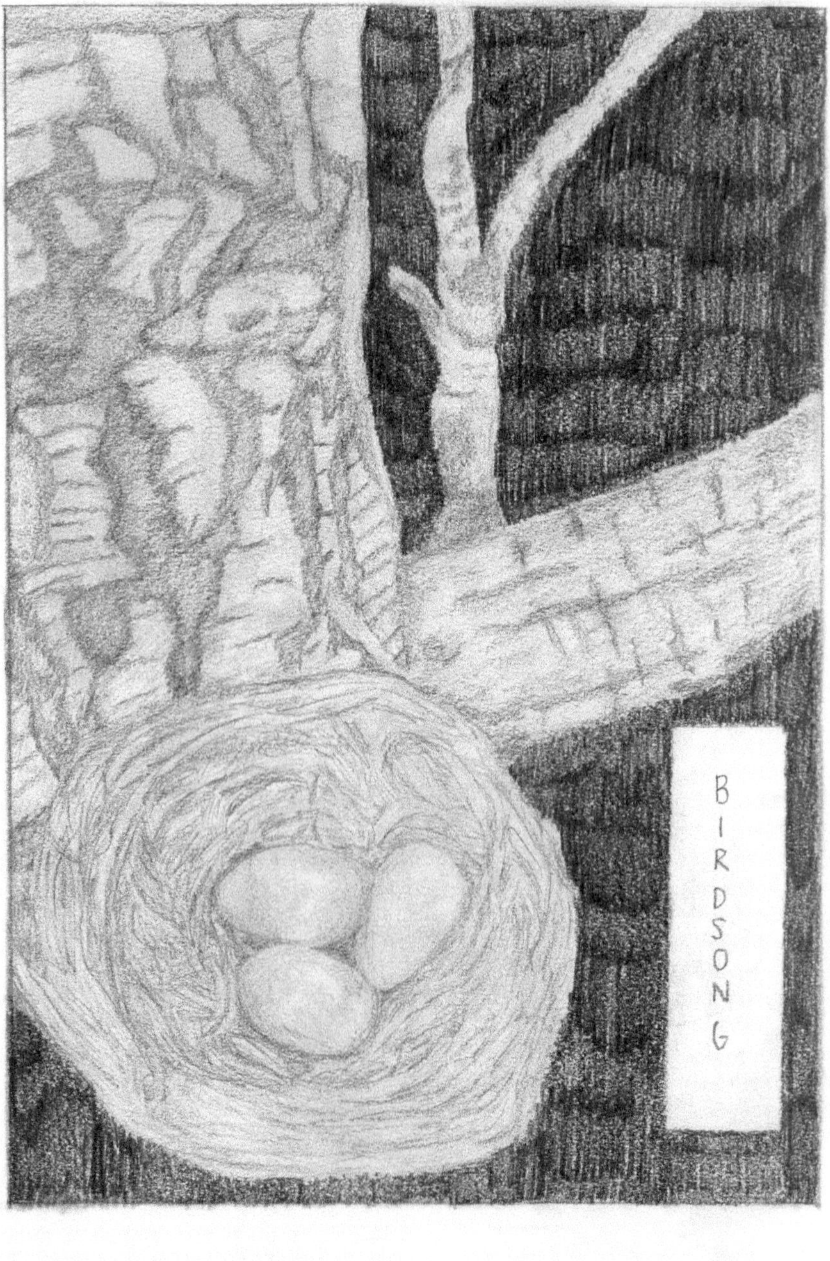
BIRDSONG

I PUKE,
MOLTEN SLUSH DRIBBLING DOWN MY CHEEK,
MOUTH SLACKED AS MY INTESTINES HOLLOW OUT.

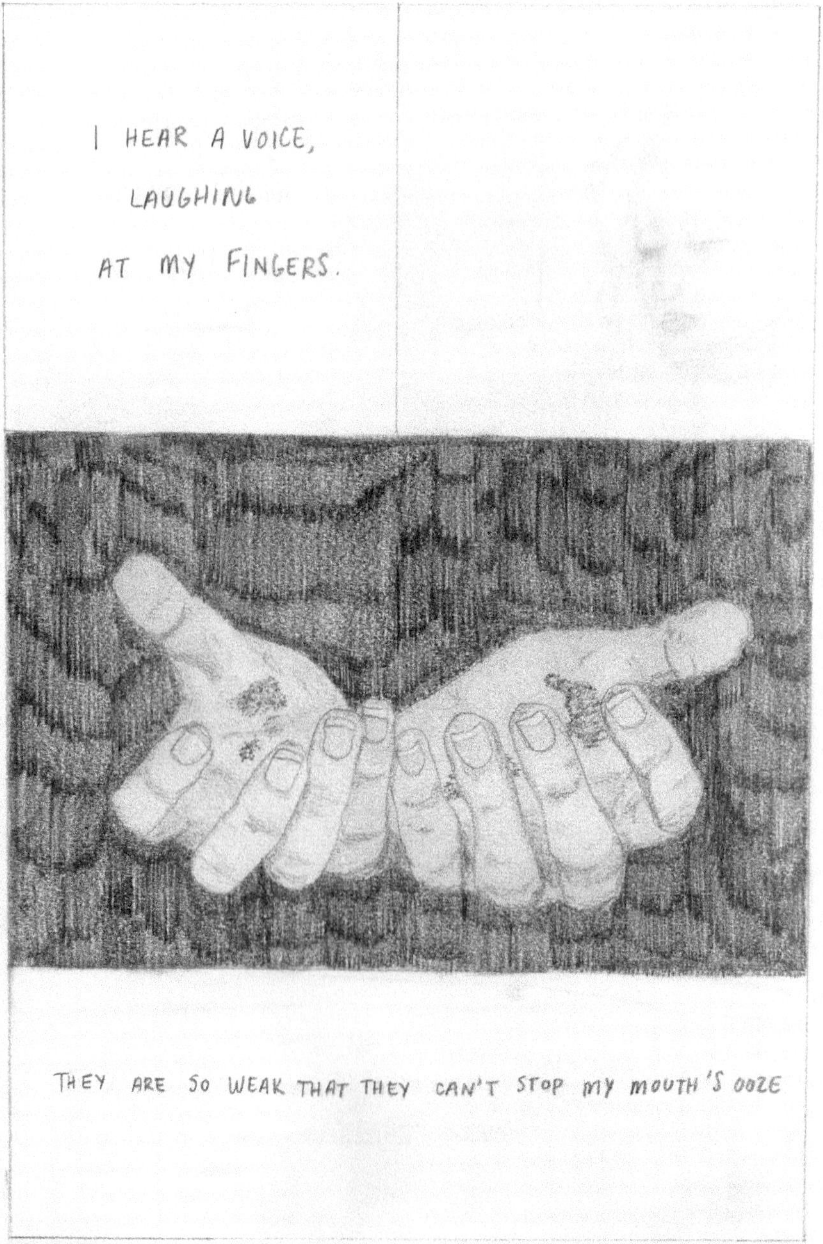
I HEAR A VOICE,
LAUGHING
AT MY FINGERS.
THEY ARE SO WEAK THAT THEY CAN'T STOP MY MOUTH'S OOZE

I PICK AT MY SKIN
AND DISCARD THE DEAD FLESH.

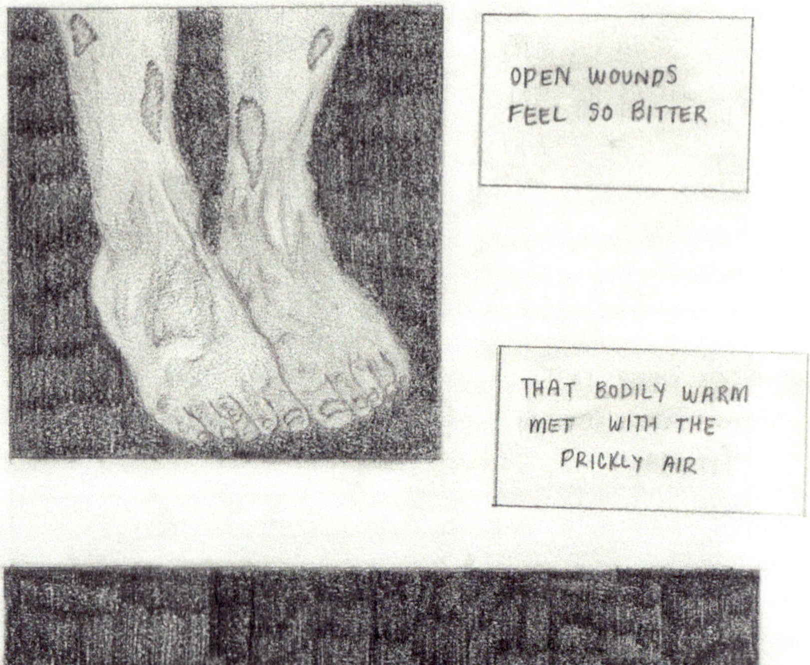
OPEN WOUNDS FEEL SO BITTER
THAT BODILY WARM MET WITH THE PRICKLY AIR

I WOULD STOP
TO CLEAN MYSELF
BUT THERE
ISN'T A POINT.
I WALLOW.

MY EAR TILTS SLIGHTLY TO THE SOUND OF A SPARROW.
HE IS LOOKING AT ME LIKE HIS MOTHER.
I HAVEN'T FELT THE URGE TO MAKE LIFE
SINCE THE LAST TIME I BLED.

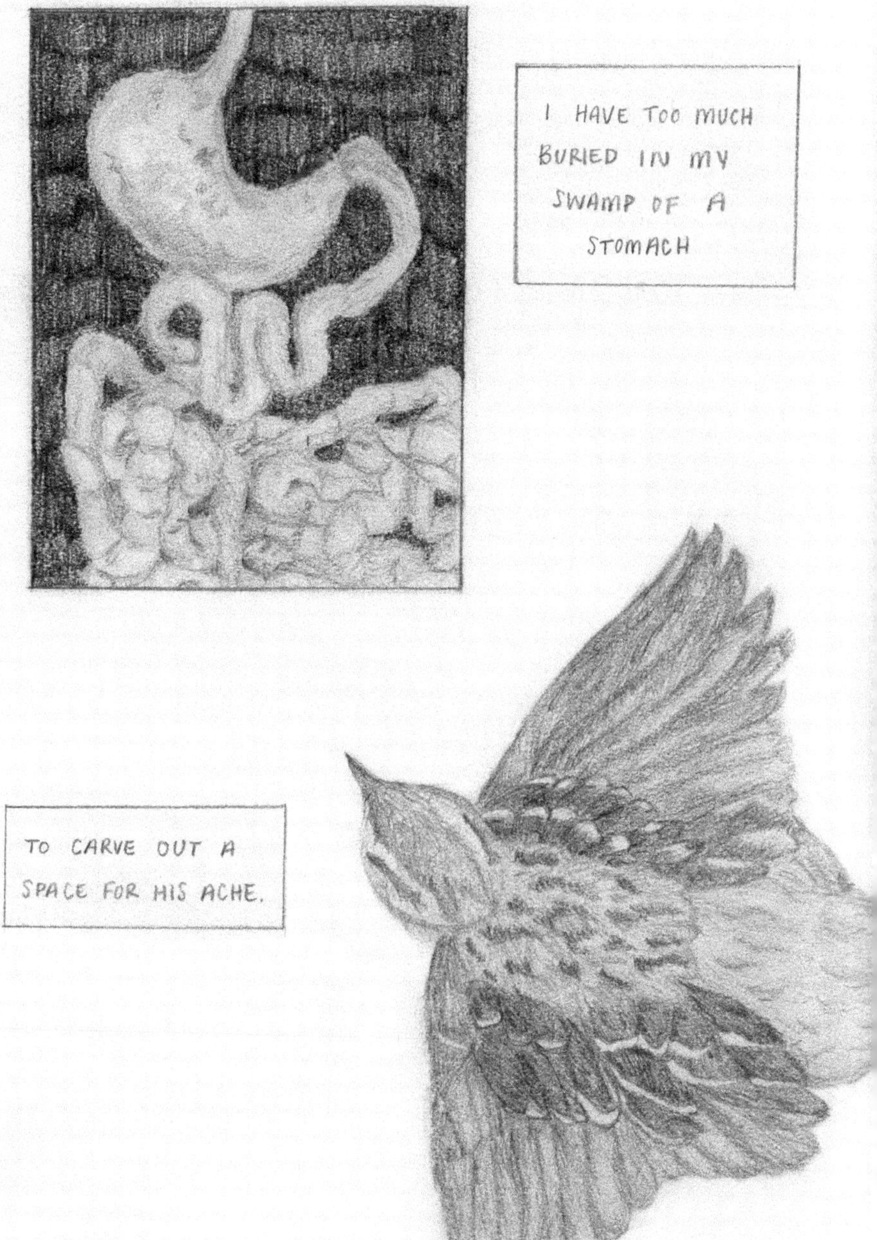
I HAVE TOO MUCH BURIED IN MY SWAMP OF A STOMACH
TO CARVE OUT A SPACE FOR HIS ACHE.

CONTRIBUTORS

Ajith Thangavelautham is a writer based in Toronto. His stories have been published or are forthcoming in *Driftwood Press, The Malahat Review, Seventh Wave*, and *Paloma Magazine.* He is currently at work on a novel about ghosts.

Devin Choudhury is a writer from Cincinnati, Ohio. He is currently a Mellon Postdoctoral Fellow in the Center for the Humanities at Wesleyan University. He received his PhD in Rhetoric from the University of California, Berkeley and his BA in English from Columbia University.

James Gianetti's stories have been published or are forthcoming in *Phoebe, Driftwood Press, SmokeLong Quarterly, Stanchion, Emerge Literary Journal*, and *The McNeese Review* (Boudin). His short story "Anastasia" won the 2024 *Driftwood Press* Adrift Short Story Contest judged by Dean Bakopoulos. He was a runner up in the *Phoebe Spring* 2025 Fiction Contest judged by Halle Hill. He is also the author of the novelette, "Calvin Klein" (*ELJ Editions*). He is currently working on a novel and short story collection.

Raphael Stigliano writes fiction, directs theater, designs games, and runs a dinosaur adoption agency. His fiction has appeared in *Qu Magazine, Half and One,* and *Story Unlikely.* His storytelling tabletop *RPG Murder Gently* will be out later this year.

Joseph Rakowski's short stories have been published by *Grist, The Carolina Quarterly, Witness Magazine, New South, Litbreak Magazine, The Antigonish Review*, *The Normal School, New Ohio Review*, and elsewhere.

Thea Nguyen received her MFA from the Creative Writing Workshop at the University of New Orleans and was the managing editor for *Bayou Magazine*. Her work has been published in *Red Cedar, Collision, Prairie Margins,* and is forthcoming in *F(r)iction.*

Anastasios Mihalopoulos is a Greek/Italian writer from Boardman, Ohio. He received his MFA in poetry from the Northeast Ohio M.F.A. program and his B.S. in both Chemistry and English from Allegheny College. His work has appeared or is forthcoming in *Scientific American, Ninth Letter, Fairy Tale Review, Pithead Chapel,* and elsewhere. He is currently a PhD candidate in Creative Writing and Literature at the University of New Brunswick.

Susan Jardaneh holds an MFA from the University of North Carolina at Greensboro. She's been published in *The Southern Review, Carve, The Berkeley Review*, and other magazines.

Porter Leland Huang grew up in North Carolina, Florida, and New York; he holds a BA in English and American Literature from New York University, and he is currently an MFA Candidate in Fiction at The Ohio State University. From 2018-2021, he served as a Global Writing and Speaking Fellow at NYU's Shanghai campus. His work focuses on everything from translation and the modern Chinese nation-state, to queerness and Drag art in the American South, to bridging generational gaps within strained familial relationships.

Andi Myles is a Washington DC area science writer by day, poet in the in between times. Her favorite space is the fine line between essay and poetry. She is the author of the chapbook *Fractured Symphony* (*Cathexis Northwest Press*) and her work has appeared in *Michigan Quarterly Review, Chestnut Review, Rattle,* and *Tahoma Literary Review,* among others.

Annette C. Boehm is the author of *The Apidictor Tapes* (April 2022) and *The Knowledge Weapon.* A queer, Autistic writer from Germany, she has served as a poetry reader for *Memorious* and has two intertextual chapbooks available from *Dancing Girl Press.*

Emily Stokes is a writer based in Philadelphia, PA. Her work has been featured in *The Boiler Journal, Pioneertown, Tupelo Quarterly, SLICE Literary Magazine, Nimrod International Journal, The Westchester Review,* and *PANK.* She received her MFA in poetry from Sarah Lawrence College.

Mathieu Cailler is the author of seven books: a novel, two short story collections, two volumes of poetry, and two children's titles. His stories, poems, and essays have appeared in over one hundred publications, including *Wigleaf, The Saturday Evening Post*, and the *Los Angeles Times*. He has received several prestigious awards, including a Pushcart Prize, a Short Story America Prize, and accolades from the Paris, Los Angeles, and New England Book Festivals.

Joshua Garcia is the author of *Pentimento* (*Black Lawrence Press* 2024). His poetry has appeared in *Ecotone, The Georgia Review, Passages North, Ploughshares*, and elsewhere. He holds an MFA from the College of Charleston and has received a Stadler Fellowship from Bucknell University and an Emerge—Surface—Be Fellowship from The Poetry Project. He lives and writes in Brooklyn, New York.

Mary Ardery is the author of *Level Watch* (*June Road Press*). Her poems appear in *Beloit Poetry Journal, Best New Poets, Poet Lore, Prairie Schooner, RHINO*, and elsewhere. The recipient of a Lifelong Arts Fellowship from the Indiana Arts Commission, she was born and raised in Bloomington and now lives in West Lafayette, Indiana.

Arvinder Kaur Johri is an Indian-born educator and poet who resides in Northern Virginia. Her poems have appeared/are forthcoming in *Sahitya Academi, The Shore, Solstice, The Inflectionist Review, Driftwood Press,* and *Dialogist*. Johri's poems explore memory, death, relationships, and displacement. Her academic interests include inequities in education, intersectionality, and writing identities.

Melissa Dias-Mandoly is a writer, artist, and book designer living in Pittsburgh, PA. She was a finalist for the Poetry Society of America Chapbook Fellowship, Submerging Writer Fellowship, Jake Adam York prize, and Noemi Press Book Award. Her poetry & artwork have been published in *Pinwheel, Cordella, Nat. Brut, Gesture, PANK,* and more. Her design work has been featured in the annual *AUPresses Book, Jacket,* and *Journal Show*, as well as *Electric Lit, Lit Hub,* and *Spine magazine*. She currently works as the Design and Production Manager at the University of Pittsburgh Press.

Dustin Brookshire is the recipient of the 2024 Jon Tribble Editors Fellowship awarded by Poetry at the Sea, and his chapbooks include *Repeat As Needed* (*Harbor Edi-*

tions, 2025), *Never Picked First For Playtime* (*Harbor Editions*, 2023), *Love Most Of You Too* (*Harbor Editions*, 2021), and *To The One Who Raped Me* (*Sibling Rivalry Press*, 2012). Along with Julie E. Bloemeke, he is the co-editor of *Let Me Say This: A Dolly Parton Poetry Anthology*, and the editor of the forthcoming chapbook anthology *When I Was Straight: A Tribute To Maureen Seaton* (*Harbor Anthologies*, 2024).

Kerry Trautman has served as a judge or workshop leader for the Northwest region of Ohio's "Poetry Out Loud" competition annually since 2016. Her work has appeared in various anthologies and journals, and her books are: *Things That Come in Boxes, To Have Hoped, Artifacts, To be Nonchalantly Alive, Marilyn: Self-Portrait, Oil on Canvas, Unknowable Things*, and *Irregulars*. Her newest poetry collection *Things to Say When You Have Nothing to Say* is forthcoming from *Roadside Press.*

Leticia Priebe Rocha is the author of *In Lieu of Heartbreak, This is Like* (*Bottlecap Press*, 2024). She earned her bachelor's from Tufts University, where she was awarded an Academy of American Poets University Poetry Prize. Born in São Paulo, she immigrated to Miami, FL at the age of nine and currently resides in Greater Boston. Her work appears in *Here to Stay: Poetry and Prose from the Undocumented Diaspora, Salamander, Rattle,* and elsewhere. She is a 2025 Undocupoets Fellow and her work has been supported by the Fine Arts Work Center, Mass Cultural Council, and Cambridge Arts. Leticia is an editor for *Yellow Arrow Publishing*, teaches various poetry workshops, and loves the moon.

Katherine Irajpanah is a writer and postdoctoral fellow at Dartmouth College, where she conducts research on political violence. Her poems have been featured in the *Colorado Review, Peripheries, Only Poems*, and *the Harvard GSAS Graduate Review*. She is originally from Santa Monica, California, where she was proudly raised by an Iranian-Mexican-American family.

Cixous LeComte is an artist from the Mojave Desert, who seeks to find duality and disruption in her work. She first began performing in the community theater in Victorville, where she discovered her love for creating. Since then, she has received a Master of Fine Arts from the University of California, where she wrote a collection of poetry. Her poems can be found in *Apricity Press* and *Driftwood Press.*

Karla Myn Khine is a writer from South Texas, currently residing in Oakland. She is a graduate from San Francisco State's MFA program, where she was a recipient of an Academy of American Poets University Award, the Daniel Langton Poetry Prize, and a Marcus Graduate Scholar. Her work has appeared or is forthcoming in *Poetry Online, Driftwood Press, The Pinch, Poets.org, Sho Poetry Journal,* and *ANMLY.*

Abbigail Baldys is a poet living in Boston, MA. Their work has appeared in *Tupelo Quarterly, RHINO, The Laurel Review, BlazeVOX, ANMLY*, and elsewhere. They write and perform avant-pop music under the name vaste.

Zach Bartles was raised in the Shenandoah Valley of West Virginia. His writing appears or is forthcoming in *Poetry Ireland Review, The Iowa Review, The Missouri Review, Southeast Review, Northwest Review, Brink,* and *Tupelo Quarterly*, among other journals. He was a finalist for the 2024 Brink Literary Journal Award for Hybrid Writing, shortlisted for *The Masters Review*'s 2024 Featured Flash Contest, and has been nominated for a Pushcart Prize. He lives in East Texas with his wife and daughter.

Winshen Liu's poetry has appeared in *Cincinnati Review, Electric Literature, The Malahat Review,* and *The Rumpus*, among others. She is grateful to the University of Mississippi faculty for their mentorship and the de Groot Foundation for supporting her work. In addition to writing, she loves long-distance train travel, baking and bakeries, and stickers.

Michael Prior is a biracial yonsei poet and teacher. His most recent book of poems, *Burning Province*, won the Canada-Japan Literary Award and the BC & Yukon Book Prizes' Dorothy Livesay Poetry Prize. He is a recent recipient of fellowships from the Amy Clampitt Residency, the New York Public Library's Cullman Center, the Jerome Foundation, and Hawthornden Literary Retreat. His poems have appeared in magazines and anthologies across North America and the UK, including *Poetry, The Believer, The New Republic, Kenyon Review,* and *the Academy of American Poets*' Poem-A-Day series. He edits the *Véhicule Press* poetry imprint,

Signal Editions.

Vaneeza Sohail is a Pakistani writer whose work explores memory, intimacy, and the shifting architectures of city life. Her writing has appeared in *Diode Poetry Journal, Wildness, Lakeer Magazine* and *Stone Circle Review.* She enjoys tracing how private wounds mirror urban landscapes.

Madeline Rosales has publications with *Onyx Publications, Querencia Press*, and *Wingless Dreamer.* Her work has been critically recognized in contests and awards by *Pigeon Pages, Literature Across Horizons*, and *Calyx Press.*

Kinsale Drake was a winner of the 2023 National Poetry Series for her debut poetry collection *THE SKY WAS ONCE A DARK BLANKET* (*University of Georgia Press*, 2024). Her work has appeared in *Poetry Magazine, Poets.org, Best New Poets, Black Warrior Review,* and elsewhere.

Corrie Williamson is the author of three collections of poetry: *Your Mother's Bear Gun* (*River River Books*, 2025), *The River Where You Forgot My Name* (*Southern Illinois University Press* 2019), and *Sweet Husk* (*Perugia Press*, 2014). She is also the co-editor of *A Literary Field Guide to the Rocky Mountains*, forthcoming from *Mountaineers Books.* Her poems have appeared widely in venues such as *The Kenyon Review, AGNI, Ecotone, The Missouri Review, Prairie Schooner,* and elsewhere, as well as numerous anthologies. She lives in Lewistown, Montana.

Sara Iacovelli is a poet and a preschool teacher based in upstate NY. She has gone to grad school too many times, though never for writing; she holds degrees in comparative literature and special education. Her work has appeared in *Milk Press, Pine Hills Review, *82 Review*, and *The Dawn Review,* where she was awarded the 2024 Dawn Prize for Poetry.

Ayendy Bonifacio is a Dominican American writer and associate professor of U.S. Latinx literary studies at the University of Toledo. He's the author of *To the River, We Are Migrants, Dique Dominican: A Memoir*, and the forthcoming novel *Bless Me, Papi.* His work has appeared in *The New York Times, Slate*, and *The Los Angeles Review of Books,* among other places.

Erin McCluskey is an artist living in Toronto, Canada. With a background in Illustration and Theatre, she creates images that exist on paper, walls, objects, spaces, and stages.

Bella Stevens is an illustrator, comic creator, writer, and multimedia visual artist based out of Richmond, VA. Bella graduated from the University of Richmond, VA with a BA in Studio Art and Creative Writing. Her work has been featured or is forthcoming in numerous magazines, including the *Virginia Literary Review* and *The Messenger*.

Ío Wuerich is an Argentinian illustrator who lives in Spain. Ío loves plants, cats, and watches cartoons all day. They also like to draw with ink, watercolors, and gouache, and loves making small digital animations.